Three reasons why
Willi... S0-AWM-876
was awarded
Three Edgars by the
Mystery Writers of America:

1.
Killed in the Ratings

2.
Encyclopedia Mysteriosa

3.

THE
HOG
MURDERS

WILLIAM L. DeANDREA

THE HOG MURDERS

WITH A NEW INTRODUCTION BY JANE HADDAM

IPL LIBRARY OF CRIME CLASSICS®
INTERNATIONAL POLYGONICS, LTD.
New York City

THE HOG MURDERS

Previous library of Congress Card
Catalog # 79-52460
ISBN 1-55882-030-2

Printed and Manufactured in the
 United States of America.

First IPL printing November 1999
10 9 8 7 6 5 4 3 2 1

For Joann and Mary, two good kids

INTRODUCTION

When Bill DeAndrea was dying, he told his mother that the only way he would allow her to have a funeral Mass said for him was if she could guarantee that the first hymn would be Leader of the Pack. She was holding a rosary at the time. He was close enough to dying that he was almost never himself any more, almost never turned on and alert, almost never out of pain. I was a walking catatonic. We had been together over thirteen years by then, and less than a month before it looked as if he were going to beat it: this strange cancer that he had, so rare that one of his doctors once told him there were better odds he'd win the New York lottery jackpot two weeks running than that he'd get what he'd got. Now there were times when he was himself only in body, times when the things he did made no more sense to him than they did to me. Once, he woke up everyone in the house, sure that the smoke alarm was going off. Once, he came to me and told me with great urgency that we had to get in touch with my mother right away if we wanted to have wild turkey for Thanksgiving. I can tell you exactly how long it lasted, that very bad time. It started on the day after Labor Day, 1996, and went to one twenty two in the afternoon on October 9th. October 9th, 1996, was the day he died.

The first time I ever heard of William L. DeAndrea, it was March 21st, 1980, and I was standing in the Open Book Annex in Grand Central Terminal in the middle of the evening rush hour. I was twenty nine years old and scared to death. A week before, I had resigned from my doctoral program, ditched my teaching job, and got on a plane for New York City, convinced that if I didn't do something right now, right that minute, I would be stuck forever in academia and never be a writer at all. I had fifty dollars to my name and a place to stay on the floor of a friend's apartment in Greenwich Village. I was on my way home to Connecticut to tell my father what it was I had done with my life. Mostly I was having trouble finding air to breathe.

"Don't go home if it scares you so much," my friend with the apartment told me--but I couldn't do that. I didn't know how to do that. So I went to Grand Central instead, and bought a ticket to Danbury, and went into the Open Book Annex to find something to take my mind off the horrendous scene I was sure was about to blow up. I found the book you are holding now, in almost the identical cover. That cover must be one of the most effective pieces of book art ever designed. I was surrounded by a cloud of tension the way some people say they are surrounded by an aura. The man with the pig's head pierced right through that--and half an hour later, as the train made its way past Fordham and Greenwich and Noroton Heights, so did the words on the pages inside. Bill DeAndrea had a very distinct narrative voice, in life as well as in his work. It always commanded my attention.

Some of the people who are reading this book will have read everything Bill ever wrote: all the Matt Cobb novels, all the Benedetti novels, the two short works he published as Philip DeGrave, the short stories that appeared in one anthology or another over the course of two decades, even the last two historical mysteries about Quinn Booker and Lobo Blacke. Others will never have heard of him at all, or be familiar only with his nonfiction: the Encyclopedia Mysteriosa, say, or the columns in The Armchair Detective. For that second group, this novel may come as something of a surprise. As a columnist and an historian of the field, Bill was known for the sharpness of both his insights and his criticism. His columns in TAD tended to provoke flame wars on the Letters to the Editor page. Some of his analyses in the Encyclopedia resulted in fellow mystery writers threatening never to speak to him again. Politically, he was a passionate and radical libertarian, a foe of all things Politically Correct. Personally, he was the product of the great Baby Boom social shift, the son of a factory worker and a nurse who got scholarships and Made Good, the second person in his family to go to college and the eventual winner of more awards than he could keep track of, including three Edgars. He lost two of his friends to drug addiction before he was eighteen. He lost half a dozen to AIDS before he was thirty-five. He never smoked a cigarette, or touched a drug of any kind, not even in the early- Seventies craziness about the transformative power of marijuana. In the end what mattered to him most--his marriage, his family, his friends, his work--seemed to him to lack some grandness of vision, some great romantic gesture that would provide him with a suitable summing up. He could only manage small things, he thought, but those small things were what I found so breathtaking. Once, in the middle of winter, convinced that I was going to run out of money and be unable to buy our older son a new winter coat, he lied to me about how many painkillers he had left in the bottle he kept by the side of his bed. He rationed them out to himself, at less than a quarter the prescribed dose, for two solid weeks before I realized what was going on. The pills were expensive--$150 for a month's supply--and we'd run through the prescription drug allowance on his health plan. He wanted desperately to do the right thing.

"Sometimes all I can do is nothing," he said, when I confronted him with what he'd done. I was angry about it, although I knew I shouldn't be. It frightened me when I thought he had given in to the pain

The novels are written in Bill's personal voice, the one he used at home, the one he used with the people he was closest to. That is true whether they are written in first person or third, as is the fact that there is always one character who is Bill himself. In The Hog Murders, that character is Ron Gentry, who would go on in later Benedetti novels to marry the woman of his dreams, the oh-so-intellectual Janet.

In The Hog Murders, Ron is what Bill thought himself to be: single and at loose ends, happy with his job but not very happy with his life. Nicolo Benedetti is The Great Detective, in the tradition of Poirot and Nero Wolfe. In real life, Bill loved Wolfe and couldn't stand Poirot. He always knew what the problem with The Great Detective was, though: nobody could approach him straight on without making him laughable. Rex Stout never wrote from Wolfe's point of view, and Bill never wrote from Benedetti's. Benedetti was always to be seen through the eyes of other people, mostly of people who worshiped him.

As a Great Detective, Benedetti is necessarily eccentric: a painter in his spare time with the ego of a Picasso if not the talent; a first class old goat with a penchant for chasing middle-aged women in restaurants and airports; the kind of person who is likely to insult the clients before the check is even in the mail. Genius has its privileges, and one of those privileges is to live without resorting to common sense. Ron Gentry, on the other hand, is common sense personified. He has so much common sense that, without Benedetti, he would be in a rut.

I sometimes think of Bill writing this novel, on the kitchen table in his parents' apartment in Port Chester, New York, while his first book was out in the void, making the rounds of agents and publishers. That was Killed In The Ratings, and eventually it would win him his first Edgar, for Best First Novel, in 1979. Bill didn't know that while he was inventing Benedetti. He only knew he had a plan, and that was to have two books circulating that were as different as possible from each other while still being mysteries. One--Ratings--would be in first person, set in a major city, and focus on an everyday working guy with a job (as network troubleshooter) that gave him a franchise to investigate crime. The other--Hog--would be in third person, set in a small town, and feature a larger-than-life sized, mythically-proportioned genius whose life and works would be more important than the cases he solved.

Like a lot of other writers, before and since, he had no idea if either of these books was any good. He was too close to the work, and too emotionally committed to it, to make an objective assessment. He just knew that he loved Matt Cobb and Benedetti both.

He didn't love Sparta, New York, the fictional setting of The Hog Murders, any more than he loved Syracuse, New York, the real town on which it was based. Syracuse was where Bill went to college--at Syracuse University--and although he loved the people he met there and the life of the university, he'd had enough of upstate New York by his third week in residence. For one thing, it was cold, too cold, and the weather was awful. When it wasn't raining it was snowing, and when it was snowing it went on for hours and covered everything. For another thing, it was in something like a media black-out. In those days before cable and satellites, being outside the ADI of a major metropolitan area meant getting four channels on your television set and all of them depressingly fuzzy. It also meant "weird lacunae," as Bill sometimes put it. You could get decent bagels but had to import lox. You could get Miles Davis but had to go south to hear Thelonius Monk.

Most of all, what bothered Bill about Syracuse-- and what bothers Ron Gentry about Sparta--is the emptiness there, the sense that there are vast stretches of land with nobody and nothing in them. A lot of people are looking for exactly that, but Bill was an urban animal, and Ron Gentry is too. There was something about the silence of the country that seemed ominous to both of them.   In the city there are almost always people around, witnesses, people to call on for help. In the country, there may be nobody at all. The old cliche might really come true. Nobody would hear you if you screamed.

Bill did a few books with serial killers in them, and all of those serial killers operated in rural or near rural areas. In The Hog Murders, where the first killing takes place in the first chapter and nearly on the first page, the backdrop to the murders is almost brutally conventional and light. A carful of college girls driving down an Interstate, pine trees and withered grass, houses put up from supermarket stock plans and looking too much alike: what was ordinary to those of us who grew up in small towns was exotic to Bill, who grew up thinking that Armonk was "the sticks."

"Syracuse isn't the sticks," one of his dorm mates informed him, his first week in college. "The roads are paved."

Bill had never lived on an unpaved road in his life until I dragged him out to rural Connecticut, and would cheerfully never have lived on one at all. All three Benedetti books would eventually be set in very small towns, and all of them would have that same quality of underlying unease, of a vision of the Garden of Eden as rotten to the core.

It was a good trick, really--a kind of professional sleight of hand--because The Hog Murders is most assuredly a humorous mystery. Humor was important to Bill DeAndrea, in everything he did. He never understood the conventional wisdom that said that a crime novel was not really "art" unless its tone was unrelentingly grim.

Oddly enough, he never understood the use of humor to wound--in his books. He was very good at using humor for just that purpose in his nonfiction, especially when he was angry or outraged. But even when he dealt with outrages beyond number, the tone of the humor in his fiction remained good-natured, even if it was sometimes incredulous. He found a lot to be incredulous about in Sparta, New York, and everywhere else. The self-absorbed cluelessness of so many members of the human race gave him a lot of material.

"Nobody lives forever," a character in one of the last of the Matt Cobb novels says.

"Yeah," Matt Cobb answers. "But have you ever noticed, everybody tries?"

The Hog Murders is a gateway into Bill DeAndrea's and Ron Gentry's and Nicolo Benedetti's world--a world where the good guys at least would like to live forever, because they're having such a very good time; where most people are basically good if also basically nuts; where the bad guys are bad because they can never see anybody or anything outside themselves.

It's not a bad place to live, and it comes with a few extras in the way of humor, and compassion, and solid, inspired prose.

If you have never read a novel by William L. DeAndrea, I hope you will like this one. I can still see myself sitting on that train, thinking how incredibly good it was, and not knowing that, in less than five years, I would be married to the man who wrote it.

Things happen to Ron Gentry that do not happen to you and me--but then, things happened to Bill DeAndrea that do not happen to you and me, either. Once, in the fall of 1984, he took me to the Burger King on the Champs Elysses and Kareem Abdul Jabar was there, carrying a plastic tray loaded down with Whoppers and large-sized fries. If I'd gone into the Burger King on the Champs Elysses on my own, all that would have happened to me was that I would have been insulted by the check-out girl.

"I just want to make sure you think I was worth it," he said to me, pulling himself into lucidity less than twenty-four hours before he died.

He was worth it. This book is worth it. So is every book he wrote.

I hope you read them all.

—Jane Haddam

ONE

❖❖ ❖❖ ❖❖ ❖❖ ❖❖ ❖❖ ❖❖ ❖❖ ❖❖ ❖❖ ❖❖ ❖❖ ❖❖ ❖

EVEN IF NO ONE HAD BEEN MURDERED, IT'S A SAFE AS-
sumption that the citizens of Sparta, New York (population approx. 191,000), would have been a long time
forgetting *that* winter. Even for Central New York State,
where (as the saying goes) the year is divided into winter
and July, there was some memorable weather. From October to April, an even fourteen feet of snow fell on
Sparta, including the thirty-inch blizzard on Ground Hog
Day.

At the time, the date of the blizzard seemed like a
particularly grim jest of fate. Sparta residents compared
the Hog's day weather that stifled the activity of the community, with the mysterious individual who signed
"HOG" on his notes boasting of the deaths; they told
each other it figured. "He's tired of killing us off one at
a time," an anonymous old woman told a local radio station. "He's gonna wipe out the whole city at once." The
city laughed along with her. It was a way to hide the fear.

There had been mass murderers in the past—London's
Jack the Ripper, New York City's Son of Sam, the L.A.
Slasher, and Zebra and Zodiac in San Francisco. But these
were big cities. The people of Sparta *expected* that kind
of thing from a big city. But Sparta was only a nice, good-
sized town halfway between Syracuse and Rochester,
with a bunch of subassembly plants and a university in it.
Why pick on us? they asked the powers that be. They had
no answers.

And another thing. Jack the Ripper carved up whores.
The Slasher took a razor to helpless derelicts. Son of Sam
shot attractive young couples. Zebra and Zodiac, along
with the other serial murderers of history, all had their
preferences in victims.

But Hog would kill *anybody,* in any way, for no ap-

9

parent reason, then laugh about it afterward. In a city like Sparta, where twenty homicides a year is a lot, six in the span of three short weeks (all apparently committed by the same hand, one that seemed to have God-sure control over people and events) were sure to provoke more than a little uneasiness in the population.

Benedetti took the case, though he proclaimed loudly (as always) that he was a philosopher, not a detective. He charged the usual stiff fee of course, but there is no doubt an affectionate regard for the city, Ron Gentry, and Inspector Joseph Fleisher, had something to do with the professor's decision.

The average Spartan didn't care. All he knew was that if Benedetti couldn't catch Hog, Sparta's own mass murderer would join most of his famous predecessors among the ranks of the uncaught.

As the professor was later to remark, if that woman in Oswego hadn't reached her 118th birthday, it would have been a different case.

Buell Tatham was composing his daily column for the *Courant* as he drove back to Sparta, mentally filling in the blanks in the standard centenarian-plus birthday story—I owe my long and productive life to——, ——has changed most since I was a young boy/girl. You could get a computer to write it as well. A columnist's curse, he thought wryly—human interest starts to get boring.

It wasn't always like that, of course. During the civil rights struggles of the early and mid-sixties, Buell, as a bona fide expatriate southern liberal, had put the *Courant* on the journalistic map with a series of sensitive articles about the suffering and anguish he'd seen racism cause blacks and whites, and why it had to stop if the South were to survive. Some of the columns had even been picked up by the wire services, though he was sure the *Knox County Register* had never run any of them. He laughed at the idea of the home folk reading his words and never knowing it was his work hidden behind a new name.

He'd had offers to move up to papers in Boston, Philadelphia, and New York, but had turned them down. It left scars, he had discovered, to leave the land his fam-

ily had owned since George I granted it to an adventur-
ous ancestor, and to leave behind the ancestor's privileges
and name as well. He couldn't face the idea of leaving
Sparta, when it had taken the better part of ten years to
make *that* feel like a home.

Now, he had been in the North country twenty-five
years, and was a kind of institution, a middle-aging
champion of the little guy, and a slightly jaded celebrant
of his small, heartwarming (Buell winced) triumphs. Oh,
there was still good to be done, he knew, and he fully intended to do it. If they didn't muck it up on him. If they
just didn't—

A blaring horn cut into his thoughts, and brought his
attention back to his driving. He had been drifting out
into the center lane, almost cutting off a yellow Volkswagen beetle carrying three young girls. *Careful, boy,*
he heard the voice of the past scold him. *You get
in trouble when you think too much.*

He brought his mind back to the road. It was too
early for the evening rush hour, but it was dusk, and the
sky was overcast, so he decided to switch on his head-
lights. His mirrors showed nothing behind him. The VW
had gone by, and it was the only other car he could see
on the highway, so Buell risked a look at the surround-
ing landscape.

Over the years he had come to enjoy the look of Sparta
in the winter, the aluminized art deco look the snow and
ice gave to everything. He enjoyed contrasting it with the
red soil of Knox County. He'd enjoy it even more when
he went back there. The red dirt would be there, but
everything else would be different; and a lot more would
be *made* different after he got there.

For one thing, he'd have Diedre and her little boy
with him. That was the one thing above all he owed
Sparta—Diedre Chester. He never knew how much he
needed a woman to *really* love; you never know how deep
a need is until you start to fill it.

He saw a highway sign indicating Downtown Sparta,
and knew he was about twenty minutes from his exit. It
used to be about ten minutes of driving, but last summer the county had started to build a new overpass and
approach ramp, and had only managed to get the skeletons up before the first blizzard of this incredible winter

hit, in early October. Further work was impossible until
the thaw, assuming the part already built wasn't washed
away by a flood of melted snow.

There was the incomplete overpass just ahead, with the
temporary wooden DANGER—CONSTRUCTION sign hung on
it, faded by the elements but still discernible.

He was about a hundred yards behind the girls, who
were just about to drive under the incomplete structure.
At that precise moment, the sign gave way.

There must have been a snap, but Buell never heard
it. The heavy wooden sign suddenly came free at the upper left-hand corner, swung heavily down and to the
right, then came free all together. Buell watched, horrified, as it fell some fifteen feet, corner first, onto the
hood of the yellow Volkswagen.

The young girl driving could not have known what hit
her. The car went crazily out of control and crashed into
one of the overpass's concrete supports. The car, nose end
now with a huge concavity, as though some giant had
taken a bite out of it, spun once, then turned turtle.

Buell pulled his car to a stop. He looked at the wrecked
car and shivered for a few seconds, but he soon realized
what he had to do. The steps he should take came like
diagrams to his mind, sharp and clear.

Buell raced around to the trunk of his car, got his fire
extinguisher, a blanket, and some other things he thought
he might have use for, and ran to the crippled car.

The Volkswagen's wheels were still spinning uselessly
in the air. Buell got down on hands and knees on the
freezing asphalt, reached in through a crushed window
to turn off the ignition, sprayed the extinguisher on the
car, then turned his attention to the girls.

Buell had first seen death at his father's wake, but he
didn't count that—it had been sanitized, almost sissified.
He saw men shot and blown apart in Korea, though, and
since then had seen death in all its forms—every reporter
does. But this was different, for a lot of reasons.

The driver of the Volkswagen was obviously dead. She
was a small, delicate-looking Oriental girl. The steering
wheel was pressed into her stomach, apparently bent
down from the force of the falling sign. Its pressure held
her tight against the seat, dangling upside down in the
overturned car. The girl in the passenger seat, a blonde,

was tangled up with the instrument panel. Her hands clawed at the padded dashboard as though it were a lover's back. Buell thought her lips were unnaturally red, and he wondered about it, until the girl's feeble cough produced a fine red spray.

She needed more help than Buell could give her, he knew, so he concentrated on the girl in the back seat, a tall brunette. She was bleeding from the scalp and trying to crawl through the back window. Buell went around and got her out, covered her with the blanket, and made her as comfortable as possible.

Then, after making sure he had nothing left to do at the scene of the accident, Buell went up the road to try and get help.

It didn't take long before a state trooper drove by.

"Call an ambulance!" Buell told him. "Some girls are hurt pretty bad."

The trooper had intended to ask a couple of questions about Buell's abandoned car, but the nature of the reporter's request, along with his aristocratic appearance and distinguished "suthun" accent, changed the trooper's mind. He radioed for the ambulance, he radioed for more police, *then* asked Buell what happened.

Buell told him; later on he told the trooper's superior, and after that he told the *superior's* superior. He didn't mind. The longer he hung around the scene, the more facts he picked up. After all, he *was* a reporter. He found out the dead Oriental girl's name was Beth Ling, the blonde's Carol Salinski, and the tall brunette who appeared to be least hurt was Barbara Elleger. Later, he learned the Salinski girl died on the way to the hospital, but that the Elleger girl would survive.

He looked over the cops' shoulders as they checked the contents of the girls' purses. They all had G.O. cards from Grover Cleveland High. Beth Ling had an autographed picture of Erik Estrada. Barbara Elleger had a brand-new diaphragm, and instructions from a gynecologist on how to use it.

And just before he told the story for the last time, he learned something else. A state police captain called Buell over to him.

"That girl that survived owes her life to you, the hospital tells me, Mr. Tatham."

Buell was truly glad. " 'I'm just a humble man, tryin' in my own way to serve the Lord,' as my daddy used to say," he said.

The captain smiled, and started to say something, but was cut off by a yell from one of his men, a technician who'd been looking at the wooden sign.

Buell turned and looked at the man, a fat guy holding a magnifying glass. He was standing in the middle of a world that no longer was a clean art deco fantasy—it was a lurid nightmare, painted police-flasher blue and blood-red.

Buell followed the captain to where the technician was standing over the sign, being careful not to step on any splinters. "This is why the sign fell, Captain. See this clamp?"

The sign had been held to the overpass structure by two U-shaped metal clamps. Both were still bolted to the wood. One was twisted and broken, but the other remained straight, with a gap of about three quarters of an inch where the curve of the U should be, leaving a metal structure that looked not unlike a caterpillar rearing up at his reflection in a mirror.

"I saw it go," the reporter reminded the captain. "I knew it had to be something like that."

"Yeah," the expert said bitterly, "but look. Of course I'll confirm it in the lab, but look at this." He ran his fingers over the broken part of the clamp. It narrowed from the roundness of the metal's regular thickness to a straight edge, rather like an extremely blunt-bladed screwdriver. "This metal didn't snap," the technician said. "Somebody was at it with a bolt cutter. This is a murder, Captain."

The captain commended his man on his good work. Then he swore. Then he radioed the Sparta Public Safety Building, and told someone to tell Inspector Fleisher that he had a murder on his hands, that the crash occurred three tenths of a mile inside Sparta's city limits.

That was Thursday, January 15. On Saturday, January 17, Buell Tatham, author of the "Human Angle" column in the Sparta *Daily Courant,* found a note in his mail at the office.

It was in a cheap, plain white envelope with no return

address. It had been mailed at a dropbox somewhere in downtown Sparta. It was addressed in uniform, well-formed, untraceable block capitals, written with a nineteen-cent ball point pen.

There was a single piece of paper inside, with a message in the same letters and the same ink. It read:

BUELL TATHAM————

YOU WERE ONE OF THE LUCKY ONES THURSDAY EVENING. SINCE YOU WERE THERE AS A WITNESS, YOU WILL DO AS WELL AS ANYONE TO PASS ON MY MESSAGES TO THE POLICE. THE POLICE WERE LUCKY TOO. I WAS SLOPPY ON PURPOSE SO THEY'D KNOW WHAT I CAN DO. IN THE FUTURE, NO ONE WILL KNOW I'VE STRUCK UNTIL I TELL YOU SO. THE TALL GIRL WAS ALSO LUCKY. SHE WILL LIVE TO USE THE DIAPHRAGM SHE HAD IN HER PURSE. THIS WON'T BE THE LAST NOTE. MORE DEATHS ARE COMING. TILL THEN.

————HOG

This is it, Buell thought, holding tightly to the letter in one hand and dialing the police with the other. This is where it starts for real. Because outside of a few law officers, Buell, and the gynecologist who gave it to her, nobody knew Barbara Elleger and her friends were on the road that afternoon to drive to a nearby town and pick up that diaphragm. It hadn't been printed. The girl's *parents* hadn't even been told. Barbara herself was still unconscious.

So, Buell thought, anyone with any intelligence will have to concede the probability that this note came from the killer.

TWO

◆◆ ◆◆ ◆◆ ◆◆ ◆◆ ◆◆ ◆◆ ◆◆ ◆◆ ◆◆ ◆◆ ◆◆ ◆◆ ◆◆ ◆◆ ◆

DIEDRE ROSE AT DAWN, THREW HER COAT ON OVER HER nightgown, and took a quick trip to the newsstand for a copy of the *Courant*. She could hardly wait to get the details of the latest development in the Hog case—Buell only had time to give her the barest sketch when he phoned last night. She raced back to her apartment, threw aside her coat and shoes, and bounced down on the bed.

"HOG CLAIMS NEW MURDER" the headline said. Buell had gotten the note yesterday, that was why he had to cancel their dinner and spend all day and night with the police. The story went on to say that Hog's note, which was identical to the first one in paper and printing, said the death of eighty-one-year-old Stanley Watson, at first believed accidental, was really the work of Hog. "Watson didn't fall down those stairs," the note stated, "I gave him a little push."

Again like in the note following the first two deaths, the writer knew something no one outside the investigation was supposed to know: Watson had been found with an unopened can of Miller High Life beer clutched in his dead hand.

Watson had about seven hundred dollars in small bills stuffed in a cookie jar and two vases in his house; it didn't appear to have been touched. Watson had retired twenty-two years ago from his job as a welder in the General Electric plant in Sparta. The police were baffled.

That last fact wasn't in the article, Buell had told Diedre that, personally. It was horrible, of course, but still very exciting. Buell was very important to this case. He was helping the police.

Diedre took anything good that Buell accomplished as a personal compliment. It made her feel special. Sure, she

16

had natural platinum blonde hair, and deep blue eyes, and the face and figure of a movie star (which she once had been, almost, until she found out about the movie), but *all* the girls in Fogelsberg, Minnesota, where she had grown up as Diedre Swenson could say that, almost. But could they say they had once been the *very* good friend of the president of the second richest bank in the country? Had they married the Liberian ambassador to the United Nations, and had a beautiful son who was a citizen of *two* countries? Were they engaged to a reporter who was so respected in his town that the police asked him for help? Of *course* they couldn't. They were all still back in Fogelsberg, working in the public library, or married to summer-wheat farmers. It took a special kind of woman, a *remarkable* woman to be loved by such fascinating men. Diedre only regretted that Ricky was with his father in Africa, and couldn't share the excitement of his future stepfather's importance.

And Buell was going to become more important when he came into his money, which would be soon. He had all kinds of wonderful plans and projects for the poor people back home. It was thrilling to be with such a man, even more thrilling (she admitted secretly) than sleeping with him. She angled her body so the rising sun streaming through her window fell on the front page of the *Courant,* and read Buell's article again.

Ron Gentry was reading that same article with the same sunlight, although he had to assist it with a desk lamp. The management of the venerable old Bixby Building in which he had his office was far less conscientious in keeping windows clean than Diedre's landlord was. Besides, Ron thought, even if Sparta *was* in the midst of a heat wave, with the temperature yesterday soaring to thirty-four degrees, the winter sun over Sparta was a feeble thing at best.

Ron felt pangs as he read Buell Tatham's article, the first straight news that good old boy had written in years, probably. Ron and the columnist had become acquainted when Buell had done a column on the professor shortly before Benedetti left Sparta University three years ago. He envied the reporter his "in" on the investigation, felt like a kid looking at a ballgame through a schoolyard fence. It wasn't as though he couldn't help them for heaven's sake. After all, he *was* a duly licensed private investigator, not to mention the only Benedetti-trained investigator in the entire world.

A clicking sound from the outer office distracted him for a second, until he recognized the step of Mrs. Goralsky, his secretary. Mrs. Goralsky was the kind of smart, resourceful, efficient office manager a private eye needs, especially when he's running a one-man operation. Ron couldn't see her through the glass door of his private office, but he could hear her going through her morning routine—the muffled thump as she put her two Sparta telephone directories on her chair, the ratcheting noise of a fresh sheet of paper going into the typewriter, the phone call to the answering service to tell them she was on the job.

The next thing he heard was the sharp rap on the floor as Mrs. Goralsky leaped from her perch on the phone books to the polished hardwood. Ron heard her little feet click rapidly across the outer office, and saw the top of her head through the glass in the door as she pushed it aside and walked in.

"Good morning, Mr. Gentry," she said. "You're here early, this morning. Couldn't you sleep last night?"

The late Mr. Goralsky, a high school football coach, was often known to say, with a grin and a guffaw, "Good things come in small packages. Take the little woman for example." He made up for his lack of originality with love—and accuracy. The "little woman" in this case was, in fact, a midget—technically a pituitary dwarf—a fraction of an inch less than four feet five inches tall. Actually, that's pretty tall for a midget. And since Mrs. Goralsky's body proportions were perfect (even sexy), it wasn't uncommon for visitors to the office to wonder why Gentry had bought such enormous furniture.

"Good morning, Mrs. Goralsky," Ron said. "No, I slept fine. I got up early to get the paper."

If Ron had any complaint about his secretary, it was her tendency to want to mother him. The fact that Mrs. Goralsky *had* a son of her own, an All-America candidate at linebacker for the Sparta University football team, seemed to make no difference at all.

"The Hog case?" Mrs. Goralsky wanted to know. "I

heard on the radio he sent another note." She walked around his desk and, over his elbow, skimmed the article. "Think we'll get a shot at the case?" she asked eagerly.

Ron, as always, was amused at the gleam in his secretary's eye when the talk turned to violence and murder. He was aware of a similar feeling and was frank enough to recognize it as not quite wholesome, but (he told himself) he had the excuse of long exposure to the celebrated Professor Niccolo Benedetti, after which nobody could be expected to remain entirely normal.

"We might at that, Mrs. Goralsky," he said. "Even if they don't invite *me* in, there may come the time when they're so disgusted with themselves they'll float a bond issue and raise enough money to get the professor. Then I'll be in on it automatically, as his flunky."

"Well, I hope so," Mrs. Goralsky said, and left the office. Ron hoped so, too. He took off his glasses, polished them, then read the article again.

Indirectly, it was poor eyesight that had resulted in Ron's becoming a private detective. Ever since the Sunday he first laboriously sounded out a Dick Tracy episode in his local newspaper, he had wanted to be a cop. But by the time he finished high school, he knew he'd never be able to pass the vision test.

It was a shame. Tall, athletic, blond, Ron would have looked good in uniform. Women always said so. But those pale gray eyes they also admired let him down.

He'd accepted it as philosophically as he could, and compromised on college and law school. Maybe some day he could become district attorney or something.

But, during his junior year at Sparta University, he literally bumped into Professor Niccolo Benedetti in a crowded hallway during class-changing time. The professor took one look at him and said, "You. You have the look. Come to my office. What is your name?"

Ron answered that, and thousands of other questions during the next few days. He did nothing but talk and write for the professor; who listened or read with that Mona Lisa smile of his, and said nothing.

Finally, when Ron was seriously considering seeking a writ of habeas corpus for himself, the old man said, "Congratulations, Ronald Gentry. I choose you, if you wish, my sixth protege. You will accompany me, and assist me in my research during my stay in this place."

Assistant to the world's greatest detective? That was better than law school. He accepted immediately.

The professor shook his head. "Do not be hasty, *amico*. The position is not without risk, to your body and your soul. Of my five previous students, one is dead; one controls a billion-dollar corporation; two are in prison, one justly and one unjustly; and one is the virtual dictator of a Pacific island. If you join me you will be dealing with evil, and evil has its attractions."

Because to Benedetti, the investigation of crime was merely a tool of research. His lifework was nothing less than an inquiry into the nature of human evil. He hunted down criminals more to study them than to punish them.

All the same, in the three years he served as Benedetti's assistant, Ron had learned more about the art of detection than he had thought existed, and at the end of that time, with the help of a good word from Inspector Fleisher, and a few favors collected in the State license bureau, Ron had gotten his license and gone into business for himself, using Benedetti's methods as well as he could.

When he got the chance, that is. Opportunities for real challenging work were rare enough, and now, when what looked like a great one *had* come along, he was on the outside. It was frustrating.

Well, there was no law that said he couldn't do some figuring on his own, just to keep in form. All it would cost him was the price of a newspaper, and he bought that every day anyway. Ron picked up the *Courant*, and brought the Benedetti method to bear on the case.

The professor had summed up his technique in two words: analyze and imagine. He likened a crime to a story, not an original idea in itself, but Benedetti put the *detective*, not the criminal, in the author's place. "In theory, it is simple; like all good theories," the professor had explained. "We are confronted with the ending of a story; that is, the situation as it stands now. This person is dead, that person is richer, *etcetera*. Remember, we must be as certain as possible that we know what the present situation really *is*, which is not always an easy task.

"Next, we know certain facts, or during the survey of

the current state of events they come to light readily; the man's wife hated him, his business partner had dinner with the Pope at the time of the crime. These we remember, but disregard for a time.

"Third, we postulate beginnings for the story, saying to ourselves, 'Such a person decided to kill the victim,' substituting the name of each person involved, in turn, for the phrase 'such a person.' Then, we create the middle of the story, the how and why of our living *romanzo,* ch? Some of the resulting stories, most of them, will be absurd, or (better still) impossible. But some will not.

"Then all that remains is to look again for facts that escaped our notice the first time, and try again and again, until we have one story that cannot be controverted by events, in short, until we have imagined the story of the truth.

"Of course, life laughs at theories, Ronald. Others besides the criminal will hide things and hinder you, you will find in life. The very presence of an investigator inevitably causes changes in the investigation. And of course, even the greatest of us is human. It takes true humility to cope with evil, *amico,* security within one's self, and acceptance at the same time of one's limitations.

"Still, my theory is a tool, a good one, to be used with patience, and talent, and humility."

As far as the Hog case was concerned, though, with its multiple victims and myriad complications, Ron was aware (in all humility), that he needed a lot more facts before he could even *begin* to write a "living novel" of the crime. The newspaper accounts were not enough. Still, some interesting questions did present themselves.

For example, the two girls died on the fifteenth of the month, and Buell Tatham received the note on the seventeenth. Stanley Watson had died last Sunday, the twenty-fifth, and the note arrived yesterday, the twenty-seventh. Was this to be a pattern? Was there some ten-day cycle, natural or man-imposed, that governed Hog's activities? For example, could he be a crewman on some ship that plied the nearby Great Lakes?

For another, it seemed apparent to Ron that Hog made intimate studies of his victims before he struck. He knew where those girls were going; he *had* to have found out the purpose of the girls' trip beforehand, he certainly couldn't have learned it after the crash, not with Buell Tatham there immediately afterward. And *that* can only mean, Ron thought, that he followed them around, eavesdropped on them—that he had those three girls and no others marked for slaughter that afternoon. Barbara Elleger had escaped through pure good luck, both for her and the police. She might be able to shed some light on the matter when she regained consciousness; any minute now, according to the *Courant*.

And how about old Watson? Sure, it was conceivable that a lonely old man might let a stranger in the house just to have someone to talk to, but what circumstances could explain his letting the stranger get behind him at the *top* of the stairs, as the medical examiner's report said had to have happened. To Ron that could only suggest that Hog had taken the time and effort to make himself known to the old man.

It was disconcerting, frightening, that someone should go to such pains to set up the murders of strangers; to make the deaths look like accidents, then proclaim them murders.

The phone on Ron's desk rang, but he ignored it, knowing Mrs. Goralsky would pick it up on the third ring. No need to seem eager.

"Gentry Investigations," he heard her say. "Yes, yes, I'll see if he's in."

Ron picked up the phone at the buzz of the intercom. "Yes, Mrs. Goralsky?"

"Mr. Harold Atler calling. Are you in? He says it's urgent and confidential."

"This is Atler of Atler, Pauling, Efter and Bass, the brokers? Hell, they could afford Sherlock Holmes. Put him on, Mrs. Goralsky." After a click, he said, "This is Gentry."

"Gentry, this is Harold Atler. Do you know who I am?" Atler's voice had a tone of habitual command that immediately set Ron's teeth on edge. It was an unfortunate fact of a private detective's life that any client or prospective client who could afford to pay a fee of any size had that attitude as part of his basal metabolism.

Realizing, though, that one must work to eat and eat

to live, Ron stifled his hostilities and said, "Yes, I do, Mr. Atler. How may I help you?"

"I want you to get over here right away, and I'll tell you when you arrive. It's a . . . delicate matter."

"I don't do divorce work," Ron cautioned him.

Atler was irritated, practically insulted. "What?" he said, then, "You don't have to worry about that, Gentry, I've never been married. There's a situation here I want assessed by a professional, but I don't want the police, do you follow me?"

"Very clear, sir. I get two hundred dollars a day, plus expenses. Is that agreeable?"

"My God, that's a thousand dollars a week!" Money was a topic Atler could get emotional about.

"I don't get work every day, Mr. Atler," Ron told him. "And I don't have enough loose capital to join you in the commodities market. Two hundred dollars a day."

The remark about the commodities market seemed for some reason to do the trick. "All right, Gentry, consider yourself hired."

"And expenses," Ron reminded him.

"Yes, yes, how soon will you be here?"

"That depends on where 'here' is. Where are you?"

Atler became really flustered. A subordinate of his would have suffered mightily for an omission like that. "Sorry, Gentry. I don't know what's wrong with me. I'm on the campus of the university. Sumter Hall. Do you know where that is?"

"Very well." Ron's first encounter with the professor had taken place there.

"Room 119. Hurry."

Ron got his coat, and stopped in the outer office to tell Mrs. Goralsky where he was going.

"He didn't want to pay our price, huh?" she asked.

"Rich people always look for bargains. That's how they get rich. He came around, though."

"Does it sound interesting?"

"Well, it's two hundred bucks, at least," Ron said. "Even if it isn't the Hog murders."

THREE

◆◆ ◆◆ ◆◆ ◆◆ ◆◆ ◆◆ ◆◆ ◆◆ ◆◆ ◆◆ ◆◆ ◆◆ ◆◆ ◆

PARKING ON OR NEAR THE CAMPUS, RON KNEW, WOULD be impossible. Some things never changed. He tucked his car in a small space in a commercial area nearby and cut across a field of frozen mud that someday was supposed to become a students' activity center. Gaining the main quadrangle, he couldn't help smiling at the sight of bundled-up coeds chasing their breaths to their next class. No woman could help looking cute and innocent in a snorkel coat and mittens.

Sumter Hall was a squat, ugly building of native limestone, with the bare skeletons of ivy vines clinging to its walls from ground to roof. Ron ignored the shoveled walks, and cut a diagonal path across the quad, his steps crunching on gritty week-old snow.

Ron liked the university and cherished the ivory-tower atmosphere most of all. It was a place where people scrambled more and changed less than anything else he could think of.

The sweltering heat inside of Sumter Hall was one thing that could use a little changing. The heat, and the smell of ozone and burning dust wafting from white-hot radiators, was like a brick wall after the near-freezing temperatures outside. Ron's eyeglasses fogged over as soon as the door closed behind him. If he tried to wipe them he knew there was a good chance they'd snap in the middle and leave him blind, so he stepped to the side and waited patiently for the temperatures to equalize and the lenses to clear. That accomplished, he headed for room 119.

It was a faculty office, in the basement. Atler was standing outside the door, amid pieces of broken glass. He was well groomed, and well, if a little too conserva-

24

tively, dressed. He gave Ron the impression of being ready to take off on a long business trip.

There was nothing wrong with the face under the broker's carefully trimmed salt-and-pepper hair, except an uncomfortably long upper lip. A mustache would have helped, but Atler had never considered growing one. He'd never even couple mustaches and himself in the same thought. Mustaches were frivolous. *Actors* and the like could grow mustaches, brokers were *important*.

The fellow walking down the hall toward him, the blond fellow with the glasses, *he* looked like a businessman, or would if he cut his hair a bit. Not like the sons of dead partners, who wore *green* suits to the office and talked (seriously) of buying marijuana futures, just in case, and kept bringing up the topic of retirement and similar ridiculous ideas.

This fellow wouldn't be like that. Excellent-looking young man, probably on the business school faculty. Be a credit to any firm, probably—

But then he stopped, nodded, and said, "Mr. Atler? I'm Ron Gentry."

Everything was a disappointment these days. Atler said, "Well, Gentry, what do you think?"

Astonishingly, the young man was grinning at him. Atler was about to put him in his place, until Gentry said, "About what, Mr. Atler? You were a little vague on the phone."

"Oh . . . ah . . . yes, of course. There's been a robbery."

It irritated Atler to see that this *snooper* wouldn't look him in the face, but instead kept gazing at the floor. "I thought that might be it," he said. "What's missing?"

Now Atler looked at the floor. He cleared his throat and said something. Unfortunately, he did both at the same time.

"What?" the detective asked.

"I said five thousand dollars!" Atler bellowed. When he heard himself, he looked up and down the hall to see if he had attracted any unwanted attention.

"Cash?"

Atler nodded.

"You kept five thousand dollars in an office in Sumter Hall?" To Atler, the young man sounded as though he felt he knew better, just like that Efter upstart. He wondered why young people these days were so cynical and mistrusting.

"See here, Gentry, do we have to discuss it here in the hall? Why don't we go upstairs to the snack bar and get a cup of coffee?"

"Okay, just let me take a look around first." Ron stepped gingerly across the broken glass, and nudged open the office door. It differed from a typical faculty office only in that it lacked the usual wall-covering blizzard of mimeographed memoes and bulletins. The usual gray steel desk, the green fake-leather swivel chair, and the two chrome and plastic kindergarten chairs for visiting students, were all present. All the drawers of the desk were standing open. He looked questioningly at Atler, and was told he found them like that. A quick look at the desk told Ron the drawer locks had not been forced.

Who is he trying to kid, Ron thought. This is amateur night, strictly page one from the Detective's Handbook: "When broken glass is found *outside* the premises, then this burglary was in fact an inside job." Surely Atler could have figured that out for himself.

"I've seen enough," Ron said. "Let's go get that cup of coffee."

When Ron saw the price of a cup of coffee he was glad Atler had paid for it. The broker selected a table in a far corner of the nearly deserted coffee shop, and the two sat down.

"Well?" Atler demanded.

Ron took a sip from his Styrofoam cup. "I have a few questions first, all right?"

Atler was resigned. "If you must," he said.

"Good. First of all, what was the money doing in that office? In fact, what are *you* doing in that office?"

Well, Atler thought, *that* one wasn't so bad. He felt decidedly more like himself as he answered.

"Well," he said. "The dean of the School of Business is an old friend of mine, and at his request, for the past five years or so, I've taught a course in applied marketing, for seniors, each fall semester. It's for young people who are *serious* about getting out there in the *real* world. We *need* eager young people to preserve the free enterprise system that made this country great." He gave Ron a look that dared him to make something of it.

Ron just smiled pleasantly and nodded. Benedetti had taught him, "Never, if you can avoid it, rush a witness. Listen to all he has to say, if there is time. A man's words when he is stalling are often more revealing than what he would say if he cut straight to the point. Besides, *amico,* only the future can say what the point really is." And because Ron believed that, and because he knew he was being paid by the day, he was content to listen.

Atler continued, though less confidently. Up to now, all he'd had to do was give Gentry a close paraphrase of a speech he'd delivered to the DAR last month. Now he was on his own.

"Now I'm no schoolteacher, I'm a trader, you understand. So the best I can do for the kids is this: I limit the course to fifty students, and each contributes twenty dollars to the class fund. Then, they study the market and tell me what to do with the money. I advise them, of course, but the decisions are all theirs. Do you follow me, Gentry?"

Ron assured him he did.

"Good. Then, at the beginning of the next semester, I liquidate everything and distribute the money, each student taking his share of the profit or loss."

"Why cash? Wouldn't checks be safer?"

Atler reddened. Ron knew they were getting close to whatever was bothering the broker.

"I . . . er . . . I wanted to impress upon them the idea that we deal with *real* things—real grain, real soybeans, and most of all, real money."

"Fifty students at twenty dollars apiece is a thousand dollars the way I figure it, Mr. Atler," Ron said. "The kids seem to have caught on about the real money."

Atler beamed with pride. "They certainly did. Brilliant group, brilliant! Picked just the right commodities for the time period, coffee and meat by-products, just before the prices went through the roof." The memory warmed Atler's heart. He loved making money on the market; it was his only passion.

Ron sipped his coffee again with new respect. Four hundred percent profit was nothing to sneeze at. "Some-one did a whole lot better than that, though," he said.

"Somebody made a profit of over two thousand percent. Who knew that money was there, Mr. Atler?"

"You won't get anywhere that way, Gentry." Atler was brusque. "The entire class knew they were to get their money today. And of course, they'd have told their friends."

"Of course. But you still haven't told me what five thousand dollars was doing in the office overnight."

To Ron's great surprise, Atler's long upper lip started to quiver, and his shrewd eyes moistened. Ron watched him struggle with himself, and, with great effort, bring himself back under control. "This is why I can't have the police, Gentry," he said at last. "And you must keep this in strictest confidence." Atler wiped his brow and cleared his throat. Ron waited for the revelation.

"I made a mistake," Atler said. "There can be no excuse for what I did. You see, I had to take the money out of the bank yesterday, because today is Founder's Day."

Founder's Day was one of those local half-holidays some communities have. It celebrated that long-ago January 28, when Cicero McCracken broke camp on the site that would later become Sparta. Public schools and banks were closed; the university and most businesses were open.

". . . and I wouldn't have been able to get the money. Foolishly, I had already announced today as the payment date. So I left the money here."

"There must have been safer places to keep it," Ron said.

"Of *course* there were! Haven't I told you I made a mistake? I could have left it overnight in the safe at the firm's office! I could have brought it to my apartment. There was no reason not to do either of those things, except I thought it would be more convenient to leave it in the office. The point is, Gentry—" Atler suddenly realized he had been shouting. He lowered his voice and began again. "The point is, *I was careless with money.* Harold Atler—careless! That would do irreparable harm to my reputation, Gentry, and I expect you to prevent it from happening. Now go to work!"

Ron downed the rest of his coffee, cool now, and crushed the Styrofoam cup. "I can find out who took it," he told the broker, "and I can get back what's left of the money, probably. I make no guarantees about what happens to your reputation."

Atler found that despicable of him. No guarantees! Couldn't this fool see what young Efter could do with this? They'd try to force him out of the firm. They'd *been* trying. He wasn't ready to retire; sixty wasn't old. His hair wasn't even all gray yet. He'd show them. He'd—

"Did you hear what I said, Mr. Atler?"

"What? Oh, yes. Now see here, Gentry. I don't expect guarantees, but I want the thief caught without the police knowing about it. *I* will deal with him when you find him."

Ron said that was fine with him. "Now," he said. "Who had keys to that office and desk?"

"What difference does that make?" Atler demanded. "If the room was broken into—"

"It wasn't," Ron said flatly.

"How do you know that?"

"It's my profession, Mr. Atler. If someone tried to pass off a carload of horse manure as strawberries and cream, you'd know wouldn't you? Well, me too. I know horse manure when I see it, I had a good teacher. Take my word for it, Mr. Atler, that money was taken by someone who had a key. Who had a key, Mr. Atler?"

Atler was silent. He looked like a man who was facing a particularly nasty fact.

Ron thought he'd help him out. "Look, you don't teach the course all by yourself, do you? You have a graduate assistant, right, to grade papers and things? I'll bet *he* has a key."

Atler looked stunned. "She," he said. "A young girl named Leslie Bickell. Of the Providence Seafood Bickells." This was quite the worst day of Harold Atler's life. He had rather liked Leslie.

"But she has a key?" Ron asked. He'd never heard of the Bickells.

"Yes," Atler said, "yes, she does."

"Where does she live?" Ron asked. Atler gave him her address, in the Albert-Runyon apartment complex, a residence for grad students north and west of the campus.

"Listen, Mr. Alter, is there any reason you'd want me to be gentle with this girl's feelings?"

Atler exploded at him. *"What is that meant to insinuate, Gentry?"*

Ron met his eye and stayed calm. "Just what the words say, Mr. Atler. Is there?"

"No, none at all."

"Then I think I'll head over there right away, see if she's home. I'll report to you later, Mr. Atler."

Ron left, already thinking over the case in retrospect. The easiest two hundred dollars he ever made, but a bore, a real bore.

FOUR

◆◆ ◆◆ ◆◆ ◆◆ ◆◆ ◆◆ ◆◆ ◆◆ ◆◆ ◆◆ ◆◆ ◆◆ ◆◆ ◆

THE WEDNESDAY MORNING SUNRISE HAD MEANT NOTH-ing to Inspector Fleisher. As far as he was concerned it was still Tuesday night. If he had to be away from his wife of thirty years, though he still loved her as much as ever, he almost wished it was because of an affair with another woman—at least then he could lie down.

He rubbed his bloodshot eyes and glared at the reporter across the desk from him. Tatham was as fresh as a hint of mint, for Christ sake. How does the bastard do it? Fleisher wondered wearily. He's been with me every minute since yesterday afternoon, why hasn't it gotten to *him?*

You fall apart when you let down, the inspector knew. When the wacko parade finally stopped, he had a chance to remember how exhausted he was.

He wanted Hog. Oh, how he wanted Hog. Actually, Fleisher was a tough, shrewd, dedicated cop, who wanted *every* criminal. But not as bad as he wanted *this* fruit-cake. It had gotten to be a personal thing . . .

The town was going nuts, and it was Hog's fault. Lit-tle boys were sneaking up on little girls and scaring them with pig masks, which some shitheel was selling down-town. Requests for gun permits were setting all-time records. Two nights ago, a young housewife heard a noise at the window, so she did what her husband had told her and grabbed the shotgun. She wound up blowing away that same husband who had lost his keys and was trying to get in without waking the wife. Things like that were go-ing to zoom, Fleisher knew.

Also, he, Fleisher, was going nuts, and that too was Hog's fault. If his thirty-three years on the force had taught him anything it had taught him the necessity of getting a jump on an investigation, to start gathering

31

facts before the victim's blood stopped dripping. If you could. With Hog, though, since he made each death look like an artistic little accident, the only way to accomplish that was to start in on *every* accidental death, visit *every* scene, and treat *every* victim as though Hog had been waiting just to kill him.

Which meant, among other things, tons of useless work for Joe Fleisher. Like tonight (to Fleisher it was still tonight). Three car wrecks. Two fires. Fifteen, count 'em, fifteen drug overdoses, and, to even it up, the beating, by person or persons unknown, of the prominent drug dealer Jorge Ruiz Vasquez, aka Juan Bizarro, aka the Pope of Dope. No fatalities (thank God), but Bizarro was a near thing. He was technically under arrest since he had a quantity of cocaine on him when he was found. They had him in the hospital, next door to the Elleger girl in what was becoming a de facto police ward.

It didn't make sense. Nothing made sense.

"It doesn't make sense," Fleisher said. He looked at Sergeant Shaughnessy and Tatham for agreement. They both agreed. Shaughnessy always agreed, which suited Fleisher fine, at least for now. He wasn't in the mood for an argument.

"Shaughnessy," Fleisher said, "call the lab and find out if they've been able to find out anything about the latest note." Fleisher pushed some limp strands of hair off his forehead as the sergeant set to work. Grasping at straws, he thought. The lab won't be able to tell me anything new.

As far as Fleisher was concerned the last useful thing the lab *had* been able to do was clear Tatham. In spite of everything, he had his suspicions of the reporter; that was why he decided to keep him around. Then the lab decided that there was no way Tatham could have gimmicked that sign and gotten back down to the highway without leaving traces on the hillside. No one had gone in either direction between the highway and the overpass, that much was certain.

Of course, now that he knew Tatham was okay, he could have thrown him out of the case, but what the hell, the guy had gotten the notes and probably would continue getting them, so why not have him handy? Besides, he was a good guy. Fleisher liked him.

Shaughnessy finished his call. "Looks like a washout, Inspector," he said, "though they haven't finished all the tests yet. They'll call us back."

The phone rang. Shaughnessy said, "That was fast," and picked it up. After a couple of seconds, he said, "Inspector, I think you better get this one."

The water that had refrozen during the night, after having melted yesterday, was melting again in the morning sun, making the roads as slick as though they'd been coated with silicon. A car sledded through the intersection of Vale Avenue and University Place, barely avoiding doing a rhinoplasty on the unmarked car. Shaughnessy, at the wheel, cursed with profound sincerity.

"Keep your mind on your driving, Mike," Fleisher warned him.

"Yes, sir," Shaughnessy agreed.

The inspector sat back again, mumbling to himself. He tried to decide whether that phone call had ruined his old day, or his new one. The question would have been academic if that skidding car had hit them, he realized. He was sorry he told Shaughnessy to be careful.

He didn't know he'd been mumbling so loud. Buell Tatham said, "Can I quote you on that, Inspector?"

Fleisher turned a bleary eye on him. The bastard had a kind of sick smile on his face. Things aren't so bad yet, Fleisher thought, I can at least *recognize* a smile.

"No, you can't quote me. I'm a career cop. I love my job. I love the mayor, and the city council, and I love tooth decay just as much. I love everybody, Tatham, in this whole goddamn city. Except the Hog. I don't love the Hog. That you can quote."

"Sorry, Inspector," the reporter's deep voice drawled. "Just trying to ease the tension a bit."

The inspector seemed not to have heard. "A *kid*, Tatham, a little *kid*. Eight years old, the patrolman said. A mess, he said. Not some high school girls trying to make it safe to get laid, no, that ain't enough. Now it's some little kid. *Damn!*"

The inspector's last word was so vehement and explosive that it startled Shaughnessy into not agreeing. "Excuse me, sir, but we don't know our boy is responsible for this. We haven't even seen the body yet."

Fleisher was so surprised at Shaughnessy's sudden independence that he cooled off immediately. "You're right, Mike, you're right. But I got a hunch, you know? You mark my words, Tatham, you'll get the note on this one before too long."

"Come on, Inspector—" Buell began, but Fleisher cut him off.

"You mark my words," he repeated. "In thirty years on the force I've learned this if I learned anything: crooks will lie to you; honest citizens will lie to you; the brass will lie to you; sometimes fellow cops will lie to you; your *wife* will lie to you. But hunches never lie. That don't mean they're always right, but if your gut is telling you something, it's probably for a good reason you can't think of at the moment."

Buell nodded wisely. He knew what the inspector meant. Reporters had hunches, too. "Well, Inspector, until and unless that note comes in, all you can do is the same things you've been doing. You've got to investigate, think, make out reports in triplicate . . ."

"Fourplicate," Fleisher corrected him. "The lady shrink gets one of everything now."

"Think Dr. Higgins can come up with anything?"

"Ha," Fleisher said simply. Over the years (many years) Fleisher had grown to respect, or at least tolerate, Dr. Jacob Issel, of the university hospital, who had been the consultant on those rare occasions the Sparta Police needed one. Usually, it was to talk to a suspect and give a horseback opinion on his sanity.

But this wasn't like that, not by a long shot, and worse than that, it wasn't even Issel. He had retired and moved to Israel. So now, the mayor's gopher sends in Issel's successor on the campus to consult, a lanky, spinsterish bimbo that couldn't be any older than Fleisher's own daughter. Well, carbon paper was relatively cheap, so Janet Higgins, Ph.D., could have all the reports she wanted, as long as she stayed out of the inspector's hair.

If they wanted to *help* him so badly, why didn't they find out where the hell the Wonder Wop was, and bring *him* in? Sure he came high, and he was, in Fleisher's humble opinion as a layman, a wacko. But this *case* was a wacko, and the record showed Benedetti got results. Who cared that part of his fee was two hours alone with a perpetrator after the arrest was made? The *criminals* hardly ever objected, they seemed to think it was an honor. They could have their lawyer present, too, if they wanted, so the DA was safe. So what was the administration's gripe? Benedetti had to *catch* the guy to collect, for crysake.

As Shaughnessy turned off the main road on to the sub-urban cul-de-sac the squeal had come from, Fleisher made himself a promise. If this *did* turn out to be a Hog murder, he would lock the goddamn city council in their chamber and pump tear gas through the air ducts until they came up with the dough to hire Benedetti. He didn't care where the money came from, Fleisher thought de-cisively—then, an afterthought: as long as they don't touch my pension money.

The house they were heading for looked to Buell as if it had been designed for hunchbacks. The huge snow drifts at curbside, and the accumulations on the lawn gave the house an out-of-proportion low-roofed look that added to the feeling of unease he had come to feel when-ever he was confronted with what might have been Hog's latest victim.

There was a young patrolman waiting for the inspector. He had his jacket unzipped and was taking long con-trolled breaths. Buell saw him take off his hat, then wipe his brow with the back of his hand. The reporter won-dered why. It was relatively warm, today, sure, but it was still only in the low thirties.

The inspector looked the young cop over intently. "Are you okay, Fiali?" he asked.

Officer Fiali gulped, but said, "I'm fine, Inspector."

Fleisher still looked suspicious, but he went on. "Okay, then, where is it."

"It's uh, in the driveway, sir." Fiali's complexion, which had been bright red, was now turning pale. "The boy's mother found the body, Jefferson is inside with her. She—she's pretty broken up. We've called her family doctor, managed to get that much out of her at least."

Buell and Shaughnessy reached for notebooks at the same time. Both started scribbling as the inspector said, "Who's the victim?"

Fiali referred to his own notebook. "Reade, R-E-A-D-E, Davy, I guess David, the mother was pretty incoherent. Age eight."

"Mother's name?"

"Joyce Reade, Mrs. John. They're divorced, he lives in California somewhere, according to what the doctor told us on the phone."

This will get them back together again, Buell thought bitterly, at least long enough to have the funeral.

"Okay, Fiali, let's see the body. Medical Examiner's men are on the way."

Fiali gulped again, said, "Yes, sir," and led them up the curving macadam drive. About halfway to the house Fleisher stopped to point to a foul-smelling patch of yellow-orange that lay steaming on the snow.

"What's this, Fiali?"

The patrolman reddened. "I did that, sir. I—I couldn't help it." Which, thought Buell, explained Fiali's appearance when they'd first seen him. He needed the air.

Fleisher told him not to worry about it.

Because of the curve of the driveway, and the high walls of snow on either side, Buell didn't see what lay in the driveway until he was quite close to it. Now he could understand why Fiali had had to vomit. Even though he'd been steeling himself, the sight forced Buell to fight down a gorge of his own.

He looked at it, said "Dear Lord!" closed his eyes and spun away. Shaughnessy whistled, long and low. The inspector kept clearing his throat.

Buell forced himself to turn back to the scene, to look at it intently, to burn the details in his memory. He felt obliged to do that much.

Someone, or something, had caught Davy Reade on his way out of the house to go to school. Sheets of paper with pale blue lines from his burst spiral-binder were floating on the surface of the blood-pool that surrounded the boy. The blood was bright red and had left its mark not only on the macadam, but as far as ten feet straight up the front of the garage door. The blood had probably spurted from an artery in the boy's neck when whatever had hit him had nearly severed his head from his body. Whatever had hit the boy had hit him close to the garage door; one foot was almost touching it, with the boy stretched out down the drive the other way.

"Watch that piece of ice, Shaughnessy," the inspector said, pointing. Buell took his eyes off the body long enough to see the sergeant standing guard over something that gleamed dull gray, a heavy piece of ice that had built up on the garage-roof overhang through the course of that wicked winter until it had become a weapon; a pronged guillotine blade, hard and heavy and deadly.

No one could ever prove this wasn't an accident, Buell knew. No one could ever prove that chunk of ice hadn't just grown so much since the first snow fell last fall that the first time it got above freezing for more than a few hours it had to break loose from its hold on the edge of the roof. But Buell also knew, with a horrible certainty, that a note signed "HOG" would be on his desk before too long, gloating over the death of Davy Reade. Fleisher's hunch would be right.

This death had the right elements to be a Hog case—the pitiful inoffensiveness of the victim, and the frightful way the victim had died.

Buell rubbed his eyes and turned away from the body. He felt weary. His Uncle Willy had warned him about keeping late hours. *"Your daddy tried to preach too much in too many places, boy,"* Buell could hear that deep voice say. *"He didn't get him enough sleep. That's why that accident happened. It was the Lord's way of gettin' him to take a rest."* Then Uncle Willy would try to hold his laughter until he got out of the room. Sometimes, he even made it, but Buell heard the laughter anyway; Uncle Willy had the loudest laugh in Knox County.

Good old Uncle Willy, Buell thought. May he fry in hell. Soon.

The morgue wagon turned up, and the reinforcements he'd had Shaughnessy call for, and the lab boys, and the victim's mother's doctor. So the inspector had his hands full.

The ME's boys and the lab boys knew what to do, so Fleisher ignored them. He sent the g.p. inside to minister to the hysterical mother, told his detectives to start a canvass of the neighborhood to try to find a witness who saw, heard, or smelled *something* (and fat chance of that, he told himself bitterly), then devoted his attention to Dr. Dmitri of the Medical Examiner's Office.

For all the emotion Dmitri showed, he could have been making a ham sandwich. All right, Fleisher didn't want him to burst into *tears* for crysake, but couldn't he at least look grim? Grim, Fleisher knew, was the proper expression for the investigation of a murder case.

Also, Dmitri clicked his tongue while he worked, a habit that had gotten on the inspector's nerves for years and years. What was he doing it for? To reassure his patients?

After a few minutes of listening to the clicking, Fleisher said, "Do they teach you to do that in medical school, or what?"

Dmitri looked up at him blandly. "Teach me to do what?" he said, with a click of his tongue.

The inspector waved it off. "What can you tell me?"

Dmitri shrugged. "In a horseback opinion, nothing that isn't obvious to anybody. The boy is dead. He died from exsanguination—loss of blood."

"I know what exsanguination means, for crysake."

"Good. Maybe I wasted my money going to medical school. Anyway, he lost that blood from his neck, and it's not a bad guess that frozen machete over there is what hit him. As for the agency that caused him to get hit with it, I can't say. All I know about ice is keeping cadavers fresh. Of course, I'll do the complete job back at the shop; you never know when you're going to be surprised in this business."

"Rush him through, will you, Dmitri? I got a hunch about this one. Maybe I can get a head start on the bastard."

Dmitri shrugged again. "I'll do my best. I've got bodies down there stacked up like cordwood—traffic fatalities, people frozen to death, electrocuted by space-heaters—this is a good winter for dying."

Fleisher caught Joyce Reade in those twilight-world moments when the tranquilizer her doctor had given her was just taking hold, with her mind still feverish and hysterical, but the slowing effect of the drug giving her the appearance of being in calm reasoned control.

So when the inspector walked in, she looked up at him and said, "Have you come to arrest me, Inspector?"

Her doctor told her to stop being foolish, and patted her hand. The inspector said, "Now, why would you think that, Mrs. Reade?" He said it very gently, like a favorite uncle.

"Because I killed Davy."

The doctor, a steely looking old gent who bore a remarkable resemblance to Lionel Barrymore, said, "Inspector, as you can see, Mrs. Reade is hardly in a condition to answer questions—"

His patient cut him off. "No, no, no," she said, as though explaining something to a child. "*I* usually take Davy to school, but this morning, he wanted to leave early, to mail a letter before the mail pickup . . ."

"Was the letter to his father?"

"Oh, no, Davy was joining the Superman Fan Club. He—he's very excited about it."

"How does that make you guilty, Mrs. Reade?"

"Because I should have gone with him. There's a crazy person in this town! But I wanted to sleep another half hour. *If I was with Davy this wouldn't have happened!*"

This, the inspector knew, was not logical, but this was not the time to tell her that Hog made kills in bunches as well. *If* this was a Hog murder at all, he almost forgot to remind himself.

Mrs. Reade was very close to a relapse. The doctor gave Fleisher a fierce look, and after Fleisher's nod, took Mrs. Reade into another room, to soothe her and put her to bed.

It took a long time. The inspector used the interval to talk to Officer Jefferson, ask Buell Tatham (who, as usual, had tagged along in the inspector's footsteps) to go easy on the confession stuff when he wrote about it, and look around the room.

It was a nice room, not tidy. There were a pair of boy's sneakers in the middle of the floor, and a boy's heavy woolen sweater lying on an ottoman, where it had been thrown, discarded by its owner, by virtue of the warmer weather. There were five comic books on the sofa, and a picture of a ruggedly handsome man on the mantlepiece in a crudely made frame with "DADDY" burned crookedly into the wood.

Fleisher sighed and turned to talk to the doctor, who

had returned to the room. From him, the inspector learned some more facts: the Reades had divorced amicably a year ago; Davy's father had moved to San Francisco, where he operated a successful motorcycle dealership; John Reade had the boy for six weeks in the summer and every other Christmas.

The doctor volunteered to notify the father of Davy's death, and Fleisher was just accepting, when officer Fiali burst into the house, saying, "Inspector, we just got a squeal. Body's just been found, less than ten minutes ago."

Fleisher turned his eyes to the sky and prayed for strength, found some, then looked at the officer and said, "Where now?"

"Down by the university," Fiali told him. "In the Albert-Runyon Apartments."

FIVE

❖❖ ❖❖ ❖❖ ❖❖ ❖❖ ❖❖ ❖❖ ❖❖ ❖❖ ❖❖ ❖❖ ❖

HERBIE HAD HAD A BAD NIGHT. NO SLEEP. HE JUST LAY in bed, watching his eyelids, and trying to stop his brain from racing like the Machine on an open-ended run. It was just no good. As far as Herbie Frank was concerned, no study, no sleep. Just as some people need warm milk before they turned in, Herbie needed the soothing effect of working La Place transforms and allotting core space for his latest program.

But last night was no good, that fight upstairs had ruined his concentration. And then there was that damn faucet. Herbie would just have to tell Leslie that people were trying to study, and if she and that townie boyfriend of hers. that Terry Wilbur jock, couldn't get along, they should do their fighting somewhere else. A fellow had to get some work done, you know? Computer engineering is no gut, not by a long shot.

He called her a whore, that was the thing that kept coming back to Herbie. It was about one o'clock, Herbie was trying to condense his pollution control program by a few steps, when he heard Wilbur's big feet make *clong!* noises on the metal steps, that echoed in the concrete cave that sheltered the entrances to four of the so-called garden apartments in the Albert-Runyon complex. You couldn't *help* but hear, with the thin walls, and crazy echo-chamber effects in the entranceway.

Herbie heard Terry Wilbur enter Leslie's apartment (without even *knocking*); just a short while later, he heard the big, muscle-bound idiot start yelling at poor Leslie. "Jesus Christ!" Wilbur had yelled, and "Leslie!" and then he started saying "Whore! Whore! Whore! Whore!" and that made Herbie mad.

That moron had no *right* to be calling Leslie names—he didn't even graduate high school, despite all his muscles,

41

and good looks, and height, whereas Leslie was a student in the grad school at the university. Okay, so it was a gut major like business, but Leslie was a beautiful girl. You couldn't expect good-looking people to be more than adequate intellectually; they didn't have the mental discipline.

It was enough that Leslie was so nice. That day in September, when he offered to help carry her stuff up to her apartment, she just said thank you, instead of wondering if he was strong enough to carry anything, the way other people did. She always said hello with such a nice smile; *she* didn't make fun of people just because they were smarter.

Herbie could talk to Leslie about things he never wanted to talk about with anybody else. She really brightened those dreary rides on the campus bus in the morning. Like one morning, the subject of acne came up, Herbie never knew how, and that afternoon, Leslie came and knocked on his door and gave him a bottle of some stuff a dermatologist had recommended for her, and he tried it, and it really helped him, some.

So Herbie considered himself Leslie Bickell's staunch friend, especially now, when anybody could see she hadn't been feeling well for more than a week, at least. He didn't like her casual dates walking in and calling her names, but he had to listen. He sat at his desk downstairs, making fists, and thinking, *if he doesn't stop, I'll—I'll—*

And abruptly, he did stop. Herbie let his breath go.

The next thing he heard was the water screaming in the plumbing as somebody upstairs turned on the water in the bathroom. To wash away tears, Herbie figured. Leslie had taken the whole thing and never said a word.

The poor kid, he thought sadly, the poor, poor kid. Her taste in men was so terrible. She let them do all kinds of terrible things to her. Herbie felt so sorry for poor Leslie, he snapped his pencil, crumpled up his useless notes, jumped in bed, and buried his head under the pillow.

But not to sleep. The water was still running upstairs, with a whining that cut to the very center of his brain. You'd think *they'd* hear it upstairs, but no. He thought of going upstairs and saying something about it, but he knew Leslie wouldn't want Herbie to see her in her humiliation. So he stayed where he was. And tossed. And turned.

Which brought him to this morning. The hell with it,

Herbie thought, I'm getting up. There was time to do some work before he had to be back at his terminal, punching away at the keyboard again.

Herbie got out of bed, rubbing his face. His fingers found no new blemishes, which he took as a good sign. He was still rubbing when he stepped over the threshhold of the bathroom door into half an inch of tepid standing water.

After the initial shock, it was easy to see what the problem was—the damn sink upstairs. It was *still* going. And something had clogged it up, and it had overflowed, and the water was seeping through the ceiling/floor into Herbie's apartment! This was too much. This was just too much, even for Leslie. It was the school that owned these apartments. Herbie was *damned* if he was going to get in trouble with the *university!*

Quickly, Herbie got into pants and shirt, shoes and socks. The idea of just slipping on his overcoat over his pajamas occurred to him, but he rejected the idea when he remembered that was how *perverts* ran around.

Herbie stepped outside his door, locked it behind him, walked up the stairs, walked over to Leslie's door; he hesitated for a second, then knocked.

No answer.

He knocked again, with the same result. He called Leslie's name, but there was still no answer.

Before he could even think about it, Herbie's hand shot for the doorknob and turned it. To his astonishment, the door wasn't locked. He eased it open and poked his head around the edge. No one was in the living room.

"Hello?" he piped in his reedy voice. "Leslie?"

He shrugged, to show himself he wasn't nervous about entering someone else's apartment unbidden. He stepped quietly inside and closed the door behind him. And then he saw her.

She had been in the corner, in the beanbag chair, hidden before by the open door. Leslie was sitting with her head thrown back, eyes closed, mouth wide open, in the expression of ecstasy, or relief. She wore blue jeans, but her torso was naked, and the sight of her nipples peeping through the strands of her long black hair aroused in Herbie some piercing emotion he was unequipped to recognize. The feeling lasted until he saw the hypodermic dangling by its silvery needle from the fair skin and pale blue vein on the inside of Leslie Bickell's left elbow.

Herbie didn't stay to notice any more details. He ran trembling from the apartment, down the stairs to his own door, threw it open, leapt inside, locked it behind him, picked up his telephone and called the police.

Inspector Fleisher noticed the details. Like the girl's Sparta University sweatshirt, lying in a heap on the floor where it had been tossed aside in the rush to get at the tender flesh of her arm.

She hadn't been on the stuff long enough to know that junkies don't like sweatshirts—too hard to roll up the sleeves. That was another detail the inspector noticed—this girl was a real rookie. So few hit marks on her arm, she hadn't even collapsed that first vein yet. She could still shoot up with her right hand. The veterans at the game were all switch hitters—they used up their left arm, then moved to the veins in their right arm, then to their thighs, between their toes, under their tongues, everywhere.

Another OD, the sixteenth, the first death. Goddammit, Fleisher thought, if it isn't the Hog, it's the Horse, for crysake.

If that pimple-faced runt downstairs had been coherent when he called headquarters, Fleisher wouldn't have even been there. He had enough on his mind without this.

Well, at least no one could say the police weren't right on the job. Fleisher left a skeleton crew at the Reade place, then led patrolmen, detectives, lab boys, ME's boys and the rest from there to here. In the car on the way over, Buell Tatham had remarked, "It's a regular caravan, Inspector," and Fleisher had answered sourly, "What it is is a goddamn circus parade, for crysake."

Well, he wasn't going to stay for the whole show. He was dead beat. For example, he couldn't even remember the name of the detective that walked up to him with an evidence report.

"This is what clogged up the sink," Detective Anonymous said. He was holding up what looked to the inspector exactly like an empty plastic evidence bag.

"What the hell is it? Air?" he asked grumpily.

"Oh, no sir, it's a plastic bag—"

"I know it's a plastic bag, for crysake! There's *supposed* to be evidence in it, Hawkins!" *That* was it. Hawkins. Funny how he couldn't remember it until he got pissed off.

"Yes, sir," Hawkins went on, unperturbed. "What I got here is a plastic bag *inside* a plastic bag. See, there was a plastic bag in the bathroom sink that covered over the hole, and made the sink overflow later on. There was a candle and spoon in there, too, so I think that bag had the dope in it. I think she loaded the needle in the bathroom."

Fleisher eyed him redly. "Know what happens if you keep thinking, Hawkins?"

Hawkins beamed at him. "Yes, sir. I make sergeant."

Fleisher laughed. The day was saved. "Good work, Hawkins. Keep it up. Now look, I'm taking Shaughnessy and getting out of here, maybe get some sleep. I want you to—"

"Inspector!" It was the voice of Officer Fiali calling from his post outside the door. "Some guy out here wants to see Leslie Bickell!"

The inspector also heard another voice saying, "Hey, watch it, huh? No need to get rough, I only want to *talk* to her. Have you busted her already? How'd you find out? Look—"

Fleisher recognized that voice. What the hell was *he* doing here? Well, only one way to find out.

"Send him in," he bellowed.

The newcomer was tall and handsome. He had blond hair and expressive gray eyes behind big square eyeglasses. He followed Fleisher's pointing finger with those eyes, and saw the corpse. "Jesus Christ," he said, then turned a puzzled face to the inspector.

"What's the matter, Gentry?" the inspector asked, gently.

SIX

❖❖ ❖❖ ❖❖ ❖❖ ❖❖ ❖❖ ❖❖ ❖❖ ❖❖ ❖❖ ❖❖ ❖❖ ❖❖◆

THE PROFESSOR ARRIVED ON THE 10:36 P.M. FLIGHT from New York on February 1; it was the last plane to arrive at Gwinnett Field before the blizzard hit and closed the place down for two and a half days. Ron was late to the airport—he hadn't had much notice. The old man could cover ground when he had to; he couldn't have gotten Ron's message at his hotel in Lesotho more than a day and a half ago; it had taken the better part of a day just to track him down.

True to his tradition of springing surprises, the professor hadn't bothered to respond to the telegram—he just showed up, and phoned Ron to come get him. Ron told him he'd be there in a half hour, but it took almost twice that long because of the constantly worsening snowfall.

At the wheel, fighting skids and slides, Ron had to laugh. He knew what Benedetti was up to, If the professor had answered the telegram, there would have been reporters at the airport. Cameras. Worse than that, politicians would be there, shaking his hand, putting their arms around his shoulders, making smiling statements about how they had "every confidence the proffesoree would bring the fiend to bay."

Fat chance. Ron Gentry knew he'd never live to see the day Niccolo Benedetti allowed himself to be used as a publicity gimmick by a politician.

The airport terminal was a huge green barn with a glass front. Ron parked the car, and dashed inside. When his glasses cleared, he scanned the big open floor in the center of the building for the distinctive shape of the professor. He didn't see it. Hoping the old man hadn't done anything impulsive, Ron went looking for him.

He found the professor (finally) in the cigar shop, exercising his Florentine charm on an attractive, plump

46

middle-aged lady behind the counter. Ron noted with an almost paternal pride that he already had her smiling and blushing. It was Gentry's considered opinion that the professor was a rake.

Ron knew that whatever made the old sinner such a scandalous success with the ladies had nothing to do with looks. If Niccolo Benedetti was not punctilious about his daily straight-razor shave, or about having his wardrobe of shapeless tweeds kept spotless, or about sporting a different bow tie each day of the week, he could easily pass as a derelict. His body was massive, but loose; under his baggy suit, he looked as though he were made of I-beams welded together at obtuse angles. His hands were large and knobby, and hung a long way from his sleeves. When he walked, he thrust his small head forward and glided, as though he were on tracks. Somehow, he not only got where he was going, but managed to leave the observer with the impression that he'd been graceful while he was getting there.

Ron had always thought the professor looked like an El Greco painting, with that small skull on that powerful body. It wasn't always easy to believe that skull housed one of the great brains of the century.

The professor's face was hard to describe. He was high of forehead, a little short on chin, with bright black eyes and a surprisingly delicate nose and mouth. "Weasel-faced" would be accurate, but misleading—the professor had the air of nobility, even royalty. He resembled an imperial weasel—an ermine, if you will.

The professor was too involved in small talk to see or hear Ron's approach. The young detective walked quietly up behind him and said, "Welcome back to Sparta, *Maestro*."

The professor beamed at him. "Ah, Ronald, *caro amico*, it is so good to see you again! I was speaking of you to Mrs. McElroy, here, who has shown me that the women of this city are fully as charming as I had remembered. The sixty-three minutes I waited for your arrival simply *flew*." Irony was Benedetti's best blade; somehow that precise pronunciation that is the last trace of an Italian accent only added to its effectiveness.

The time was long past, though, that the professor's irony could bother Ron Gentry. "I'm sorry, *Maestro*," he said. "You should have taken a taxi, or hired a limousine."

"Bah! And lose the pleasure of your conversation for the duration of the ride? You hurt me, Ronald, to think I would do such a thing." He shook his head in disappointment, but the black eyes twinkled. Ron knew the old skinflint just didn't want to pay for a cab. Professor Niccolo Benedetti was world renowned for (among other things) never paying for anything.

Right now he was holding up a box of $1.75 cigars. He handed them to Mrs. McElroy, and said, "So, *bellissima signora,* I shall take these, and I shall think of you with every puff." He turned to whisper to Ron. "Ronald, I must go now to answer the call of nature. You will take care of this purchase for me, will you not? And then we will leave."

He gave Mrs. McElroy a parting smile that had her squirming like a little girl. Just as the professor was about to step out of the shop, she blurted, "Don't forget you have my phone number!"

Ron looked at the box of cigars he had just paid for, and at the red and breathless widow behind the counter, shook his head and grinned. Two new triumphs for Benedetti, he thought. He does it every time.

Ron stowed the professor's things in the trunk, taking extra care with his painting kit. The professor painted to help him think, and, quite unconsciously, turned out canvases that hung in some quite well-known art museums, credited to half a dozen aliases.

Ron joined the professor in the car, brushed some fat wet snowflakes from his hair, and started the engine. He asked the professor if he had had a pleasant trip.

"Quite pleasant, indeed. This spectacular display of nature is the best part of all." He gazed out the window at the storm.

Ron grunted. Their respective arguments about the merits of snow, and Sparta snow in particular, had all been placed on the record before.

But Benedetti felt like talking, so he changed the subject. "You know, my friend," he said, "I have not always been a supporter of the so-called 'women's movement,' with their attempts to minimize the glorious differences between women and men, but I have recently learned of one accomplishment which I must applaud.

"On the flight from London to New York, I discovered that instead of silly, insipid little girls, many airline stewardesses are now beautiful, mature women. I met one on this trip (which, by the way, I instructed the airline to charge to you, not knowing which city official is responsible for my expenses)—as I say, I met a stewardess—or rather a 'flight attendant' as they prefer to be called—who introduced me to a charming custom called so quaintly, 'the layover.' It was a revelation . . ."

Ron was aware the story could go on for hours, so *he* changed the subject this time. "How much do you know about the case, *Maestro?*" He was careful to pronounce it the way the professor had taught him: not "MICE-tro," the way Americans usually said it, but "ma-AYSS-tro."

"The case," the professor said. He said it slowly, as though he were tasting it. "Quite interesting, from what I was able to gather from the New York City papers. I see a possibility that *real* evil is at work here. I am very happy you and our friend Inspector Fleisher have offered me a chance to deal with this 'Hog.' Very happy." The professor looked off into the storm again.

After a few seconds, he shook himself, and said, "But, *amico,* I remind myself that there is another case of which we first must speak."

"Another one?"

"Certainly, the case of cigars you were so kind as to purchase for me. I must reimburse you."

Ron would have told him not to mention it, especially in the face of the fact that a box of cigars one way or another didn't amount to much compared with the Lesotho–Nairobi, Nairobi–London, London–New York and New York–Sparta plane fares the professor had stuck him with, but he was so surprised by the unprecedented prospect of Niccolo Benedetti parting from *any* money, he forgot to say anything.

It was all Ron could do to keep his eyes on the road as the professor took out his wallet. Ron half expected a moth to fly out, and didn't want to miss it. Out of the corner of his eye, Ron saw the professor remove a wad of money. "Here you are, *amico,*" he said pleasantly.

Ron stuck out his hand, and actually felt money touch

50 *William L. DeAndrea*

it before the professor said, "I trust you will have no trouble negotiating these Moroccan *dirhams?*"

Ron laughed at his own gullibility. He should have known.

"No? Ah, well," the professor said, hastily folding the money and returning it to his wallet. "I travel so frequently I often forget what currency is valid where. Of course, I would not *dream* of putting you at an inconvenience. Let us leave it for another time then, agreed?"

"Agreed, agreed."

"Where am I staying, while I am here?" the professor wanted to know.

"Only you would show up at eleven o'clock on a Sunday night, unannounced, in the middle of a blizzard, and ask that. The city hasn't had a chance to arrange anything for you, obviously. Therefore, you will stay with me."

"Excellent, excellent. That will suit me perfectly, *amico.*"

Sure, Ron thought, you don't have to *tip* anybody.

Ron's house had been a hunting lodge, before the city had grown southward to meet it. It now sat with its back to the railroad tracks and its front to an alternate-route state highway, but the house was surrounded by magnificent old oaks and chestnuts that helped to keep the twentieth century at bay. Inside, it was all rich woods and ornate carvings; they helped Ron escape from the concrete that so often seemed to be closing in on him when he was at work.

As usual, the professor wanted to go right to work. Benedetti steadfastly refused to dally with women while engaged on a case—a rule, he said, that encouraged him to bring his cases to speedy conclusions. Ron had obtained copies of the police reports covering the events up to the time of the discovery of Leslie Bickell's body last Wednesday, and the professor sipped at a tumbler of red wine and read them, while Ron laid a fire in the big granite fireplace.

They finished about the same time. The professor said, "Inspector Fleisher's disappointment begins to shine through his reports." He wore a sly smile.

"You're reading about the Elleger girl's boyfriend, young Carlton Muntz? Bright young man."

"He is indeed," the professor said.

"Yes, indeed. Fleisher had him in for questioning after the first deaths, and young master Muntz not only tells him where to take it, but when Fleisher makes threatening noises about the diaphragm the girl had, Carlton has an answer for that, too."

"Yes, I read that with some interest," Benedetti said. "Muntz points out that since Miss Elleger is several months older than he, and has turned eighteen while he remains seventeen and a minor, the only one who can be charged with a crime is Miss Elleger, who (technically) is guilty of endangering the welfare of a minor. You know, Ronald, the younger generation is no more sexually active than yours or mine, but at least we had the good grace to act as though we were ashamed of it —even if it was only to comfort our parents.

"Incidentally, I find myself intrigued by the method in the first murder. I presume the police have retained that sign?" When Ron confirmed it, the professor said, "*Va bene*. I will see it." He took another sip of wine.

Ron said nothing as he made a note of Benedetti's request. Usually, Benedetti took a look at the scene of the crime, then left the physical evidence to the lab, saying, "There is nothing I can do with it."

"But none of *this*"—the professor tapped the reports —"explains what finally moved the city fathers to summon me—at the usual fee for murder?"

"Yes, *Maestro*, all the money, plus two hours with the culprit when and if."

Benedetti smiled benignly on him. "Excellent, *amico*. But next time, remember to allow for inflation. Now you must tell me the rest; if I plan to start my inquiries tomorrow, I must be up to date."

Ron agreed. "Well, *Maestro*," he began, "it's quite a story . . ."

The afternoon of Wednesday, January 28, had proceeded pretty much according to routine. A horde of detectives assigned to the Hog case, playing Fleisher's hunch, canvassed the neighborhood Davy Reade had died in and came up with negligible results. No one had seen anything

("Listen, officer, I'm lucky if my *eyes* are open that time of the morning, you know?") Veteran detectives, realizing that any person inflicting that slice to the child's neck would have been literally showered with blood, came pretty much to the opinion that the boy's death had indeed been an accident.

After the scene cleared at Leslie Bickell's apartment, the inspector left another detective team at work, and went home to his wife. Buell filed his story at the *Courant,* made one more brief stop downtown, then ran to the comforting arms of Diedre Chester. Ron Gentry, having had a good night's sleep, hung around. He was present when the city detectives turned up the interesting fact that Leslie Bickell's connection had been one George Ruiz Vasquez, aka Juan Bizarro, aka the Pope of Dope, currently in the hospital after having been beaten up for presumably selling some fifteen doses of too-potent heroin. Miss Bickell's remains were moved to a low priority on the autopsy list.

Meanwhile, attempts to find Terry Wilbur (who according to witness Herbert Frank was Miss Bickell's current boyfriend, and had been present and angry the night of her death) met with no success. Wilbur was a gardener, so he wasn't working during the winter months, and he was not at his apartment on Henry Street. The police would keep looking.

Meanwhile, Ron Gentry went to the office of his client, broker Harold Atler. He said, in part, ". . . so, Mr. Atler, after a quick once over, this is what it looks like. Your grad assistant has, within the last couple of months, started to mainline heroin. Now, normally—"

"But why?" Atler protested. "I don't understand!"

"I don't *understand* either, Mr. Atler. I don't think there's *ever* been a narcotics case that made sense. Some people have to punish themselves.

"Anyway, up until now, she'd had no problem with the money part of it—her father is a rich man, and he sent her a generous allowance.

"But this month, for whatever reason, her allowance was late. I checked her records; the money should have been here over a week ago. For all we know, it was on that mail truck that was buried in the avalanche in the Berkshires.

"So Leslie's money ran out; and her dope ran out. And dope is the basic reality of a junkie's life. She *had* to have it. Then you came along with the five thousand dollars in cash, and Leslie took you for Santa Claus. With that, she could take care of her immediate needs and have some as a cushion for a rainy day.

"She probably took the money and connected right away, then dashed home as fast as she could. Then a couple of unfortunate things happened: she left the stuff on or near the sink with the water still running, it fell in, and went away; and the dope itself was a little too strong—OD strong."

Atler was inestimably relieved. Five thousand dollars could be replaced; the evidence of his carelessness with the money was restricted to Gentry, the police, and himself, none of whom would be likely to spread it around. It *was* a shame, though, that the girl could be so foolish. She'd been a big help in teaching the course, too. Well he'd learned a lesson for his five thousand dollars. The green-suited vipers at the office would never have a chance like this again, you could be certain.

He sighed, and was philosophical. "It's ironic, eh, Gentry? Leslie took the money for a bad purpose, and it literally went down the drain." He shook his head.

"No, sir," Ron told him, "on the bathroom floor. The plastic bag clogged up the sink."

"Oh. Of course." Atler wasn't equipped to deal with interruptions. Ron's correction threw him, for a second.

Finally, he said, "You're, eh, sure this is what happened?"

Ron scratched his head. "Well, I'm not mathematically certain. Any digging I do now, though, will only tend to bring up what you want quiet—like if I talk to her supplier."

"Then you think I should stop here?"

"I think so. The money's gone beyond recovery. I won't bill you, I didn't do anything. Yes, I think it's a safe bet that this business won't go any farther."

When Buell Tatham got the next note, though, all bets were off.

It reached the *Courant* late in the morning of Thursday, January 29. As he had been instructed, Buell called the police as soon as he recognized the blue-ink block printing that none of the thousands (yes, *thousands*— some postmarked as far away as Miami) of bogus Hog notes had been able to duplicate for sheer nondescriptness.

Fleisher came running, trailing a fingerprint man in his wake. No fingerprints on the envelope but Buell's, not even the mailman's—they all wore gloves in weather like this. No fingerprints on the letter itself at all. The usually self-effacing Sergeant Shaughnessy felt himself moved to comment. "Shit," he said.

But the message itself was different. Hog had outdone himself. He had written:

TATHAM—

TELL THE POLICE I GOT TWO IN ONE DAY THIS TIME, THOUGH I COUNT IT AS ONE AND A HALF. THE GIRL STARTED DYING THE FIRST TIME SHE PUT A NEEDLE IN HER ARM. WHERE DID THE COLLEGE SWEATSHIRT LAND? I DIDN'T NOTICE WHEN SHE THREW IT AWAY. THE LITTLE BOY TOLD ME HE WANTED TO BE LIKE SUPERMAN. TOO BAD HE WASN'T INVULNERABLE, ISN'T IT? MAYBE I'LL GO FOR THREE NEXT TIME. TILL THEN.

—HOG

After he read that note, Fleisher was furious. For the first time in thirty years, he wished he was back on traffic detail so he could hand out tickets and make the whole city as miserable as he was.

"All *right!*" he said at last. "All right. Back to square one. Tails on everybody—Muntz, the pimple-faced kid, Gentry, everybody. And tell the mayor I'm coming to see him."

The mayor, at the moment, was in conference. The mayor was young, handsome, had a pretty wife, a cute kid, and had never been caught doing it to his secretary, the dog, *or* the public. He liked being mayor, but he would have liked to be a senator even more.

So the mayor was in conference with Harry Lanagan, who could deliver a large chunk of downstate delegates. The mayor had to see him now. It wasn't that the mayor wasn't conscientious—he wanted to catch Hog with all his heart and soul—the voters remember things like that. But Hog would still be there this afternoon, and Lanagan was going back to New York, and from there on a Sentimental Journey to the Auld Sod, which he had last seen in 1911, when he was two years old. He could see Fleisher later.

The mayor's secretary had the looks and personality of a yeast cake. The mayor hired her so he wouldn't be tempted. But she was competent, and fiercely loyal. So, when she relayed her boss's instructions to the inspector, and he gave her a poisonous look, and got black in the face with rage, she was ready to give her all in a shouting match.

But when the inspector bit his tongue to get himself under control, then said calmly, "Very well, I'll wait," she didn't know what to do. She certainly couldn't bodily remove two big policemen and a fair-sized reporter. She couldn't call the police. She wasn't about to interrupt the conference that could make her the secretary to a United States senator. So she let them wait.

Fleisher, Shaughnessy and Tatham used the time to discuss the case.

"You know something," Shaughnessy said, "this time is the first time the note came the next day. Ain't that right?"

"Hey," Buell said. "That is something."

"What the hell are you talking about?" the inspector groused. "The first two times, Hog struck in the late afternoon, evening, after the pickups at the dropboxes had all been made. This time, he was finished with both murders by eight o'clock in the morning."

Shaughnessy went back to his policy of effacing himself. There was silence in the mayor's anteroom. It lasted until Dr. Dmitri walked in.

Dmitri had been freed from a very busy morning down at the morgue by the urgency of what he had to tell the inspector. He was in a good mood that clashed badly with the gloom of everybody else. Dmitri didn't care. He'd rather face a dozen angry Fleishers than cut into one more corpse before lunch.

"They told me you'd be here," he said to the inspector.

"What's on your mind, Dmitri?"

"I just finished the post-mortem on the Bickell girl."

"Yeah. Can't possibly be proved it wasn't an accidental overdose, right?"

"Wrong. Apparently, the girl broke some glass about an hour before she died."

"We know that."

"Yeah. I found tiny slivers embedded in the skin of her right hand. But that's not all she broke."

"What do you mean?"

"When she broke that glass, she gave herself three separate hairline fractures in the bones of her hand. Must have hurt like hell."

Fleisher caught on, and was suddenly excited. "So from the needle being in the veins of her left arm, we know—"

"We know that unless she's a contortionist with talented toes, it's extremely unlikely Leslie Bickell administered her own shot. Impossible, in fact. We've got a provable homicide for you, now."

"About *time,* for crysake," Fleisher said. "Now we can get a little *action.*" He started stalking toward the door of the mayor's office, paused to brush the horrified secretary aside, and burst in.

"That's where he called me from," Ron told the professor. "The mayor's office. Of course, the mayor couldn't chew Fleisher out with the downstate money man there, so Fleisher had him. And us."

The professor grinned. "And us indeed. You are happy to be in on the case at last, are you not?"

"Of course, *Maestro.*" .

"There is no 'of course' about it. Of all my pupils, you are the only one who has not taken what he has learned and turned it to his own profit at the expense of his fellow beings. You are an interesting and complicated man, Ronald."

"I'm a struggling private eye," Ron said. "Nothing special."

"A struggling private eye who could grab wealth or power in politics or commerce! You must either be complicated, or a fool, and you are no fool, *amico.* Niccolo Benedetti does not have truck with fools.

"*Ma, va bene,* we have business to discuss. Tomorrow, I wish first to see the physical evidence. They have it all?"

Ron nodded. "They even have the ice in a deep freeze."

"Good. I will also begin seeing witnesses. I am especially eager to see this Terry Wilbur."

"As soon as Fleisher finds out, *Maestro*," Ron promised.

"Of course. The police have consulted an alienist in this case?"

"A Dr. Higgins."

"Very well, tomorrow I will also confer with him."

"Her," Ron corrected.

Benedetti showed as much surprise at this as he ever did at anything. "So even our friend the inspector must bow before the might of the political women, eh?" He stroked his chin as though he had a beard there. "Is she competent?"

"She's enthusiastic," Ron said, "and Fleisher doesn't make it easy. Take his opinion of shrinks, divide by his opinion of working women, and that's his opinion of a woman shrink. She's young, and acts cool, but I think she feels the pressure. She keeps dropping things when I see her in the library."

The professor smiled. "You amaze me, Ronald. I don't remember you as one who spends time with books when there is a killer to be caught."

"I've been chasing him through the library, *Maestro*. I took one little piece of the picture the cops haven't had time for, that's all."

The professor lit up one of the expensive cigars from the airport, holding the flame from the wooden match away from the tip and puffing gently until it glowed redly through the aromatic smoke. "Have you found anything?"

"So far, only some coincidences. But they make for interesting speculation. After I hear from my correspondent, it may be even more interesting."

Benedetti leaned back in his chair, with the cigar pointing straight up in the air, like a signal beacon. It was his favorite position for receiving reports. When he had attained complete comfort, he said, "You may begin, Ronald," as he listened to his favorite pupil recite.

SEVEN

◆◆ ◆◆ ◆◆ ◆◆ ◆◆ ◆◆ ◆◆ ◆◆ ◆◆ ◆◆ ◆◆ ◆◆ ◆

IF YOU ASKED JANET HIGGINS WHY A PERSON LIKE SHE WAS, who had gained some acclaim as a musical child prodigy, should toss that aside to become a psychologist, she could give you lots of reasons, like service to humanity, and the chance to do something really important. The *real* reason was a closely guarded secret—she had become a psychologist to avoid the humiliation of having to consult one.

When Dr. Higgins analyzed herself, as she frequently did (every time she was nervous, for example), she saw herself as a classic inferiority complex, for which she compensated by tremendous drive to prove herself, first in music, then in her work. She excelled at both.

But Janet was faking it (she told herself)—somehow or other, she kept fooling them all. In the back of her mind was the constant fear that someday they would find out what she was—a woman in her late twenties, rapidly approaching spinsterhood (if not there already), pinetree tall, broad of shoulder and shallow of chest; with a bump on her nose, and hair the precise color of mouse fur; looking at the world with brown eyes that had needed bifocals since childhood; and faking it.

Running up the steps of the Sparta Public Safety Building, Janet tripped and fell, sprawling, scattering her notes to the wind. *Good work, Janet!* she hissed at herself as she scrambled after the papers. Her coordination vanished at times like this—klutziness was the partner of self-analysis in her nervousness.

And today promised to hit new heights—she had to expound her theories on the case to Professor Niccolo Benedetti, recognized as the world's top authority on cases like this. What could Benedetti possibly learn from her? Could he *suspect* her? Janet told herself savagely to cut it out. Her conduct was not becoming to a trained scientist. She'd allow herself the inferiority neurosis, but she drew the line at paranoia.

Still, she couldn't help speculating about the behavior of Benedetti's assistant, Gentry his name was. Ever since the professor had been called in, this Gentry had been haunting the library, where Janet did most of her work. He *said* he was researching a theory of his own, but if that was true, why did she always catch him *looking* at her? It certainly wasn't for her beauty.

Janet would have never believed it, but at that moment, in the corridor of the PSB that lead from the evidence room to Inspector Fleisher's office, Ron Gentry wore a small smile of pleasure at the thought of seeing Dr. Janet Higgins again. The smile had come, unbidden, as soon as Benedetti had stopped cooing over the evidence—the twisted splintered sign; the beer can; the ragged but deadly edge of the ice; and the hypodermic needle. Ron had no time to think of anything but the case, because the old man showed all the signs of actually *learning* something and Ron wracked his brain trying to figure what it might be.

After that, though, his mind was free to choose its own subject, and it chose Janet. And it *was* for her beauty. Where Janet saw a bumpy nose and weak eyes, Ron saw an irresistible wistful smile. Where she lamented the nondescript color of her hair, he saw how thick and glossy it was. Where she despaired to see her boyish torso and extreme height, he gloried in the sight of broad, womanly hips and spectacularly long, shapely legs.

Another thing Ron liked about her was that he seemed to be the only one who realized how good-looking she really was. It made him feel like a great detective, and it made him feel superior to all the other clods who hadn't noticed. He'd have to make sure that the end of the case didn't mean—

Benedetti was holding open the door to Fleisher's office. "Coming in, Ronald? Or do you plan to daydream in the hall all day?"

Buell looked out the window as the snowflakes sped by on their way to becoming the nineteeth inch of accumulation. It wasn't that he enjoyed the sight of the

snow so much; it was just that Fleisher's face was too
painful to contemplate. Buell had been the last to arrive,
because Diedre, a relative newcomer to Sparta, had
used the storm to play "Baby, it's cold outside," and had
won. He smiled at the memory.

A scowl from Fleisher brought his full attention back
to the matter at hand. The inspector was summing up the
lines of investigation the police had been following.

"Suspects. Every case brings a new load of suspects.
So far, we can't tie anybody we've come across with
any of the other incidents. And there isn't anybody
that doesn't have an ironclad alibi for at least one of the
crimes."

"Including Terry Wilbur?" Ron Gentry asked him.

"Including him. He was at the YMCA when that car
crashed and killed the two girls. Which isn't to say we
don't want to talk to him, bad.

"Witnesses? The only things resembling witnesses we
have are Buell, here, the Elleger girl, and this Herbert
Frank. We all know what Buell saw; Barbara Elleger
remembers the noise when the sign crashed into the
car, period; and all the Frank kid can do is tell us Wilbur
is our boy."

"He was there, Inspector," Benedetti reminded him.

Buell was surprised at the almost deferential respect
the inspector had for Benedetti. Fleisher's expression
changed from irritated to quizzical as he said, "Are you
saying it might be Wilbur after all, Professor?"

"I haven't gone that far *yet,*" the old man said. "But
I would consider inadequate any explanation of this
case that cannot account for the behavior and disappearance of Terry Wilbur. I can only echo Mr. Frank,
and say *find Wilbur.*"

"Well, we'll keep doing all we can." Fleisher picked
up his dissertation. "Now about the victims. We can't
find *anything* they have in common. In age, they run
from eight to teenage, to early twenties, to old age.
Socially, the Bickell girl was from a rich family; the others
are middle class. Religion, Ling was a Lutheran,
Salinski Roman Catholic, Watson an all-over Baptist,
and Bickell, Episcopal. The Reades don't go to church.
Interests, history, accomplishments, hobbies, jobs? Noth-

ing. Nothing sixteen good detectives can turn up, any-way."

At the same moment Buell said, "Are you sure, In-spector?" Benedetti said, "No?" Fleisher, naturally, jumped on the professor's comment. Buell was just as happy. For a lot of reasons, he didn't want to be the one to make any suggestions to the hard-working in-spector.

"What is it, Professor? Have you spotted something?"

"*I* haven't," he said, "but my young colleague has. A rather intriguing discovery. It concerns more than the victims, too."

The inspector demanded an immediate briefing from the blond detective, and Buell had his pencil poised, ready to take down the story for page one, but Gentry couldn't be persuaded to talk.

"I want to check it out first," he kept insisting. "It's weird, and it probably doesn't make much difference, anyway."

Still, Fleisher kept urging Gentry to spill it, until the professor rescued him by asking Fleisher to go on, which he did, although reluctantly.

"Well, it seems to me there are three possibilities. One: Hog has a grudge against each victim seperately, a different reason for each."

"He must have a wide circle of acquaintance," mur-mured the professor.

"Exactly," Fleisher said grimly. "And besides, what could he have against an eight-year-old kid, for crysake? So that one seems to be out. Two: Hog hates all his victims together, all for the same reason. Even more far out. These victims never *did* anything together.

"So that leaves just one possibility: Hog has nothing against his victims, outside of the fact they belong to the human race. So, smart as he may be (and believe me, anybody who can fake two accidents perfectly and two more almost perfectly is *smart*), he has to be a nut. Dr. Higgins, I guess that's your department?"

"Yes," the professor said. "I am eager to hear your evaluation of the case."

Janet spilled her notes as she started to stand up, and felt her face and neck go red hot. As a child, the words she came to fear most were, *Play something for us, Janet;*

and now here she was, giving a recital in a matter of life and death.

Well, she'd learned the only way to get it over with was to go ahead and do it.

"This case," she began in a voice so clear and confident that she surprised herself hearing it, "differs in some ways from similar cases of the past, and I have to admit I'm not completely sure what those differences mean. But I think I can give some idea of the kind of person we're looking for.

"The one thing I think we can be sure of is that Hog is a man."

The professor clapped his hands softly. *"Brava!"* he said, "an excellent start; we agree already. I have known woman murderers, of course—even woman mass-murderers. But I have never known of one who felt the need to show bravado, to boast of her crimes. Again, *brava."*

Janet thanked the professor warmly. She felt that Benedetti couldn't be faked out—therefore his praise meant she had genuinely accomplished something, though she knew the idea was pretty obvious.

"Physically," she went on, "the killer is probably less than normal height. DeSalvo, Manson—and Hitler, Napoleon, and Franco, for that matter—all were small men. In certain cases it can reinforce feelings of inadequacy."

"Inadequate?" Fleisher asked. "You say Hog feels inadequate?"

With her initial nervousness past, Janet had become too involved in her subject to catch nuances like the tiny breath of sarcasm in Fleisher's voice. She went on.

"Yes, inadequacy, inferiority. It's very often the pattern of the lives of men who become mass murderers. Hog is probably in his mid to late twenties, or older, the time a man comes face to face with the fact that he's not a child any more.

"Hog is probably single," she said. "Either he's *never* had a successful relationship with a woman, or he's too easily successful, and holds them in contempt. If he's employed, he probably does menial work; work he considers beneath him. He probably has no close friends— his co-workers probably don't think much about him one way or the other.

"He's from a broken home, or a bad one. His father may have beaten his mother in his presence, or beaten him. He's either been forced to participate in, or forced to watch some sex act he would consider humiliating.

"So, to sum up," she said as she polished her glasses, "past cases show that Hog is someone who is a male, between, say, twenty-five and forty, undersized, from a broken home; a loner, doing work he considers beneath him, unsatisfied sexually, and carrying a massive inferiority complex."

Benedetti cleared his throat. "Ronald," he said, "do we know anyone who fits that description?"

Buell answered him in a tone that almost said he was sorry to interrupt. "Well," he drawled, "I can't say about his sex life, but physically, that boy Herbert Frank seems to fit the description. And he certainly seems to have it in for this Terry Wilbur, who all the neighbors say is so handsome and charming."

"You wanna know who feels inferior, for crysake?" Fleisher growled. "Me, I feel inferior."

Everybody laughed, more or less good naturedly, except the professor. He took a cigar from a case that had been a present from one of this former students, lit up, and said around puffs, "That makes at least two of us, Inspector. This Hog has awakened in me a healthy respect."

"Why?" Buell wanted to know.

Benedetti made a sign for the inspector to explain.

"Well," Fleisher said, "with all respect to Dr. Higgins, here," and now there was more than a breath of sarcasm in his voice, "Hog is something new. Something else.

"I won't even *worry* about what he looks like, or why he's killing these people; let's just take a look at what we know he's *done*.

"He scouted this girl Barbara Elleger, maybe all three of them, right down to what they had in their purses, for crysake. He had to know beforehand; he never had a chance to look afterward. He knows about when they're going to be under the construction work, and he cuts the sign loose just in time to crash on the car. And he did it *without* leaving a readable track.

"Two. He makes the acquaintance of old man Watson, gets to know him well enough that he gets to see the upstairs, too. One time, with Watson coming down ahead of him, Hog gives him a little push, and that's that. And nobody ever sees him. Of course, that's a neighborhood where minding your own business is the thing to do, but still.

"Three. He gets into Leslie Bickell's apartment, some-how—"

Buell Tatham interrupted him. "Of course, if it *is* this Terry Wilbur, there's no mystery about how he got in."

"Yeah," Fleisher conceded, "but there's still his alibi for the first murder."

"He *did* disappear," Ron chimed in, strictly in the interests of fairness. "And don't forget what we found in his room."

Janet was puzzled. "What did you find in Wilbur's room."

"Oh, I forgot," Ron said, "the police didn't think it was important. I'm going to take the professor out there this afternoon for a look, care to come along?"

"I—I'd be glad to, if the professor doesn't mind."

"It will be my pleasure," Benedetti said. The professor never spoke loud, but there was something about him that made people feel what he had to say was more important than what they had to say. With five words, he had stopped the conversation from running away with itself. Now he said, "I don't believe the inspector was finished."

Fleisher grunted. "Thanks, Professor. Now, about Wilbur. He doesn't feel right to me as Hog. I can't see him killing three people just to kill his girl friend, then kill an innocent kid, and then disappear."

"Nevertheless, he did disappear," the professor said, "and he must be found."

"I know, I know," Fleisher said. He was starting to get irritated. "Anyway, to pick up where I was before, he gets into Leslie Bickell's apartment, gets her half naked, loads up that needle, and lets her have it; and it looks like she cooperated the whole way.

"Now that's not so hard to believe, if you know junkies. Her right hand was out of commission, that vein in her left arm was the only one she'd found yet, Hog must have looked like a fairy godmother to her. That all adds up.

"But what Hog got away with next is a goddamn *miracle* for crysake! Leslie Bickell's body isn't even cold yet, when Hog spots the Reade kid heading to school early, because he wanted to mail a letter to the Superman fan club. Then, *in broad daylight*, he gets behind the kid in his own driveway, breaks off that piece of ice, lets him have it, and gets away. *In broad daylight*. Even though Dmitri says he had to be covered, literally soaked, with blood.

"So, Dr. Higgins," Fleisher concluded with scornful deference, "if Hog feels inferior, I sure would like to meet the person he feels inferior to. In my book, he isn't inferior to anybody. He's only nuts."

Janet was hurt. She had worked hard on that profile of Hog. If Fleisher thought she was wrong he could just say so. He didn't have to *humiliate* her like that. She was about to tell him so, in no uncertain terms, but the professor spoke first.

"Well spoken, Inspector Fleisher," he said. "You have outlined the problem admirably. But you haven't mentioned the most remarkable thing Hog has done."

"What's that, Professor?" It was everybody's question; Buell was the one who got the words out first.

Benedetti, Ron saw, was smiling his Mona Lisa smile. He only did that when he was pleased. The professor was also scratching the back of his right hand, slowly, with the fingers of his left. Ron had always found that a feline gesture, like what a cat does before he pounces.

"Well, Mr. Tatham," the professor said, "at least once, to my knowledge, Hog has taken a souvenir away from the scene of his crime."

EIGHT

◆◆ ◆◆ ◆◆ ◆◆ ◆◆ ◆◆ ◆◆ ◆◆ ◆◆ ◆◆ ◆◆

FLEISHER WAS SPUTTERING. HE WAS TRYING TO PROMISE dire consequences to whichever of his men had muffed finding that lead, but he couldn't get it out past the rage that was choking him.

Ron Gentry was none too pleased with himself, either. He *knew* the old boy had spotted something, he'd known it earlier; and while he didn't claim to be a Benedetti, with that much to go on, he should have spotted it. Damn. He was slipping.

Janet Higgins was aware she was a mildly split personality. When spindly, awkward Janet couldn't cope; competent, professional Dr. Higgins could jump in and bail her out. That's what had just happened, but the fight she was ready for didn't materialize. So it was with a much more detached eye than usual that Janet was able to look at the reactions to Professor Benedetti's bombshell.

She noted Fleisher's impotent rage with a kind of good-natured spite; and sympathized with Ron Gentry's self-directed irritation. Buell Tatham's reaction she noted with a mild scientific surprise; she hadn't expected him to be such a sensitive individual. He looked almost sick. She soon found out, though, that Tatham was as much sensitive as well read.

He asked her, "That fits the pattern, doesn't it, Doctor? Didn't Jack the Ripper take away one of his victim's breasts?" He pulled himself together, and turned to the inspector. "We've got to find him, Fleisher, this is going too far!"

Benedetti chuckled softly. "Please relax your southern sensibilities, Mr. Tatham. I'm not speaking of that kind of souvenir. Hog has been content to kill his victims, however horribly. At least to date.

"No, what Hog took away inspires no horror or disgust

—at least not in me, though I am certainly jaded—but only curiosity. Ronald," and Janet was surprised at how fast the young man snapped to attention, "show the inspector and the others those photographs we obtained from the laboratory technicians."

Ron started leafing through a folder. "Which ones, sir?"

The professor's grin widened. "You can't say?" He clicked his tongue. "Ah, *amico*, you must keep your mind on your work, eh?" He made a noise that might have been a chuckle.

Janet saw a little-boy look of stubborn determination appear on the young detective's face. He was going through the photographs more slowly now, not exactly studying them, but giving each a thorough look before passing on to the next one. She saw his eyes light up as he removed a photo from the folder. "This one," he said. "And this, and . . . this. Right?"

Benedetti beamed. "Excellent, Ronald, I knew you would see it. Please, pass them around."

When they came to her, the pictures did less than nothing for her. They showed the clamps that had once held the wooden sign to the unfinished overpass on the state highway. She'd seen them before; one showed the distressed, twisted and bent shape of the clamp that had given way from the weight of the swinging, dangling sign. The second showed the one that had been tampered with —the incomplete arch, the two legs ending in the marks of Hog's bolt cutter. The third photograph was a split-composite of both.

After everyone had a look, the professor said, "Well?" His response was shrugs and head-shakes and bewildered looks. "It must be explained, eh? Very well. Explain it, Ronald."

"Thanks, *Maestro*," he began, and Janet was surprised to find that Dr. Higgins was gone, and with her all sense of detachment and restraint. She leaned forward in expectation, breathlessly eager to hear the great deductions.

My God, Ron thought as he began his explanation, I'm reacting like a patted puppy. He told himself he would have seen it on his own, in time.

He held up the first photograph. "This is the clamp that held the upper right-hand corner of the sign as Buell saw it. You can see by the shape it's in that it broke because of the stress put on it when it had to support the entire, swinging weight of the sign. It did swing, right, Buell?"

The reporter nodded. "One more swing, and they would have been by it and safe. Hog has the devil's luck."

"Indeed," said Benedetti, taking a contented puff on his cigar. "He does indeed."

Ron went on, holding up the second photograph. "Now this one," he said, "has been cut by a bolt cutter—it's obvious from the edges. As we've all read in the lab reports, it would have been no surprise if the clamp had *snapped* naturally. It was only supposed to be on overnight, and instead had to last through an extremely cold and windy winter.

"But if it snapped, the cross section would be round and rough, not tapered and smooth the way it is."

Sergeant Shaughnessy spoke for the first time all afternoon. He said, "Yeah?"

"A bolt cutter makes that kind of mark because of the way it works," Ron said. A look from the corner of his eye at the professor told him he was doing okay. "It works by *wedging* a notch into the metal that's being cut, directing the force into a wider and wider channel in the metal, until it breaks apart."

From the look on her face, Ron could tell Janet was having some trouble understanding him. He tried to explain. "It's like . . . like . . ."

"Biting a Tootsie Roll in half," Fleisher said, helpfully.

Benedetti chuckled. *"Buonissimo,* Inspector. A perfect example."

Fleisher looked a little sheepish. "That's how the lab boys explained it to me."

"It's a perfect example," Ron said. "But think about it, now. If using a bolt cutter is going to have *any* effect on the total length of the metal being cut, it can only make it *longer.* You're not wearing away the metal, like you do when you use a hacksaw; you're just pinching it together in the middle until it gives.

"So, *these two pieces of the cut clamp should equal at least the length of the two pieces of the clamp that snapped*. And as these pictures plainly show, they don't."

Ron wasn't supposed to hear Fleisher's whispered "I'll be a son-of-a-bitch," but he did.

"Knowing the professor," he concluded, "I'm sure he can prove what I've just said with actual measurements. Right, *Maestro?*"

"Of course, *amico*. The cut clamp is missing a fraction less than three quarters of an inch . . . about sixteen millimeters. That means, of course, that *two* distinct cuts were made, cutting it into *three* pieces. Your men performed a thorough search at the scene, did they not, Inspector?"

"Hell, us and the state troopers both, for crysake. Maybe I should retire. Two weeks we've had that thing. *I* don't notice it. The *lab* doesn't notice it. *Nobody* notices it!"

"Don't feel bad, Inspector," the professor told him. "If the police noticed everything, Niccolo Benedetti would be a pauper.

"So, while I grant the possibility the piece of metal was overlooked and is buried under the snow, I think it much more likely the one who cut this clamp took it away with him. The question is why. Dr. Higgins?"

"Well," Janet said, "it doesn't fit the pattern. Usually the serial murderer will take something personal away, like a lipstick, or an article of clothing. Or, as Mr. Tatham pointed out, a piece of the victim's body."

"Well, I'd like to know what the professor thinks," Buell said. "Why would Hog take a worthless hunk of metal for a souvenir?"

"As a matter of fact, Mr. Tatham, I am toying with a particularly intriguing idea . . ." his voice trailed off, and Ron saw the professor get that dreamy look he got in his eyes when he contemplated a truly artistic piece of nastiness. Finally, he sighed and said, "But no, it has no consistency with the rest of the facts. It was a foolish notion, and I am sorry I even mentioned it."

The professor rose, and put on his gloves and hat. "Now, Inspector," he said, "if you will please give Ronald the necessary credentials, he and I and Dr. Higgins, if she still cares to accompany us, will spend the rest of the afternoon braving the elements to interrogate witnesses. *Buon pomeriggio.*"

They were the only ones crazy enough to try to drive through the snow, so they had the streets to themselves. As long as Ron kept it at a slow and steady pace, he could keep the nose of the car pointed forward. The professor was largely unconcerned with Ron's driving problems. He was in the back seat, leaning back with his eyes closed. If it weren't for an occasional brightening of the glow at the end of his cigar, you would have thought he was asleep.

"Where are we going first?" Janet wanted to know.

"Wilbur's room. It's the farthest away. We can hit the others on the way back—I don't think we have to worry about their being out." He checked his watch. "Mind if I put on the radio? It's time for the news."

"No, go ahead."

Ron tuned in. The news was grim. The city was socked in by the blizzard—in fact, the whole Northeast was, from Cleveland east to the Atlantic; from Baltimore north to Hudson Bay. Hundreds of people were snowed in or stranded; roofs had collapsed. Intercity transportation had ceased to exist. That was the lead story.

The second story was just as tragic, only on a smaller scale. A pig farmer from north of Sparta had beaten his brother-in-law to death at a family gathering; both had been drinking. The brother-in-law had been taunting the farmer with the joking accusation that he had committed the so-called Hog murders to boost business. It was a fact that pork sales in the Sparta area were running ten to twenty percent higher than usual since the first—

They heard Benedetti's heavy sigh from the back seat. "It is an ill wind indeed," he said. "Please shut that off, Ronald. I am certain it can tell us nothing." He sank back into silence when the radio clicked off.

Ron shook his head. "You must be the envy of your profession from coast to coast, Janet," he said. "There's enough hysteria in this case to make work for six psychologists."

Her laugh was half rueful agreement with Ron's remark and half pleasure because he called her Janet. "There's a book in here for somebody," she said. "Every psychologist has to write a book."

"I didn't know that. Is it part of the course?"

"They teach it by example. Publish or perish."

"Still, huh?" He wrenched the wheel suddenly to pull the car out of a skid. "Watch it," he told the car. "Where are you from originally?" he asked Janet.

"Little Rock. I thought I'd lost my accent."

"I don't think you have an accent. Go to college there?"

"Uh huh, University of Arkansas, then I took my master's and Ph.D. at Sparta. Why do you ask?"

He smiled at her. "Habit. I'm a detective, remember. But there's something I forgot to ask you in the conference.

"Is it possible that Hog isn't aware he's committing these crimes? That he blacks out, or has another personality?"

"Psychic fugues, is the professional term."

"Well?"

"I don't think so."

"Why not?"

"For one thing, the notes. The police are sure the killer is the one sending the notes, aren't they? And there's quite a time lag between the killing and the sending of the note, which would mean an extended fugue, or blackout, or it would mean the killer has a fugue, kills somebody, returns to normal, then has another fugue, and writes and mails the note. As Dr. Issel used to tell me, stranger things have happened, but a person with blackouts that frequent, or that long will probably seek help, and Inspector Fleisher has already alerted all the doctors and counselors around."

"That makes sense," Ron said. "And now that you mention it, there's been evidence that Hog scouts his victims, which would take up even more fugue time, right?"

Janet came to the sudden realization that she had just been given an intelligence test, and the knowledge that she had passed it with flying colors didn't make her like it any better.

She took a hard gaze at the wholesome profile of the young man beside her. He wasn't questioning her just from habit. From obsession, possibly; but she was sure, like his mentor, Mr. Ronald Gentry had a reason for every question, and a use for every fact. Dr. Higgins now knew him for what he was—a watcher; always poking and probing, looking, and listening for a wrong word or tone of voice.

And he was obsessed with the case, fascinated and excited by each new development, while at the same time horrified at the deaths. It was the same emotion, her training told her, that makes people slow down on the highway to get a better look at auto accidents. The deceptively mild-mannered Mr. Gentry had this in an unnaturally large degree, and had found a socially acceptable way of gratifying it.

The idea that the same thing could be said of a certain Dr. Janet Higgins never occurred to her.

NINE

❖❖ ❖❖ ❖❖ ❖❖ ❖❖ ❖❖ ❖❖ ❖❖ ❖❖ ❖❖ ❖❖ ❖❖ ❖❖ ❖❖ ❖

CRIMES COME IN ALL SIZES, SHAPES, COLORS, FLAVORS, and textures but they all have one salient feature in common: to a greater or lesser degree, every crime costs the taxpayer money.

Now, Fleisher was a conscientious cop, and more important than that, he was a taxpayer. So while he spared no legitimate expense, he tried in various ways to conserve precious tax dollars. To give just one example, he made his detectives single-space their reports in order to save paper.

But sometimes, a case comes along that's a royal pain *everywhere,* including the pocketbook, and that's how the Hog case was.

Like today for example. In response to an idea from Sergeant Shaughnessy, who apparently had a lot more imagination than Fleisher had ever given him credit for, the inspector had sent men out into the blizzard at great trouble and expense to bring to headquarters certain people they had turned up in the files. Shaughnessy's suggestion was that when the killer wrote "HOG" at the end of his notes, he was, quite simply, signing his name, or a form thereof.

It was just wacky enough not to be ignored, but nobody, except possibly Shaughnessy, had much hope it would turn up anything. For the first time in the investigation, Tatham hadn't even bothered to hang around. Fleisher missed him. He had started to feel that he, Tatham, and Shaugnessy were like Siamese triplets.

Right now, Fleisher was talking to "Piggy" Fleming, recently out of jail after doing two years on a promoting prostitution rap. That means he was a pimp. His nickname came not only from his looks (his nostrils were set almost vertically, giving him a striking resemblance to

73

Lon Chaney in *The Phantom of the Opera*), but from his now-legendary escape attempt across the ice rink in City Park.

Piggy was disappointed. He, for one, had never believed those stories about the cops rousting an innocent citizen who had paid his debt to society. He had gone straight, he asserted. They had no right to do this to him. "Even when I *did* break the law, I wasn't no freak. I supplied a needed service, that's all. I never *hurt* nobody."

Fleisher made a face. "Piggy, please, don't insult my intelligence, for crysake, okay? Your girl Pony took the stand against you wearing a neck brace that she didn't get from too much mattress bouncing. You're ugly, mean, and nasty, Piggy. The only question is are you nuts."

"Look," Piggy said. He puffed out his chest, standing on his dignity. "There's a big difference between belting a lying bitch that's held out on you three nights runnin' and chopping heads off little kids. It's a goddam insult you even think that way, and if you want to talk about it any more, you're gonna have to take it up with my attorney."

Fleisher could see he really *was* insulted. It was a surprise—he hadn't thought it was possible to insult Piggy. You never stop learning, he thought. The Hog case was full of these charming little human insights.

The inspector turned to Shaughnessy with a look that said "you got me into this." He told the sergeant, "Show Piggy the door. The outside of it."

The next interviewee was a Lester Osgood, a cashiered cop for whom, it was theorized, the word "HOG" would have resonances of the word "pig," which in turn would mean that the whole thing could be a plot by Osgood to make his former colleagues look foolish.

And by God, by the end of the questioning he *did* make Fleisher feel foolish, for thinking an animal like Osgood could ever do anything violent that didn't involve punching or kicking.

After that, Fleisher went on to talk to another Piggy (a peeping tom), a Porky (rape), a Harvey Oscar Gorman (embezzlement—he wasn't the type, but his initials were too good to pass up), and even a Miss Lavinia Hogg (child abuse). With similar results.

When it was all over, and the valuable time of more highly and expensively trained police officers was being used to take the interviewees home, the inspector summed up his feelings. "Crap!" he said. More of the taxpayers' money down the toilet, and more wear and tear on Joe Fleisher. He held it against Buell that he had missed it. Fleisher wished he was wherever Tatham was, and Tatham was here at headquarters.

Where Buell was at the moment was wrapped in the arms of a whispering, cooing Diedre Chester, on the sofa in her apartment. She tried her best, but after a few minutes she left off cooing and chuckled good-naturedly. "What's the matter, darling?" she asked.

Buell gave a tired laugh of his own in reply. "I'm getting old, Diedre, that's all. I should stick to my column and let the hungry youngsters follow Fleisher around. I swear I don't know how he *does* it."

"He probably eats enough," she told him. She took one of his hands in both of hers, and held it up in front of his face. "Look at this," she scolded. "White as that snow outside, and no meat on it at all. You remind me of Hansel."

"Of who?"

"Hansel and Gretel. The witch was nearsighted, so when she was trying to fatten Hansel up, he showed her a stick from the cage instead of his finger. Don't you remember the fairy tales you read as a child?"

"You forget my Reverend Uncle Willy raised me after my daddy died. No heathen literature in *that* house. Just the Gospel according to Willy Chandler—pamphlets like *Socialism: The Eighth Deadly Sin* and *Jesus Talks about the Inferior Races*."

Diedre tried to stifle a giggle. It was all too ridiculous. "You shouldn't make up things like that about a sick old man. How is he, by the way?"

Buell offered a sincere prayer of thanks that Diedre was so innocent she couldn't believe in uncle Willy. "My few friends back in Knox County tell me he's not supposed to live out the month."

"Is he aware? Would he recognize you?"

"They tell me he's as ornery as ever. Awake and alert, too."

"You ought to go down and see him, Buell. You shouldn't let him die with bad blood between you." She put her head on his shoulder.

"That's the way we lived, Love. From the start. It ended up with him holding a shotgun on me and giving me a half hour to clear off his land—and considering his land was about ninety percent of Knox County, it wasn't so easy."

Diedre could feel Buell go all tense, even at the old memory. "Why did he do it, Buell?"

"Run me off? He found out I went for a drive with a Mexican girl whose family worked on the farm. It wasn't even a drive, truthfully, I just gave her a lift to her grandmama's house." Buell could still hear his uncle's screaming voice. "You want some dark-meat poontang, that's one thing, but you were seen in public, boy. Now get!"

"Well," Diedre said, rubbing his shoulders, trying to get him to relax. "Soon it will be yours."

Buell nodded. Uncle Willy didn't hold with making a will—considered it sinful to try to have an influence past the grave. A free white man's property belonged to a free white man's family, and that was that. And that would be the ultimate joke on Uncle Willy. Buell would change Knox County from the last stronghold of antebellum feudalism into the showplace of the New South. There was no room in the world for Knox counties, or uncle Willys. Evil brought it's own punishment.

"There's another reason I can't go down South, Love— the case. I can hardly leave in the middle of this, can I?"

"Of course not," she said. She wouldn't want him to, anyway. It was still too exciting.

She took his hand again. "Buell, after we're married, I'm not going to be put off like this, you understand? So I'm going to make you a big sandwich, start building you up again, make sure you keep up your strength, and you're going to eat every crumb, or else."

"Or else what?"

"Or else I'll beat you up!" They both laughed; she gave him a quick kiss, and scooted off to the kitchen.

He heard her humming happily while she worked. He

listened to her as he looked around the room. It always delighted him to notice how Diedre's personality was reflected so perfectly by her environment. Feminine and delicate, but fun-loving and mischievous, too; she had put a huge black paper mustache on one of her frilly lace lampshades for no more reason than silliness. On the other side of the room, she had the framed pictures—

"Diedre, what happened to the picture of you, me, and Ricky?"

She came back from the kitchen with the sandwich. "Oh, darn, there goes the surprise. I sent it away to have a poster made of it, one-and-a-half by three feet, I think. Won't that be terrific? We'll be just like movie stars."

He smiled at her. "You'll always be a star to me."

"Eat your sandwich."

"Yes, ma'am." He took a bite. "Where'd you get the idea?"

"Oh, they called me on the phone, a new photo developing place; as an introductory offer, if I sent them two rolls of film to develop, they'd make any color or black and white print into a poster, so I—what's the matter?" Her fiancé's expression was definitely one of pain.

"Where'd you send it?"

"Oh, a box number, I've got it written down somewhere. What's wrong?"

"I don't like the idea of sending that in the mail especially in this kind of weather. It can get wet, or—or crushed . . . it's a hard picture to replace."

"Don't be such a worry wart. I've got the negative." It didn't seem to make him feel much better. To take his mind off it, she said, "Tell me about the case."

He told her all about the morning's events; Janet Higgins's profile, Fleisher's skepticism, and most of all, the professor's bombshell about the sign. Telling about it took his mind off the picture, but it didn't seem to make him feel any happier.

When he finished, Diedre said, "These people all sound so *interesting*. I've *got* to meet them. I'm going to invite them all to dinner. What's today, Monday? I'm going to make a big turkey dinner for Wednesday. Let's see, I can get fresh vegetables from—"

"Diedre, a murder investigation isn't exactly—"

"You have to make everyone promise to come, Buell."

"Love, I just can't—"

"Oh, yes you can. Don't think you're going to have all the fun."

Buell exploded. "Fun! How can you think this is fun!"

Diedre was all waving hands and urgent whispers, cutting him off. "That's not exactly what I meant, Darling, please don't be mad. Please."

Buell subsided but shook his head. "Diedre, sometimes I go sick inside when I think about this whole thing. It's *not* fun, Love, at all."

Now Diedre was troubled. "I know, I know I said it wrong, but what I meant was I love you, and I'm jealous of you. You're working with these people, getting close to them. I want to be part of whatever you're part of. I want to know the people you know, so I can share more of your life—your feelings."

Buell grinned at her, ruffled her hair. "Well, right now I feel like a rockheaded fool, if you want to share that one. I'm sorry, Love."

She forgave him. "Then you'll get them to come?"

Two pairs of blue eyes gazed at each other from a distance of eight inches. Buell said, "I'd go to hell and invite the devil himself, if you asked me to." Then the kissing started.

Janet had taken Ron Gentry's cryptic remark about Terry Wilbur's room as a challenge. Apparently there was something here to see, and she turned around once, then again, sweeping the room with her eyes trying to see it.

"Are you a child, or a teetotum?" Ron asked under his breath.

"What?" Janet demanded.

"Nothing. It just seemed appropriate considering Wilbur's taste in literature."

It did strike the psychologist as a somewhat juvenile atmosphere for a boarding house tenant in his mid-twenties. The poster of Farrah Fawcett-Majors (whom Janet hated with a cold-green passion) and the various pieces of hockey equipment were understandable; some things men like no matter *what* their age. But Wilbur's room was littered with children's literature of all kinds—

Little Golden Books, Dr. Seuss, even an old Alice and Jerry primer left over from some obsolete grade school reading program. There seemed to be everything, in fact, but a copy of *Through the Looking Glass,* from which Ron had quoted.

The professor was carefully leafing through some of the books, lost in thought. Janet peeked over his shoulder. Some of the books, many of them, had been defaced by pencil marks. Words were underlined, giving sentences bizarre emphasis, like, "No, I do not like *them,* Sam; I *do* not like green eggs and ham." Words, sentences, and sometimes single letters were copied in a strange, distorted scrawl. Often, Wilbur had inscribed a jagged, angry zigzag on a page, pressing so hard he had torn the paper.

The professor looked up, and spoke to his pupil. "You are right, Ronald. This room is important, I can sense that. Did not the police examine this room?"

"A couple of times," Ron told him. "The first time, they were looking for drugs. The second time, after the note, they tried to find something that would indicate Wilbur wrote the Hog notes. They looked all through the books, but they were trying to find something *in* them instead of something about them."

Janet was looking at a slim volume entitled *The Littlest Snowball.* She held it gingerly, as though it were dirty. Scientist or not, she was puzzled, and more than a little afraid.

"But what can it *mean?*" she demanded. "Something about these simple little books made him furious." She looked again at the book. "What could he read in here to make him so angry?"

"I wish I knew, Janet," Ron said. "Which one have you got there, *The Littlest Snowball?* That's not even the one that made him the maddest. There's one called *The Big Red Dog* that he thrust the pencil clean through, like he was stabbing it through the heart. I'm not the shrink around here, but it's my opinion that Terry Wilbur is one disturbed young man."

Janet wasn't about to argue with that. The fact that she could not *conceive* of a reason for Wilbur's behavior added to her feelings of unease. As soon as the blizzard let's up, she promised herself, it was back to the library for a look at more case histories. A book, she knew, was a vaginal symbol. She'd start her research from there.

"And yet . . . ," Benedetti said, as he looked through more books. "And yet, not all of these aroused Wilbur's ire. It seems as though the thicker the book, the less it bothered him. There are a few here that are virtually untouched."

"I noticed that, *Maestro*," Ron said. "Including this one." He handed the professor a brand-new-looking copy of E.B. White's *Charlotte's Web*. It was the thickest book in Wilbur's collection, and it was evident that he had seldom, if ever, opened it—the cover creaked when the professor looked inside. It was also the only "Children's Classic" Wilbur seemed to own.

"This is the one you mentioned to me, isn't it, *amico?*"

Ron nodded. Janet said, "What's so special about that story?"

"Don't you remember?" Ron asked.

"I never read it."

"You never read *Charlotte's Web?*" Ron sounded horrified. "Look, it's all about—"

The professor interrupted. "I believe it will be better for the investigation if Dr. Higgins reads the book for herself. She will better be able to evaluate your theory if she follows the same steps you did in forming it. Don't you agree, Doctor?"

It all sounded like mystification and showing-off to Janet, and she was about to say so, but the look in the professor's shiny dark eyes was so commanding that she agreed to his suggestion, almost meekly.

"Va bene," he said. "Now, I wish a word with Wilbur's landlady."

The landlady was hovering on the stair landing, waiting breathlessly for them to come down. Since Ron had been there twice already, and was therefore an old friend, she addressed the question to him.

"Well, Ronny? Did you find anything? Proof? Disproof? Anything?"

"It's hard to say, Mrs. Zucchio." As far as Ron could tell, nothing trivial had ever happened to Rosa Zucchio in her life. The last time Ron had visited her boarding house, he had actually heard her say "Ooh, I just had the most terrific drink of water!" (She started many of her sentences with "Ooh.") And she greeted all the common-places of life the same way—with an enthusiasm that bubbled musically through her voice, and animated her tiny and still attractive person with constant sweeping gestures.

Right now, she was torn between conflicting emotions: a genuine liking for Terry Wilbur and concern for him, and excitement at the prospect of going down in history as the Hog's landlady. A nontrivial fact like that, care-fully used, could see her through years of breathless con-versation.

When the professor asked her if she would mind an-swering a few questions for him, Ron saw her big eyes go all soft and dreamy, and chalked up another conquest for Benedetti. Mrs. Zucchio nearly floated into the living room, where she shooed out her boarders and seated Ron, Janet, and the professor in front of a roaring fire.

"That's Terry, there," she said, pointing to a row of pic-tures on the mantel. A photographer-tenant had taken them to test out some new equipment, and used his fel-low boarders as models.

The portrait of Wilbur revealed nothing sinister. It showed a clear-eyed, wholesome-looking young man with a strong build and a good, outdoor tan.

Mrs. Zucchio went to get them coffee and Italian cookies. Benedetti pronounced them *"Delizioso!"* and smacked his lips, making Mrs. Zucchio his slave.

"Now, dear lady," he said, "tell me about Terry Wil-bur."

Ron had found that the most frustrating words a pri-vate detective can hear are "I already told the police." There was no danger of that from Rosa Zucchio. Not only did she cheerfully answer for the professor the same ques-tions the police had asked, but she cheerfully gave word-for-word indentical answers.

Terry Wilbur had been boarding with her almost nine years, since he was eighteen. He had no living relatives, poor thing. He worked for Sparta Lawn and Garden, had been there eleven years, started right after he left school. Everybody liked him, nobody hated him. He was friendly, quiet, popular, bright.

Girls? He had girl friends, nice girls. Never tried to

keep them past eleven o'clock. "I don't allow opposite sexes to stay past then," she explained. "He had to see a girl, he went out."

Had she met Leslie Bickell?

"The girl who died? I met her once, but I wasn't too crazy about her if you want to know. Ooh, such a stuck-up! Like she went with Terry to do him a favor, you know? What's the matter, Professor?" she asked, suddenly concerned.

Ron saw with a degree of amusement, Benedetti was scowling a fearsome scowl. He hadn't read the police reports to hear Mrs. Zucchio recite her lines from them, he wanted to compare old answers with new and mine the differences for significance.

That wouldn't work with Mrs. Zucchio. She had a phonographic memory for the sound of her own voice. Benedetti would have to frame some questions the police hadn't asked. Ron waited for the mastermind to go to work.

"Was Wilbur a good gardener?" Benedetti asked. That's how one knows he's a mastermind, Ron thought. He can get away with a question like that.

Mrs. Zucchio answered, "I heard he was very good."

"He has lived here nine years, correct? Has he ever done any gardening for you?"

"He repotted my hydrangea . . ."

"Heh, heh, heh," the professor laughed benignly. "No, dear lady, I meant on the outside of the house."

"Ooh, no, how could he? He's busy working for the company from early early spring until way in the middle of the fall, and before and after that the ground around here is like a *rock!*"

"What did he do, then, to pass the winter?"

"Well, last year, he worked as a busboy in a restaurant downtown."

"And this year?"

"He wasn't working anywhere this winter. He said he had a project for this winter."

And that, Ron thought, is how he *proves* he's a mastermind. God alone knew what Benedetti had in mind when he started the line of questioning, but look what he had found.

"What was this project, Mrs. Zucchio?"

"I don't know, he wouldn't tell me. He said he might when he was finished."

"When did he tell you this?"

She scratched her head. "Oh, October, November. When I asked him what he was doing with that big package of books."

TEN

◆◆◆◆◆◆◆◆◆◆◆◆◆◆◆◆◆◆◆◆◆◆◆◆◆◆◆◆◆◆◆

ALL THE WAY TO THE HOSPITAL (THE NEXT STOP ON THE agenda) the professor had been talking to himself in low, rumbling Italian that was too fast for Ron to understand. In his experience, though, it always meant trouble.

In the elevator on the way up, the old man exploded. "It is *wrong!*"

Janet jumped. Ron said simply, "Yes, *Maestro.*"

"Wilbur's disappearance, I can understand, but the books, the destruction of the books—I don't like it, Ronald."

"Yes, *Maestro.*"

"Yes," the old man echoed. He rubbed his chin. "This may be a sign of an evil deeper than I had anticipated. Well, if it is, I welcome it! I will see its face! I am not a detective, I am a philosopher. There is always more to learn." He tossed his head decisively.

Now that the crisis was past (for now, at least), Ron felt safe in saying something beside "Yes, *Maestro.*"

"Who do we see first, *Maestro*, Elleger, or Vasquez?"

"Vasquez?" Janet asked.

"Leslie Bickell's heroin probably came from him," Ron told her. "Terry Wilbur went to school with him."

The professor chose to see the girl first. The uniformed policeman guarding the two rooms checked their credentials and let them in.

Despite being swathed in bandages and casts, Barbara Elleger was starting to feel better—it was obvious by her crankiness and irritability. When Ron, Janet, and the professor entered, the girl was complaining to a middle-aged couple, who reminded Ron of Grant Wood's "American Gothic," about her hospital-enforced ten o'clock lights out.

"How can I go to sleep? How can I get tired just laying here?"

Her parents sympathized, but said it was the policy for the whole hospital, beyond their poor power to change. Their daughter appeared to hold it against them.

When she found out who her visitors were, she said, "Look. Can you get that reporter Buell Tatham to come here? I want to thank him, but the big brains around here won't let me have a phone, let alone *call* anybody."

They told her they'd pass the message along.

"Good," she said, "now what do *you* want?"

At this point, Mr. Elleger, who had been silent, jumped to his feet and confronted the professor. "Now listen," he said without preamble, "I don't mind you asking Barbara about the accident itself, but I won't allow any questions about this . . . this Muntz boy, or diaphragms, or anything like that! Do you hear?"

Barbara Elleger's freedom of movement was limited, but she managed a grand gesture with just her eyes, rolling them upward in disgust and saying, "Oh, Daddy."

Ron could tell from the professor's tight smile that he was making allowances. Calmly, he said, "I hear you, Mr. Elleger, please, there is no need to shout in the hospital. But may I ask the reason for your position?"

Elleger was flustered. "I—I won't have Barbara exposed to such things."

"Indeed," the professor said. "It would seem from her statement to the police that she has already been quite thoroughly exposed to—"

Elleger swung at him. The professor seemed to pull his head into his overcoat, like a turtle, so the blow missed. Elleger was undiscouraged, and was going to try again, but Ron grabbed him by the inside of his elbow, firm but not brutal, pulled him off balance and led him to a chair.

"What's the matter with you?" Ron asked him. "You're twice as old as I am, and he's twice as old as you are. That would make for a pretty strange fight."

"I am not four times as old as you are, Ronald," Benedetti said. "I am still less than one hundred years old, I assure you."

Mrs. Elleger took the opportunity to assert herself.

She mopped her husband's balding pate and said, "I think we'd better leave now, Russell." She kissed her daughter on the small available patch of forehead, smiled at the three investigators, and said, "So nice to have met you."

When they were gone, Barbara said, "Honestly," in the manner of someone who bears a great burden. "Well, what do you want to know?"

The interview turned out not to be worth the trouble it took to get it. It consisted almost exclusively of "I already told the police" followed by negatives.

No, she had no enemies. No, she had never been aware or suspicious that anyone was watching her. No, she never told anyone but her two deceased girl friends about the diaphragm. No, she had never heard of or met Stanley Watson, Leslie Bickell, Terry Wilbur, Davy Reade, or any other of the hundreds of names turned up during the investigation of the case.

Of the crash itself, she remembered nothing but the impact, and being helped from the car.

"Anything else?" she asked, peevishly.

The professor waved his no. "Ronald?"

"Yeah, I have a couple of questions."

Barbara Elleger sighed.

"Carol Salinski was of Polish descent, right?"

"That's all? Yes, she was. Half. Her mother is French."

"And Beth Ling was Chinese."

"Good guess." She was very sarcastic.

"Poland," Ron said. "China." He stood up. "That's all, thanks."

"Good," the patient said. "Maybe I can get a little rest."

George Ruiz Vasquez, aka Juan Bizarro, aka the Pope of Dope, hadn't been in a car accident, but he was hardly in any better shape than the Elleger girl, though he did have the use of one arm.

Since he and Ron had made each other's acquaintance in the past, the detective took a more informal tone. "The professor has a few questions to ask you, Bizarro."

"No speeka Eengliss." Vasquez, where he showed through the bandages, looked handsome and intelligent. He made a lot of money, and lived well. And whatever his injuries, one thing that wasn't on his medical report was needle marks. He was no fool.

"Try again, George. Your older brother tells me in the store you wouldn't have been such a bum if you hadn't forgotten how to speak Spanish—you might have heard sense from your uncles."

"Poor me," Vasquez mocked.

"I disagree," Benedetti put in. "He would have been a bum in any case."

"But I have no interest in you, Vasquez, except insofar as you can tell me about the Hog case, particularly Leslie Bickell and Terry Wilbur."

"Why should I?" Vasquez sneered.

"Because if you don't, I'm going to circulate a rumor that the reason all those people got sick, and the girl died," Ron said, "was the fact you cut that horse with Drano. I'm sure the guy who beat you up will be back for seconds."

"I'm not worried about *him*," Vasquez said, but he flicked his tongue quickly across his lips.

"Sixteen OD's, your Holiness," Ron said. "I'll bet every one has fathers, brothers, friends—"

Vasquez shut him off with hissing obscenity. "All right, what do you want to know?"

"Did you know the heroin was going to be extraordinarily powerful when you sold it?"

"I don't admit I sold it."

"The police have you cold for the cocaine, George. The rap is the same. They don't have to know about the heroin. Come on." This was the one area in which Ron felt he was superior to the professor—Benedetti had no talent for dealing with the professional criminal.

"No, of course I didn't," Vasquez said. "If I'd known it had such a jolt, I would have cut it more, made some more money. And I cut it with lactose, same as always." A pusher lives by his reputation; Vasquez was affirming his integrity.

The professor resumed his questioning. "Leslie Bickell bought a large quantity of it from you, is that correct?"

He smiled at the memory. "Five grand, in small, unmarked bills. *Beautiful.* I sold her what I had left. Rich kids are the best customers, I swear. That's how I worked my way through college, you know. Making too much money to quit when I graduated, though. Still, it adds class to the operation."

"How did you meet Miss Bickell?" Benedetti asked.

"Old Terry Wilbur introduced us." Vasquez laughed. "Ran into him one time, she was with him. He said hello, old school chums and like that, introduced us, and let it slip he was going away on a gardening job for a couple of weeks.

"Leslie had the look, you know? The I-am-high-class, I-can-handle-anything, I-am-curious look. My meat. So when old Terry left town, old friend Georgie looked up Leslie. I think she enjoyed the contrast between somebody with a college education and a stupid dropout like Terry, you know? So I gave her the usual bullshit, and she took to the stuff like mother's milk."

"When did this happen?"

"A couple of months ago, I guess. I guess Terry found out, that's why he started this Hog thing."

"You believe Wilbur is Hog?"

"Sure, I do. The boy is crazy, always has been. He wiped out a few zeros, then Leslie, then that kid. He thought he'd get you confused, you know?"

"Why did he disappear?"

Vasquez laughed again. "Because he'd crack under questioning. He knew he'd be tempted to confess, to prove he was smart."

"You seem to know him very well."

"Look, one morning I got on a plane in San Juan at nine-thirty A.M. I was five years old. Eleven o'clock, we land in New York. By twelve-thirty, I had moved in with my uncles here in Sparta. By one o'clock I had met Terry Wilbur. He's the only one who still calls me 'whore-hay.' And he was *always* crazy.

"Look, one time in high school, there was a book report due, and Terry didn't hand one in, said he didn't do it because he was too busy, and that old queen Mr. Tim-mons said he didn't do it because he was too stupid, and Terry screamed and cried, and beat that old guy to a *pulp*, man. It took four gym teachers to pull him off. And that was the end of Terry Wilbur's academic career." Vasquez's laughter fell on the backs of his audience as they walked through the door and left him.

"Where now?" Janet asked wearily, back in the car.

"Home," the professor said around his cigar. He puffed at it heavily for a while then said, *"Terry Wilbur must be found! Or this case is meaningless!"* The Italian rumbling started again.

"I want to stop at my office first, *Maestro*. Mrs. Goralsky is probably getting ready to sue you for alienation of affection." When the professor had agreed, Ron turned to Janet and asked, "What did you think of Mr. Elleger?"

"I think," she said, "that he seems to be jealous of his daughter's lover."

Ron shook his head. "Doesn't it get depressing knowing that kind of thing about people? Carrying around that kind of knowledge in your head?"

"I wouldn't think it would be any more depressing than making a living dealing with the likes of Vasquez. We both do that."

Ron smiled. "Touché." He dropped Janet at her apartment, and drove up to his office just as the snow was stopping.

There was trouble in the Bixby building. As he walked with the professor down the gray corridor, Ron heard angry voices yelling in his office. The high-pitched, indignant voice belonged to Mrs. Goralsky. The rasping roar, Ron was astonished to realize, belonged to that pillar of commerce, Mr. Harold Atler.

"Don't give me that, you—you munchkin!" the former client screamed. "I demand to see him immediately!"

"I am not accustomed to being called a *liar*, sir!" Mrs. Goralsky yelled back. "I will tell you *one more time*— Mr. Gentry is not in!" The tiny woman's inflection implied Atler was in danger of being thrashed within an inch of his worthless life.

There was an inarticulate growl from Atler. Mrs. Goralsky yelled, "Stop! You stop that! You can't go in there!"

"This is the way out, Mr. Atler."

The broker jumped, and turned to face him. "I—I was just looking."

"I can see that. Do you want to consult me about something? I can always find time for a former client."

The broker looked relieved.

Ron said, "Now, after you apologize to Mrs. Goralsky, we can have a little talk."

Atler didn't apologize often in the normal course of his life; he didn't have to. Ron thought the experience would be good for him. The broker licked his lips, faced Mrs. Goralsky, and said, "I—I'm sorry I lost my temper."

"And you're sorry you called her a liar," Ron said.

"Ah, yes . . . I'm sorry I called you a liar."

Benedetti spoke for the first time. "The munchkin remark was in questionable taste as well."

Atler winced, but he said it. "I'm sorry I called you a munchkin."

"I accept your apology," Mrs. Goralsky told him gravely. "Now don't let it happen again."

Atler had never been so humiliated in his life. To apologize to a private detective's secretary. A midget! Still, he had to do what he came to do.

Gentry introduced the strange-looking old man as Professor Benedetti. That would make the problem more difficult, but it couldn't be helped. He got down to business. "Mr. Gentry, today's newspapers have said you— and the professor of course (he smiled)—are working with the police to find the person who killed poor Leslie."

"The papers were right, Mr. Atler. You sent me stumbling right into the case, and I've been retained to aid the professor. I *did* return your retainer, didn't I?"

"You didn't bill me." Atler wanted to be strictly accurate on matters of business. "But that's not the point. I want to hire you to protect me. At . . . shall we say a fee you may name yourself?"

"Protect you from whom?"

"My enemies. I have . . . enemies." And *that's* the truth, Atler thought righteously. The boys in the green suits.

"What did the police say?"

"I, uh, I haven't been to the police."

"What are the names of these enemies, Mr. Atler?"

The upstart was offensive in tone and manner. Why, he wasn't even looking at him! He was polishing his spectacles, looking at the desk.

"I'll tell you that when you have agreed to the offer."

"I believe you are your *own* worst enemy, *Signore*."

Now the sinister foreigner was getting into the act. "Your proposition is open to many unflattering interpretations, eh? Don't try to be subtle, Mr. Atler, you are not equipped for it. You wish to buy Mr. Gentry off the investigation of these murders. Why?"

"What do you take me for, sir!" Atler was on his feet.

"I am trying to decide," Benedetti said softly.

The *nerve*. "How *dare* you suggest I would do anything in the interests of that monster! I want him caught, and caught fast!"

Gentry replaced his glasses and stared rudely at Atler. "Then why the bribe?"

"That remark is actionable!" Atler was shrill, screaming. With an effort, he regained some control. "However, we won't pursue that. Gentry, you have a *duty* to withdraw from the Hog case immediately!"

"Oh?"

Atler leaned across Ron's desk, now frankly begging. "Look, Gentry, if you are involved with the capture of Hog, there will be great publicity. You will be a focus of interest; the newspapers will want to publish all the details of the case, including how *you* came to be involved.

"It cannot become public that I left five thousand dollars in cash unguarded in a desk drawer! I won't allow it! It would do untold damage to my career!"

Atler could not imagine a colder or grayer gaze than the one he was getting from Ron Gentry at the moment. He could feel its contempt. He should have known better than to expect understanding from *any* of that generation. They never believed they could get old, be forced to give up what they'd built, just hand it over to the green suits.

"Get out of here, Mr. Atler," Gentry said.

In desperation, the broker appealed to the older man. "Professor," he began, "surely *you* can—"

"Get out of my office, Mr. Atler," Gentry repeated, "before I do untold damage to your face. Five murders, Mr. Atler. *Five*. Three young girls. An old man. A little boy. Just look me in the eye and tell me, Mr. Atler, how your career stacks up against that."

Atler stood up and tried to bolt from the office. No one would ever see *him* cry; but he waited on a word from Gentry.

"A question, Mr. Atler. That money came from trading

in coffee beans and what?" No answer. "Meat by-products, right? What particular kind of meat by-product?"

Atler's reply was a whispering, sobbing, *"Oh my God!"* Then he ran from the office as though he was running for his life.

The door slammed so hard behind him, Ron was afraid the glass was going to break. He heard the professor offer a heavy sigh.

"So, *amico,*" the old man said. "This is how you use the training I have given you? Dealing with *pazzi* like Atler?"

"He's a frightened man. I wonder, though."

"What do you wonder?"

"What the average man on the street might say if you asked him to stack his life's work against the lives of five total strangers."

"Be quiet. *You* are a detective, not a philosopher. I also wonder."

Ron smiled. "What do *you* wonder, *Maestro?*"

"Whether Atler is such a *pazzo* after all. He is the only one, so far, to see the significance of your little questions, eh? He may surprise us yet."

ELEVEN

◆◆ ◆◆ ◆◆ ◆◆ ◆◆ ◆◆ ◆◆ ◆◆ ◆◆ ◆◆ ◆◆ ◆◆ ◆◆ ◆

IF IT WERE POSSIBLE FOR SOMEONE TO SHARE HOG'S thoughts that evening, he could never believe Hog had taken the lives of five helpless human beings. The thoughts were thoughts of nervousness, doubt, uncertainty.

Hog tried to achieve calm by composing the next note. That was a first. It had always been better to wait until *after* the deaths to prepare the taunting messages. But things were slightly different, tonight.

It was a clear night, no moon. The blizzard had moved eastward, leaving a dry, cold night in its wake. Hog noted with satisfaction that the sharp-edged wind was strong enough to blow snow over any footprints as soon as they were made.

Hog could see the light in the motel window. Hog could see, in silhouette, the man who would soon be dead. The motel was a rambling, one-storey structure; the victim had been careful to take a room far away from the office, or any of his fellow guests. Access would be no problem.

Still, Hog hesitated. It *had* to be tonight. It had to be *now*. Still . . . As had happened after every death so far, Hog toyed with the idea of stopping this madness, even agonized over it, but had come to the realization that one couldn't start something like this and just stop it. Events wouldn't bend to a human will; their outcome was in the hands of God.

But I must be careful! Hog's thought was a self-directed whip-lash. Another mistake, like the one in the case of the Bickell girl, would be fatal. It couldn't be allowed. Hog was almost at the end of the task—there could be no failure now. Benedetti was too smart to be trifled with. Did he have a whiff of the truth even now?

But Hog felt secure that there was nothing to fear. Benedetti, and all of the rest of them, would all go on searching for the wrong thing. The wrong thing.

It took only fractions of a second to cross the motel's snow-covered lawn. Hog tapped lightly on the sliding glass door of the patio. The man inside took a look, smiled, opened the door.

"About time you got here," he said. He was a medium-sized, stocky man, with slicked down hair that was too wavy to stay slicked down, ending up in a pattern of shiny ridges. He smiled a lot, showing gleaming white teeth, but he never looked sincerely happy. It was a synthetic smile, like a used-car salesman's.

"Let me in, Jastrow," Hog said. "It's cold."

"Sure, sure. We going to do business?"

Hog looked defeated. "Just write it up. I'll sign it."

Jastrow beamed his phony smile. *"That's* what I like to hear." He sat at the writing desk, took out some stationery, and began to write. "When I finish," he said over his shoulder, "I want you to copy this in your own handwriting. It's more legal that way, okay?"

"Anything you say."

Jastrow went back to writing. Jastrow considered himself an expert at sizing up people. The first few times he met the person who was in his room tonight he had taken pains to make sure there was no danger to himself. He had himself convinced he would never have to worry. He was wrong.

From an overcoat pocket, Hog produced a .32 caliber revolver. Almost absently, Hog crossed the room to stand to the right of the seated Jastrow.

Jastrow looked up. "Yes?"

"I just want to see what I'm going to be signing."

"You'll see it soon enough. People reading over my shoulder make me nervous."

"Oh," Hog said. "Sorry." Hog brought the pistol to within an inch of Jastrow's temple, and pulled the trigger. It made less of a noise, and more of a mess, than Hog had expected.

Hog raised Jastrow's still bleeding head an inch off the desk, and slid the paper out from underneath. Tenderly, almost lovingly, the pen was removed from the dead fingers, the wiped gun put in its place. Being careful to leave no fingerprints, Hog took a few seconds to look around the room. The search paid off. Hog put the bloody papers in a plastic bag, the object of the search in a pocket. For the second time, Hog was taking souvenirs from the scene of violent death. Only Jastrow's dead eyes saw Hog leave the room. Outside, soft snow filled Hog's footprints.

Ron heard the professor's pleasant baritone crooning *"Non dimenticar"* through the door of the spare bedroom. Benedetti had picked that room, he said, because it had the best light, which Ron found rather amusing, since the old man never painted in the daytime anyway.

He knocked on the door and walked in. Cigar smoke tinted the air inside a faint gray. The professor was seated at his easel, painting a picture that, to Ron's uneducated eye, looked remarkably medieval, like an old hunting tapestry. It depicted a knight (who had a definite facial resemblance to Niccolo Benedetti) riding a white stallion, thrusting a silver lance through the body of a very nasty looking wild boar. The painting was practically finished—the professor worked in acrylics, quick-drying paints; and his hand moved across the canvas almost in a blur.

Ron had learned to gauge the state of the professor's progress on a case, from his canvases. The closer the old man felt to a solution, the more abstract his painting became, until he was painting what he called "pure thought."

Ron said hello, the professor grunted a greeting in return. Ron studied the painting without enthusiasm . . . it still looked too much like something to mean anything important. He looked closely at the tusked boar, trying to spot a resemblance to someone in the case, with no success.

After a while, Ron said, *"É una pittura molto interessante."*

The professor jabbed a thumb at the canvas. *"Questa?"* He grunted. *"Questa é una pezza di porcheria."*

Ron thought it over for a second. "Is that a pun, Maestro?"

The old man smiled. "I suppose it is, though I didn't intend it that way. It is true that a literal translation of *porcheria* is 'that which is given to pigs,' but in idiomatic

English, the most accurate translation I can think of is 'shit.' "

That dampened Ron's enthusiasm for philological inquiry. He changed the subject. "Are we going to that little get-together Buell Tatham's fianceé is planning for tomorrow?"

"I think so," the professor said. He picked up a finer brush, for detail work. "It will be a fine opportunity for you to expound on your observations. It will be interesting to note reactions."

Ron was dubious. "It's not exactly right for a social occasion, *Maestro*. I heard from my correspondent today. I'd rather save it for a time we're concentrating on business."

"You will have no choice," the professor said. "Your hostess will demand it of you. I am sure the whole purpose of this dinner is for this Mrs. Chester to feel closer to the chase. In fact—"

Fleisher's phone call interrupted him.

It was a motel room, no different from countless motel rooms Ron had seen all over the country. It was done up in the same grayish pastels, with the same marshmallow-soft bed, and the same plywood and formica drawer-and-desk combination. The body was seated at that desk, in the same semimodern chair; a thin pad of vinyl-covered foam rubber stretched over a curved wire frame. It wasn't a chair so much as a basket that caught one's form before it hit the floor—it took an effort to sit in one.

Ron looked at the corpse. There was a small hole in his right temple, and a larger one where his left temple used to be. He was dressed casually in slacks and turtleneck. His sleeves were rolled up to show an eagle tattoo just below the elbow of the arm that held the gun.

Fleisher was arguing with one of the meat-wagon boys. "Leave that body right where it is," he said. "Right across the desk. I want—Oh, he's here. Hello, Professor."

Benedetti's lips showed a faint smile. "Good evening, Inspector. What is it about this murder you wish me to see?"

"Well," Fleisher began, "I—What makes you think it's a murder?" he asked suspiciously. "I said 'apparent suicide' on the phone."

Benedetti chuckled. "You have your methods, Inspector,

but you know mine. I am sure you would never think
of dragging me away from my easel just because *you*
felt obliged to visit the death scene. Therefore, something here bothers you. Since we are involved with murders that try to look like accidents or suicides, and you
have called me, what is bothering you is an apparent
suicide you believe is a murder."

"I know it's a murder," the inspector said. "In a way,
I almost wish it wasn't, for crysake. This guy would have
been a great candidate for Hog."

"You know who he is?" Ron Gentry asked.

Buell Tatham said, "I recognized him the second I got
here, from the *Courant,* and the inspector already had
the word out on him."

"Well," Ron asked, "who is he?"

"No, no," Fleisher said. "First I want the professor to
tell me why it's murder."

"You challenge me, eh, Inspector?" The professor
was amused.

"Just checking my own ideas," Fleisher said.

"Very well." Benedetti looked closely at the body,
starting by meeting the staring dead eyes. "If it was suicide," the old man said, "he was well disposed to meet it
—his face is calm, his eyes open."

He took his eyes off the body momentarily to look at
his protégé. "Don't just stand around, Ronald. Ask the
necessary questions."

"Yes, *Maestro,*" Ron said. "Who found the body, Inspector?"

"Hotel manager. One of the guests started a small fire,
a little trash can thing, but the local ordinance says they
have to evacuate the place. J—the victim had told the
manager he'd be in his room all evening and didn't want
to be disturbed—"

"That's why this room is so far out for such an empty
motel?"

"Yeah. Told the manager he'd be getting some work
done, wanted to be quiet. He's been here since January
twelfth. That's why—

"Anyway, he didn't come out when the fire alarm rang,
so the manager had to go and get him."

The professor put a bony hand on the back of the wire
chair. The meat-wagon man said, "Hey, cut that out!"

as the bloody head started sliding on the blotter toward the edge of the desk.

"I am so sorry," the professor said, with absolutely no sincerity. "Please continue, Inspector."

Fleisher shrugged. "There's nothing more to say. The manager, guy by the name of Ickes, knocked on the door, got no answer, figured the victim was asleep, used his key and found him."

"Just the way he is now?" Benedetti asked. "I mean to say, the way he was before I shifted the position of his head?"

"Yeah, just like that."

"Then you are correct, it is murder."

"I knew it!" Fleisher said. "Suicide and accidents are damn hard to fake, but Hog is good, I was losing faith in myself. Do you call it murder for the same reason I do?"

The professor nodded. "If your reason is this abomination masquerading as a chair, yes."

When Fleisher indicated his agreement, and understanding came into Ron's face, Buell said, "Well, it still isn't clear to me. Don't you all go mysterious on me the way the inspector has been."

"It's really very simple, Mr. Tatham," the professor said. "Do you see the position of the body?"

"Of course. Why couldn't he have shot himself in the head and then have fallen over on the desk?"

The professor touched the back of the chair again, eliciting a growl from the man in white when the head slid another fraction of an inch.

"This chair," the old man said, "is made of a thick steel wire. It is very springy—furthermore, it is made so that it tilts backward. This is not the kind of chair that should be placed at a desk (or anywhere else in my opinion), but especially at a desk, because in order to do any writing, you must lean over the desk, and in a chair like this, you must exert a steady effort to do so. In fact, it takes some effort merely to sit up straight.

"Now the body of our anonymous friend is found slumped over the desk. That means he must have been leaning forward when the trigger was pulled, leaning *over* the surface of the desk, in fact, so that his head fell straight *down* to the desk. Even so, this chair makes that a precarious position—you saw how just the weight of my hand started the head sliding backward. One more touch, and he will flop to the floor."

"Don't, huh?" the attendant pleaded. "I'll only have to explain the bruises to Dmitri."

The professor took pity on him. "Of course, of course. I have no further use for the remains. Inspector?"

"Nah, get him out of here."

The meat-wagon boys got busy, and Benedetti went on. "Now. If the dead man were seated straight up when he pulled the trigger, we would have found him either on the floor, or more likely, leaning back in his chair, the same way Leslie Bickell was on her bean-bag.

"That is why I say it was murder. Because if I say it was suicide, I must explain why a man will exert effort to lean so far forward his nose is perpendicular with the surface of a desk before blowing out his brain! For that, I have no intelligent explanation. And Niccolo Benedetti takes no joy in appearing stupid."

The professor did his catlike hand-scratching again. "Now, since I have explained, perhaps someone will be kind enough to tell me who the dead man is?"

Surprisingly, it was Ron Gentry who spoke. "It's Jastrow, isn't it?"

Fleisher said, "Yeah. Did you know him?"

Ron shook his head. "Buell ran his picture with a couple of columns, I remember. I was keeping a crime scrapbook at the time. High school project."

"Your academic career is, of course, fascinating," the professor said, "but it *still* doesn't tell me who the dead man is."

How does it feel to be in the dark for a change, *Maestro?* Ron thought but did not say. Instead he said, "Jastrow—I think his first name was Jeffrey—" Buell nodded "—used to be a cop, or rather a deputy sheriff for the county. Until he got kicked off, he was the terror of the county roads. He was—"

"He was crooked down to the *ground,* for crysake," Fleisher growled. "It made me sick to find out about it."

"He was a kind of Johnny marijuana seed, wasn't he, Inspector?"

"Yeah. He'd stop a car for speeding (though it didn't make any difference to him if it was really speeding or not), get everybody out of the car, search it, and 'find' just enough marijuana to mean a jail term. Especially on cars with out-of-state plates, you know? Then, he'd manage to be convinced not to haul them in, you know? He took about a hundred and fifty dollars worth of convincing."

The professor rubbed his chin. "In other words, extortion, pure and simple."

"That's about it, Professor," Buell told him. "And if they didn't have enough money to convince him, he'd haul them in anyway. He was very good at getting backroom confessions. Or, if there were girls in the car, letting them work it off, if you know what I mean."

"Indeed. A charming specimen, all together."

Ron said, "He'd still be at it, if it weren't for Buell."

"And the inspector, too, don't forget," the reporter said.

"My pleasure," the inspector said. "Bastard like that gives *every* lawman a bad name for crysake."

"Well, anyway," Buell went on, "I started hearing rumors about this Jastrow—I heard one that said a kid was hauled off to the substation and never heard from again—a runaway. So I decided to check it out. I told the inspector, and he came along with me. I got hold of a car with plates from the South, ran two miles over the speed limit, and when Jastrow stopped us I did all the talking. We almost had him to the point where he took money from us—"

"But I screwed it up," Fleisher growled. "I took my badge out of my wallet, all right, but I forgot to remove my ID card. Jastrow saw it, let on he recognized me all along, and tried to make out like it was a joke." The inspector rammed a fist into an open hand, still angry with himself. "Anyway, I said the hell with it, told Tatham to do the column anyway, you know? We didn't have enough to put him away—nobody wanted to come from out of state to testify, but we got him kicked out of the sheriff's department. Cost the bastard his pension, too. Buell got a commendation from the sheriff, for cleaning up the place."

"And you and Buell are the ones who've been most closely connected with the case," Ron said. "Is that why you liked him for Hog?"

"That's it," Fleisher said. "It could be a way at getting

back at us, you know? Also, he's an ex-cop. Now Shaughnessy's got this theory that Hog stands for something, and one of things we've been looking at is brutal cops, you know? Pig? Hog?"

Benedetti smiled. "Fascinating theory. Did you hear that, *amico?*"

"I certainly did, *Maestro,*" Ron said. "My congratulations to the sergeant."

"All right, all right, you don't have to be so sarcastic, for crysake. The guy is trying, just like the rest of us."

Ron couldn't help laughing. Fleisher gave him a disgusted look. The professor said, "I would like to talk to the manager, if I might, Inspector."

"Okay." The inspector stuck his head out the door and yelled for Shaughnessy, who returned with a man who looked frightened out of his wits. More than that—who looked so frightened, it was hard to believe he had ever *had* wits.

Ickes was a member of that relatively new economic class—the franchise manager. They are a masochistic lot who want the responsibility of ownership, and the danger of risking their own money, without sacrificing their God-given right to have someone higher up to be afraid of.

Ickes was in a virtual ecstasy of fear. He was afraid of the police, ipso facto. He was afraid of the guy with the accent—he looked like an emissary of the devil. He was afraid of not handling these people right, and winding up on the carpet in front of the regional supervisor. He was afraid the bloodstains would never come out of the carpet. When the big bony foreigner asked him if Jastrow had had any visitors tonight, he said, "I'm afraid I don't know," in his best welcome-to-the-Restover-Inn voice. "We don't lock the side doors until midnight. 'When you stop at a Restover Inn, you're just coming home again,' we like to say, and it's bad psychology to lock a person in or out of his home. The company manual says . . ."

Inspector Fleisher stopped him before he could explain what the company manual said. "Okay, okay, no visitors. Any phone calls?"

"No, sir. In the time he was here, he neither placed or received any calls. At least not through the Inn. He may have used the pay phone in the parking lot." Ickes bit his lip, trying to decide whether he wanted to risk saying what he had to say. The regional supervisor might not like his butting in on police business. Still, the company demanded all its franchise holders to be citizens of the highest caliber. He decided to risk it, for the greater glory of Restover Inns.

"Inspector," he began. "Inspector, in the accommodation industry, we get to be pretty good judges of character. You can appreciate that, can't you?"

"Oh, sure," the inspector told him dryly.

"For example," Ickes went on, reassured, "the other day, a man and a woman came in and tried to register as Mr. and Mrs. William Smith. Well, that name. Such an obvious alias. But let me tell you, the poor man was *so* self-conscious, I was sure he was telling the truth. I mean, there have to be thousands of real William Smiths in the world, right? So, I said to myself—"

Fleisher did not subscribe to the Benedetti philosophy. "What's the point?" he snapped.

Ickes had reached nirvana. He was at the absolute zenith of fear. God, he had antagonized the police! Fatalistically, he finished his thought. "Well . . . ah . . . I just thought . . . that is it seemed . . . at least to *me,* though of course I'm no expert . . ."

"Out with it!"

"Well, it just seems obvious that there *couldn't* have been a visitor here with Jastrow."

"Why not?"

"Because if someone was here with him they wouldn't have let him *kill* himself, would they?"

Fleisher groaned and rubbed his eyes.

The professor came to the rescue. He said, "Thank you, Mr. Ickes, that is very logical. It had never even occurred to us."

Hearing that, Ickes bigheartedly understood and forgave Inspector Fleisher. The police had been under a lot of pressure, after all. "My pleasure," he smiled. "Any time I can be of help."

The foreigner (who no longer looked half so sinister) said, "How kind of you. *I* have a question. How much stationery might one expect to find in this room?"

That was an easy one. "The stationery comes in sealed plastic packets of twelve pieces of Restover Inn stationery and twelve envelopes. It's terrific advertising, you know," he confided.

"I'm sure it is. How often are these packets replaced?"

"Well, if the customer hasn't opened it, the maid leaves the packet; but if it's been started but not finished, she replaces it with a brand new one. 'Everything's the best over at your friendly Restover,' " he quoted.

"It is indeed," the professor said. He turned to the inspector. "There you have it. Ronald, show him the contents of the drawer."

A young guy with blond hair and glasses, whom Ickes had thought was a cop, opened a drawer, and removed the torn plastic packet. "Eight pieces of paper," he said. "Still twelve envelopes, though."

"So," the old Italian guy said. "We have our explanation for the position of the corpse: Jastrow was engaged in writing something when he was shot."

"Like what?" drawled a voice from the Deep South. Ickes suddenly recognized him as Buell Tatham. Ickes loved his column, but wisely decided this wasn't the time to say so.

The professor shrugged. "Who can say what he was writing? Perhaps the killer's name. In any case, the papers were taken away. I would not be surprised, Mr. Tatham, if your next note from Hog came on Restover Inn letterhead."

Oh, my *God!* Ickes thought in panic. A Hog murder at a Restover Inn! The regional supervisor was going to be furious.

TWELVE

TUESDAY WAS AN EVENTFUL DAY. EARLY THAT MORNING
the professor, who had not gone to bed, finished the boar
hunt painting and started on one that looked to Ron's
bleary sleep-starved eyes like a map of New York State.
When he asked the professor and found out that was indeed what it was, he asked why.

"Because," the old man said, "I have traveled to every
continent but one, and I have dealt with evil in the most
exotic lands on earth; yet nothing I have ever seen can
match the cases this state and this city have produced for
my enlightenment."

Enlightenment, Ron knew, was Benedetti's highest
praise for criminal cleverness. "You think this is going to
be a classic, then?"

"Yes, I do, even if Hog *does* turn out to be merely a
lunatic who should be put out of his misery, but, of course
won't be. The case of the severed head in the bathroom
bowl was child's play by comparison."

Ron removed his glasses, rubbed his eyes. "It's always
a pleasure to be in on history, *Maestro*," he said. "What
do you want for breakfast?"

The old man looked up from the canvas. "If, as I think
you are, you are offering me a choice of abominable
cereal products to be eaten with cold milk, I shall skip
breakfast and continue to paint."

"Good," Ron said. "I'll see you later at my office."

Downtown, Ron found Mrs. Goralsky in a happy
mood, humming to herself as she answered some cor-
respondence. Ron wondered about it until she started
asking him coy questions about what time the professor
was coming into the office. Ron mumbled something, and
retreated to his private sanctuary.

He returned a couple of calls, one from Janet Higgins,

who was more than a little miffed at not being invited out to the motel last night, but who would still be going around with Ron and the professor today; and one from a friend in Albany, who informed Ron that a Mr. Harold Atler had filed a charge of unethical conduct against him with the State License Bureau.

Ron looked at his watch. It was going to be a long day.

Diedre Chester wouldn't have agreed. The morning was flying by; she was positively radiant. She turned up a gorgeous turkey at a little poultry shop she had never seen before, and she had turned up vegetables so fresh, it was as though it wasn't even winter. Her party tomorrow night would dazzle, especially with the new murder to talk about—oops, she thought, Buell wouldn't like that kind of thinking. And of course he was right. How would she feel if Buell or Ricky were to have something happen to them?

The morning mail brought a letter from Ricky, from his father's house in Monrovia. They'd gone hiking. Diedre thought it was wonderful that Ricky would have a background in two kinds of cultures; maybe he could be a diplomat or something when he grew up.

Diedre put the letter back in the envelope. She remembered to make a mental note to ask everyone at the party if they collected stamps.

Tuesday brought a minor triumph to Inspector Fleisher. With the written and oral consent, and the personal presence of Buell Tatham, and with political manipulations that went as far as Washington, D.C., the inspector had finally persuaded the United States Postal Service, Sparta, New York, division, to intercept the reporter's mail. The result of all this effort was to put the latest letter in his hands two hours earlier than it would have been otherwise.

Buell made the mistake of pointing this out.

"Never mind that stuff," the inspector snarled. "Every second might count, for crysake."

The envelope looked identical to all the others, with the exception of the date on the postmark. But inside, there were several differences. For one thing, Benedetti had been right. The envelope did indeed contain a sheet of Restover Inn letterhead.

Another difference was there was no message. Or rather, no *written* message. There was the familiar signature: "—HOG"; but above that there was just an irregular brownish stain that the lab later identified as the blood of ex–Deputy Sheriff Jeffrey Jastrow.

Everyone seemed to get the message just fine.

When Mrs. Goralsky summoned Ron to the outer office, he emerged to find a rather irritated man with a taxi-driver's cap holding the eminent Professor Benedetti by the elbow.

"*Amico,*" the old man began.

"You Gentry?" the cabbie snapped.

Ron toyed with the idea of denying it, but finally said he was.

"You gonna pay this fare?" the driver demanded.

Ron sighed. He asked how much, dug out his wallet, and paid the man, who walked out grumbling.

The professor shook his head. "Disgraceful," he said solemnly. "I am a visitor to this country. If taxi drivers do not wish to accept Brazilian *cruzeiros,* they should make it clear at the outset." He brushed the traces of the cabbie's essence from his tweeds.

"So, Ronald, have you had a pleasant morning? Have there been any developments?"

Ron, who had been on the phone with Shaughnessy, told him of the developments. The professor grunted, and said, "Well, then, let us pick up Dr. Higgins and get about our own work, shall we?"

Herbie Frank was pleased. His visitors today were more than just the dumb flatfoots who had been bothering him, getting in the way of his work. This was Professor Benedetti, whose picture was in the newspapers. The famous man had more sense than to try to pretend he suspected Herbie of being Hog, asking him sick questions about what he did when he thought about poor Leslie. It made him mad. Not that he *couldn't* fool the police if he wanted, they were dumb enough; but still.

But Benedetti was smart. He asked Herbie for his help on the case, he knew Herbie had a lot of ideas.

He liked the lady, too, this Dr. Higgins. She smiled at him; it was a nice smile. She understood the way things were in life, too. Like how sometimes a very intelligent person can have only a "C" average because the stupid professors don't understand what he's trying to say, or because they're jealous.

Even the young blond guy, who was obviously only some kind of chauffeur, seemed to be okay. When Herbie told him where he worked summers, the guy didn't make any cracks about him being strong enough to do it. Herbie got tired of having to explain he was there as a clerk.

The professor wanted to know if he could smoke. Herbie told him sure, although he didn't usually allow smoking in his apartment. He got the professor a Dixie cup to put his ashes in.

"Now, Mr. Frank," the old man said. "My colleagues and I are extremely interested in your opinion of the case."

"Yes, sir," Herbie said. "Well, since I knew Leslie pretty well—she kind of looked up to me, if you know what I mean—I've been very interested in the case. I'm working on a program on it, for the computer. I figure if Hog strikes only three more times, I'll have enough data to work it out."

The professor smiled at him. "I had hoped to have the benefit of your thinking before Hog struck again."

"Oh, of course, naturally. But you have to realize that however logical my mind has become, from working with the machine, you know, I can't be mathematical and certain. I can only give you, you know, ideas."

"I understand perfectly," the old man said. "At this point in the investigation, even ideas would help."

Reassured, Herbie went on. "Now, I think that even though Hog is—excuse me, Dr. Higgins—in plain English, carzy, he doesn't think he's crazy. *I think he thinks he's doing it for a reason.*

"Now, you look at all the victims, and what do we find? That the odds that Hog could have a reason to kill all those different people are, you know, infinitesimal. I could show you a formula I worked out . . ."

Herbie was pleased to see they trusted him enough to take his word for it without seeing the formula. "So," he said, "Hog must have a reason for killing only *one* of his victims, and he did the rest as, you know, a smoke screen."

They were all looking intently at him, hanging on his every word. Herbie started to toy with the idea of doing a law enforcement program for his doctorate.

The professor said, "That's certainly a possibility we are considering. Have you considered the matter further?"

Herbie nodded enthusiastically. "Uh huh. Now, look at the victims again, this time looking for an anomaly, you know, something different. That's how my program's going to work. And what do we find this time?

"Of all Hog's victims, poor Leslie Bickell was the only one who was rich. Hog thought he could gain from her death."

"But nobody gained anything from her death." It was the blond guy. He was a little slow to catch on.

"Of course not," Herbie explained patiently. "He's crazy remember? He got all mixed up. He thought he could gain by her death, but, he realized, it was too late. That's why he dropped out of sight, and he only comes back to, you know, kill somebody else to try and cover up."

"Aha," the old man said. "Then you believe Terry Wilbur is the killer."

"It seems *obvious* to me," Herbie stated flatly. "Naturally, though," he went on, "I knew him and saw and heard him a lot, and you didn't; you'll have to take my word for some things. He's . . . well . . . he's *sick!* I can prove it on the machine!"

Dr. Higgins asked him, "How did he show it?" The professor murmured, "Well worded."

Herbie said, "He did crazy things. He treated Leslie rotten—no respect, you know?"

"What exactly did he do to her, though?" the lady asked.

Herbie rubbed his face. "Oh, well, darn it." He fidgeted in his seat. "Well, he *whistled.*"

"Whistled?" the blond guy echoed.

"Yeah!" Herbie said. "When he came to see Leslie, going up the stairs, he'd always be *whistling,* like a happy little bird, or something. Sometimes he'd sing, things like

'Tonight's the Night' or some other dirty thing like that."

"Anything else?"

"Yeah, his stupid *keys*. He always came up the stairs jingling his keys, you know? Like to tell the world he could get into Leslie when—I mean into her apartment—whenever he wanted. Rubbing it in that they—that they—"

"Had intercourse?"

Herbie relaxed. Trust the professional to have the right way to put it. "Yeah, he had to brag that they had intercourse. You should have heard him run up those steps that night. Then he had the nerve to call her a *whore!* I get mad just thinking about it!"

"So," the professor asked quietly, "you think we should concentrate on finding Terry Wilbur?"

Herbie was too worked up to speak, he could only nod.

"Then I don't mind telling you, Mr. Frank," the old man said as he rose, "that I agree with you whole-heartedly. I thank you for your time and assistance."

"And," Dr. Higgins said, "if you—uh—if you have any further ideas about the case, call me about it, all right?" She gave him her card.

Herbie smiled so wide he hurt his face. He *knew* they were smart!

Outside, Ron let go a long low whistle that showed in the cold air like a smokey dagger. He looked at Janet. "How does it feel to meet your own psychological profile?" he asked. "It must feel like you *created* him, for God's sake. Is that why you gave him your card?"

There was a firm line to Janet's jaw, and a firm professional glint in her eye. "That boy is desperately in need of help."

"I'll say. He doesn't even concede the possibility that a guy could whistle or sing or run or jingle keys because he might be happy to see his girl. If you don't skulk around about it, you're a pervert."

"That's exactly why he needs help!" the psychologist said.

"Well," Ron said, "if, as a noted psychologist's report seems to imply, Herbie Frank is the Hog, then *nobody* is going to be able to help him. And even if he isn't, and you just pat him on the head once, he's going to fall in love with you! And if you try to cut him loose, he might *still* be dangerous!"

"Oh?" Dr. Higgins said. "And where did you take *your* Ph.D., Dr. Gentry?"

"Ha, ha," Ron said. "Just don't go playing cozy with someone who just might be a mass-killer, all right? As a favor to me?"

Dr. Higgins was still in control for the argument, but Ron's last sentence rang a tiny bell in the Janet part of her personality.

"You have to admit," Ron went on, "he fits your profile that you were so hot on yesterday morning."

"I am a professional!" she snapped. "I know what I am doing!"

"But he fits in, along with everybody else. You heard what he used to do summers!"

"He worked in a foundry!" Suddenly, she brought herself up short. "What everybody else? What are you talking about?"

Before Ron could answer, Professor Benedetti's voice, laden with disdain, ended the argument. "Very entertaining," he said. "And if my lifework were the study of human folly rather than that of evil, it would even be instructional. But we have work to do, eh?

"*Va bene.* Then I will settle this immediately. First of all, Ronald, I assure you that Dr. Higgins has no intention whatever of treating that poor wretch Herbert Frank herself; and that in fact she only argued with you because she would not have you think she would refer him to a male colleague because she is afraid, and because of your appalling arbitrary attitude.

"Secondly, I assure you *both* that the argument is academic. Herbert Frank is not the Hog. Despite his obvious emotional problems, he has found an outlet for himself. As long as he has access to the sterile, emotionless world of the electronic brain, he will be a danger to no one."

Despite what Benedetti said, Ron still wasn't ready to send his sister to the prom with Herbie Frank. But there was no arguing the accuracy of the old man's first observation; Janet was as red as a stop light. Ron smiled. The idea of a shrink blushing at the revelation of her innermost thoughts tickled him no end.

"All settled?" the professor asked. "Friends again? *Buonissimo*. However, I'm sure the outburst of your emotions has cost you the realization of the one significant thing that young fool *did* have to say."

If any bloodstains remained on the driveway or garage at the house where little Davy Reade had been, yesterday's blizzard had mercifully covered them. Just looking at the place brought the police photographs back to Janet's mind. She shuddered.

The man who opened the door looked like a western-movie star at the end of a long convalescence. There was a grayish tone to his tanned complexion, and new-looking hollows in his face. He eyed his callers suspiciously.

"What do you want?" he asked.

"Mr. Reade?" The professor smiled exactly like an undertaker.

"Yeah, that's me. What do you want?"

The professor had Ron produce the credentials Fleisher had given him and made the necessary introductions. When he saw that his visitors were official, John Reade's face went slack, as though the effort of registering suspicious hostility had been a great one.

"Well," he said, "come in." He led them into a room Janet recognized from police photographs. It was a lot neater now. She noticed the handmade picture frame on the mantel, and felt her throat tighten up. She made herself stop—too much sentiment was unprofessional.

Reade said, "Anybody want a drink? No? Anybody mind if I have one?" It was a rhetorical question. The cap was already off the vodka by the time he finished asking. Reade poured his drink, vodka on ice, and said, "What can I do for you, Professor? Sorry about my attitude at the door, but you wouldn't believe the people who have been here. Reporters, one guy wanted to ghost a book by my—by Joyce, telling what it's like to lose a son to a maniac. I hit him. There was an old lady that was going to contact Davy in the 'spirit' world. And relatives. People who didn't even come to our wedding came to little Davy's funeral. Ghouls." He tilted his head and drank like vodka was a soft drink. He wiped his mouth with the back of his hand and said, "I'm a louse. I've always known that. But since I've come back to Sparta,

I've been thinking that I might not be so much worse than anybody else."

Ron said, "You came out here the day after Davy's death, correct? From San Francisco? That would be Thursday, the twenty-ninth?"

"Yeah. What's the point?" Reade was gathering up the energy to become hostile again, Janet saw. He was making inferences about what the detective's question really meant.

Ron, however, was bland. "Just checking. Did you have to close the motorcycle shop to come out here?"

"No, my partner is watching the business."

"What kind of bike do you sell?" Ron asked.

"All kinds."

"Harley-Davidsons?"

"Yeah, I've a got a contract with some of the police departments, I sell a lot of the bigger ones, the real . . . oh, my God!"

"What's the matter, Mr. Reade?"

Reade's jaw had dropped open. He tried to cover it up with another long pull at his drink. Janet looked around to see Ron's face grim, and a vague smile on Benedetti's. Janet was very confused.

The old man said, "Please, do not worry, Mr. Reade. The merest coincidence."

Reade looked slightly better, though he was still obviously shaken. "I—it never occurred to me."

The professor shrugged it off. "Perfectly understandable. Now, sir, I want to ask you some personal questions. Is that all right?"

"What? Oh, sure, go ahead."

"Why did you and your wife divorce?"

"Because I'm a louse. I told you. I screwed other women."

"You had an affair?"

Reade snorted. "Not even. A bunch of one night stands I never cared a damn about. One after another, like peanuts. Joyce probably would have forgiven an affair, but she couldn't understand the peanut women." He lifted his glass and mumbled into it, "Neither can I."

"Did you make enemies doing this? Or in your business? Could someone have wanted to get back at you by killing your son?"

Reade shook his head sadly. "No. The women were all unattached, or if they were attached, there've been plenty of men besides me. I didn't even go into business until I moved West, so that's out.

"The only person I've ever given cause to hate me has been Joyce. And she doesn't even do that."

"How is Mrs. Reade taking this?" the professor asked.

"Bad," Reade said. "I've got to get her to snap out of it. She's so distant. I'm afraid to leave her alone. I've been sleeping on the couch here, to keep an eye on her."

"How long do you plan to stay with it?" Ron asked.

Janet thought she caught a spark of life in Reade's eyes. "Hey," he said. "I'm a louse, but I'm not that big a louse. As long as it takes, that's how long I'm going to stay with it!"

"May we talk to Mrs. Reade, please?" the professor asked.

Reade made a face. "I wish you wouldn't. I finally got her to try and get some sleep."

Benedetti was apologetic. "I understand, Mr. Reade, but if we are just seconds earlier in catching the killer, we may save a life, eh?"

Reade nodded resignedly, saying, "I'll go get her." He disappeared into the back of the house.

A few seconds later, he was shouting something.

Janet looked at Ron. "What is he saying?" she asked. "Sounds like 'Rig! Rig!' " he replied.

That's what it sounded like to Janet, too. The mystery was soon solved, however. Reade, frantic, appeared back in the living room yelling, "Dr. Higgins! Come quick!" She got up and followed.

Janet was a psychologist, not a psychiatrist. She wasn't a medical doctor. Still, she knew what to do when confronted with the comatose form of a woman with an empty bottle of sleeping pills in her hand. While she did it, Ron Gentry, who had followed her, called for an ambulance.

It's a drama with a small number of characters, played on one set, with one line of dialogue, and two possible outcomes. But when a doctor walks into the waiting room, no matter how often this particular stock piece is played, there is never anything less than one hundred percent suspense on the part of the audience. They played it this time with the happy ending—"She's going to live," the doctor said. Curtain.

She would not only live, she would be fine. She had been found before any permanent mental or physical damage could be done. John Reade wept; Fleisher, who had rushed out to the hospital, went home, grumbling. Buell Tatham, and the rest of the reporters, went to file their stories.

The professor had been strangely quiet during the whole thing. To Ron, it seemed that once again, the professor was showing all the signs of having learned something. Ron hinted around, trying to find out what it was, to no avail.

Finally, the old man said, "Ronald, take me home. I will see no more witnesses. I will paint. Take me home, Ronald."

Ron went to tell Janet. "What does he mean, he's seeing no more witnesses?" she wanted to know.

Ron was troubled. "It means he's mad at himself," he said. "It means he's spotted something important—he's got this inhuman instinct for knowing what's important—but he doesn't know why it's important, or, sometimes, even what it is he's spotted. He's so conceited, he holds it against himself. So he just stops working and paints until he figures it out."

"Does it take him long?"

"It took three weeks in the Entwright thing. But usually, it's only a couple of days. And when he comes out of it, he's usually got the case cracked. Are you coming along?"

"I can't," she said. "The police and the hospital want some more from me."

"Okay," he said. "See you tomorrow then." He took her hands, which were nearly as large as his, patted them, and left.

The business at the hospital took a lot longer than she expected, and it was past midnight when Janet got back to her apartment. She was worked up and tense, so she played the piano for a while, then took a sleeping pill— *one* sleeping pill—and went to bed. She completely forgot her intention to read her newly bought copy of *Charlotte's Web* that evening.

THIRTEEN

◆◆ ◆◆ ◆◆ ◆◆ ◆◆ ◆◆ ◆◆ ◆◆ ◆◆ ◆◆ ◆◆ ◆◆ ◆◆ ◆◆ ◆

If Tuesday had been eventful, on Wednesday, to use Inspector Fleisher's phrase, it *really* hit the fan.

From a variety of directions.

Ron Gentry was chagrined to find the professor daubing away at his painting of New York State (he was putting in the Finger Lakes) wearing a beard stubble that sat on the old man's nut-brown skin like fungus on a breadboard. The case had really gotten to him. Ron didn't even bother to wish his mentor a *buona mattina*. He just quietly slipped out to the office.

Up on the campus of Sparta University, Dr. Janet Higgins was involved, in spite of herself, in a heated controversy in a faculty meeting. Tired of repressive administrative policies, low pay, and class overload, and egged on by the leaders of the student government (in the interests of academic freedom and more time for ski trips), the faculty of the School of Liberal Arts had decided to strike. The question then arose whether Operation Outreach, the blanket title for university personnel lending their expertise to the community, should be struck as well. The answer was yes. Then, the radical young man from the poli sci department, who had fomented the strike in the first place, pointed out that if Dr. Higgins pulled out of the Hog hunt, the result would be bad ink in the press, and bad vibes all the way around, man. The radical young man was shouted down. He wondered why the people he had gotten all excited wouldn't calm down at the proper time. He had never read *Frankenstein*.

Janet had been a card-carrying member of the American Federation of Musicians since she was four years old. She was staunch for the rights of labor. But at that moment, she crossed the mental picket line, and quietly but

115

firmly became a scab. She left the meeting and headed for the Public Safety Building.

Things were hopping down there, too. Inspector Fleisher couldn't remember a crazier day in Sparta since the time in his youth when some Canadian rumrunners, New York City speakeasy owners, and Buffalo hijackers shot it out for six hours across Pershing Square, killing the council president's mistress on the steps of city hall in the crossfire.

But that had been crazy and exciting. Today was only crazy.

They were picketing the PSB, for crysake. Walking around out there in the cold, carrying signs with things like, "Catch the Hog—Now!" and "Make Sparta Safe Again!" What the hell were these people trying to prove? Did they think the inspector hadn't been putting out on this goddamn case? That each and every *one* of the thirty-five detectives in what had come to be known as the Hog Squad wasn't putting out? That stupid cardboard *signs* were gonna make them try harder, thank you for bringing it to our attention there's a murderer running around? Idiots.

Then that lady shrink showed up, just to tell him she wouldn't be leaving the case, even though her fellow big-domes up on the Hill told her she had to. The inspector had to admit it took a certain amount of guts. He felt a kind of grudging respect for her. Not that she'd been much of a help so far, but still.

The inspector was showing Janet the latest no-progress reports, when Hawkins of the Hog Squad barged in looking like he just found his sergeant's stripes made up in a sandwich in his lunchbox.

"You look too happy, Hawkins," Fleisher said dyspeptically. "If you don't have good news, I'm going to be angry."

"Oh, it's good, sir," he said eagerly. "Or, at least it's something."

"Well?"

"I—I mean Aronian and me—we broke Terry Wilbur's alibi for that first murder."

"Tell me about it," Fleisher said.

"We just kept going back to the witnesses, again and

again," Hawkins said, "until we got one guy who admitted he wasn't completely sure it was Wilbur he saw at the Y that night. We went back with that to the other witnesses, and all of a sudden *they* weren't so sure any more, either."

"Okay Hawkins, good work." The young detective smiled and left. Fleisher was pleased, but not overjoyed. He knew that if you ask someone, "Yeah, but are you *sure?*" enough times, you could get him to doubt dogs have hair. It was a bad sign in an investigation when the cops started doing the DA's work—Fleisher felt it was better to concentrate on arresting somebody, then letting the lawyer types worry about sowing doubt on alibis.

Dr. Higgins was frowning. Fleisher asked her what was the matter.

"I've been reading over these notes again," she said. "And there's something here I hadn't noticed before . . . another way Hog is different from the normal serial murderer."

"Normal?"

"Well, the usual kind."

"What's that?"

"These notes tell us nothing about Hog at all."

Fleisher sputtered. "What do you want, his address, for crysake?"

"Do you have to try to deliberately misunderstand me, Inspector?" she asked quietly. Fleisher, chastened, shut up.

"What I mean is this," she went on. "All the cases I've researched show the killer with an urge to reveal things about himself. George Metesky, the Mad Bomber, talked about his grudge against a utilities company—"

"He didn't kill anybody," Fleisher corrected. "But I do see your point. The New York cops found Metesky in a file of unsatisfied ex-employees. It's that stuff about they want to be caught."

Dr. Higgins nodded. "The ultimate case, of course, is the boy that scrawled 'stop me before I kill more.' "

"But Hog's notes don't tell us anything about him; they just say enough to prove they're from the killer, and sometimes promise more. He keeps himself out of the notes. Aside from the fact that he thinks drug addiction is bad, and that a reporter who stumbles onto his story is lucky, he gives no opinion at all."

Maybe there's something to this broad after all, Fleisher thought. Since he was an honest man, he was going to say so, and apologize for his earlier skepticism, but he never got a chance. Shaughnessy burst into the office, panting.

"What is it, Mike?" the inspector wanted to know.

"The commissioner's here!"

"Here?" Fleisher was shocked. Sparta's police commissioner was a hair bag, a political hack, whose knowledge of police work came exclusively from watching *Dragnet* on television. He could, however (and more importantly did), draw on his wife's substantial fortune at campaign time. He was an old crony of the mayor's; he performed best in his job (to Fleisher's way of thinking) when he went on one of his extended fact-finding missions about the police methods in the Caribbean Islands.

"What the hell is *he* doing here?" Fleisher wondered aloud.

The inspector hadn't seen that afternoon's edition of the Sparta *Express,* or he wouldn't have had to ask. The *Express* was Sparta's "other" paper. That's how everybody thought of it—"Go down to the newsstand and buy the *Courant* and the other paper." No one at the *Express* had ever minded the second-class status, especially. They were happy it existed at all. Sparta really wasn't big enough to support two dailies; the *Express* was run by a big corporation as a tax loss.

But enough was enough. The *Courant* had the Hog story all to itself. Hell, Buell Tatham had the police eating out his hand. The *Express* would see about that.

It was a front page editorial. The headline was "OF-FICIAL COVERUP IN HOG CASE?" A survey later showed not one reader in a thousand (and many more thousands than usual saw the *Express* that day) noticed the question mark. The piece said, in many more words, that they at the *Express* had wondered at Hog's seeming omniscience; how he knew so much, and could elude the police so easily. They wondered if Hog might not be "privy to the strategy of the men in blue," and they wondered if this simple idea, which they offered for what it was worth, had occurred to the police. "Or," they concluded, "can it be that it already has? If so, when we see one reporter from one source with the police day and night, and we hear reports of 'no progress' from official sources after so much time and so many horrible murders, we have to wonder whether the answer is being hidden."

Had the mayor been eating anything but yogurt when he read that editorial, he would have choked to death. He had a mental picture of the senate sinking in a hog wallow. He called his old buddy, the commissioner, and demanded action.

And action he got. The commissioner had made a rare appearance at police headquarters to inform Fleisher that he, Fleisher, was holding a press conference in twenty minutes to explain the important new developments in the Hog case, and to put to rest the vile rumor that there could be any kind of conspiracy involving his police department, or *anyone* connected with the administration of the next United States senator from the state of New York. It was not necessary for the commissioner to add "or else."

Dr. Higgins excused herself, and left. Fleisher's thoughts had to do with rats and sinking ships.

Ron Gentry, meanwhile, was going over a list of the things Harold Atler had put in his complaint to the license bureau. Gentry had made private use of information gathered while in Atler's employ. He had slandered Atler, and threatened him physical violence. One out of three, Ron thought.

He made a face. Atler had obviously flipped—the hearing he was after would make public the very things he wanted quiet. Atler probably figured he was through, anyway. Now it wasn't so much help Atler as hurt Gentry he was interested in. In spite of everything, Ron had to pity the broker.

The phone buzzed. Mrs. Goralsky's voice said, "Dr. Higgins is on the line."

Ron told her to make the connection. He heard the

usual click, then Janet's voice say, "Ron!" then a loud *clunk!*

"Hello?" he said. "Janet?"

"Hello?" Janet said.

"Are you all right? What was that noise?"

"What? Oh, I just dropped the phone. Ron, Fleisher's in trouble."

"I saw today's *Express.*"

"They're making a scapegoat out of him." She told him about the commissioner's visit. "Can't you do something? You know Fleisher would never ask for help."

"You flatter me," he told her, "but I carry no weight here at all. If anybody, it has to be the professor."

She told him to hurry.

He had Mrs. Goralsky ring his house. Useless. When the professor went into his painting frenzy, he couldn't be bothered with worldly concerns like answering the phone. Ron swore, and hung up, ran downstairs, and drove through the slush to his house.

Now, the professor did look like a derelict; unshaven, in his soiled shirt, staring with glazed eyes at the canvas. Even that looked somehow gone to seed. The wide part of New York State was wider, and more rounded near the edges. The narrow, projecting part was longer and thinner. It was a map for the wall of the mirror room in the fun house.

The professor didn't hear Ron come in.

"Maestro?"

Benedetti did not look up from his canvas. "Yes, Ronald? Are you home already? I have decided not to attend Mrs. Chester's little get-together this evening."

"I'm not here about that, *Maestro.* They're getting ready to dump Fleisher off the case."

The old man laughed. "And who can they find better? In this town?" The old man liked to pretend he was naïve about politics.

"It doesn't matter if they get someone better. They're all on the hot seat—they have to give the illusion of movement, even if they aren't going anywhere."

The professor rose from his stool. "Ronald," he said softly, "this case is an abyss. I have analyzed. I am trying to imagine. And I can find no explanation at all, *buon'Iddio,* not even the most outlandish one, that is consistent with itself, let alone evidence. I am dealing with perhaps the strangest evil I have ever found, and you come to me with the petty politics of the police. *I will not tolerate interruptions!* Had you done something like this before, you would not have lasted a day as my pupil."

Ron exploded. *"Why don't you grow up, for God's sake?"*

The professor tilted back his head and looked down his nose. "Niccolo Benedetti is not talked to in this fashion."

Ron said, "I'm sorry," in tones of no sincerity. "All right. You sit here in your rent-free studio, and paint and think to your heart's content. But as a philosopher, you should try to understand that evil today is not fought from the backs of white stallions. Evil today is tied in with all the petty, weak human things, like looking for a scapegoat when the villain eludes capture. And you might take a moment to think about who got you the opportunity to study this particular evil in the first place.

"And you might think about this. One guaranteed result of Fleisher's replacement will be a period of confusion, a slowing down of the investigation. A fine chance for a maniac to strike, wouldn't you say, *Maestro?* But at least you will have proved you're consistent in your eccentricities, won't you?"

He turned to stalk out, and heard the professor's laughter behind him. He whirled around. "What's so funny?"

"A struggling private eye who denies his complexities." He laughed again, sighed. "Once again, the teacher learns from the student, eh? If you give me a moment, I will come with you. First, I must wash and shave."

Fleisher's news conference was not going well. He had started out by giving the newspaper and broadcast reporters present a catalog of the various things an investigation of that size entailed. That was received with, at best, tolerance. Then he made the tactical error of pointing out just how many similar cases in the past, from all over the world, had gone unsolved.

"Is that a copout, Inspector?" asked a man from the Top-40 station. There was a rumbling in the room.

The trouble is, I can't think straight, for crysake,

the inspector thought. His mind was full of the thought of strangling the mayor and the police commissioner simultaneously, one in each hand.

There was only one thing to do. The inspector threw them a bone. "No, it's no copout. I'm just saying. In fact, we've made some progress just today. Detectives, ah, Aronian and, ah," what the hell was his *name?* "ah, Hawkins," that was it, "detectives Aronian and Hawkins, working under my direction," and God forgive me for that, he thought, "have broken the alibi of Terry Wilbur, the boyfriend of Leslie Bickell, the fourth victim, who as you know has disappeared. We now consider him an active suspect."

He might as well have saved himself the trouble—the press had considered Wilbur an active suspect since the first time they tried to interview him and he wasn't there.

The man from the *Express* said, "Come on, Inspector, who are you covering up for?"

Fleisher started to boil. As a thirty-three-year man, he had heard questions like that before, and knew how to handle them; but he wasn't himself today, he was the damn mayor's whipping boy. And if he did give that bastard the answer he deserved, he was through. So the seconds ticked by while the inspector stood in impotent rage.

The reporters and spectators started to yell. "Well?" "What about it, Fleisher?" "Does this silence mean you're really shielding someone?" "Who is it, Fleisher?"

Then a voice came from the door in the back of the room. It wasn't a loud voice, but it cut through the other voices and made people listen.

"I will answer those questions, if the inspector does not mind."

Fleisher could have kissed him. "Not at all, Professor," he said, quite literally from the bottom of his heart. "This is the world-famous Professor Niccolo Benedetti," he told the press, who did not need to be told.

The professor, followed by Ron Gentry, walked up on the small stage, shook hands ostentatiously with Fleisher, stood behind the podium, adjusted the microphone, and addressed the ladies and gentlemen of the press.

"Fools!" he said. "Fools of the press and fools of the administration! This man cannot be apprehending a mur-

derer if he is here defending his well-earned reputation from malicious rumors repeated and feared by fools."

Ron saw Janet in the audience. She was having a hard time keeping in her desire to applaud.

Benedetti went on. "You wish to know if anyone connected with the investigation of this case can be Hog? Do you think the inspector is as stupid as you? Everyone connected with the case, everyone, even to Niccolo Benedetti, has been tailed, at random, by policemen since this case began, and all, I repeat all, have alibis for at least one of Hog's atrocities. Are you now happy?"

A lady in a wig from a local TV station was not happy. "Why didn't Fleisher say this himself?"

Benedetti smiled, and scratched his hand. "Because," he almost purred, "unlike some, he cares more about catching the Hog than he does about his reputation. He didn't want his men to know their fellow officers were spying on them, on occasion, because if Hog *were* someone connected with the case, he would be tipped off, eh? And also, to keep up the morale of the officers. You have ruined this part of the investigation.

"But you must have something to tell your public, eh? Very well, tell them this: Today is Wednesday, the fourth of February. Niccolo Benedetti promises—at the risk of his *own* hard-earned reputation, that this *malefattore*, this Hog who wallows in human blood, will be in the custody of Inspector Fleisher within a week. Tell *that* to your public!"

Reporters have thick skins. The professor's insults were a small price to pay for his promise. They rushed to the phones to call the story in.

Buell Tatham, though, having no immediate deadline, ambled up to talk to the professor and Fleisher. "That was quite a speech, Professor," he said. "People are usually afraid to tell us off like that."

"It was not a blanket indictment," Benedetti smiled. "The word 'fool' was intended only for those to whom it applies."

Buell smiled. "I'll be sure to mention that in my column tomorrow. And don't forget Diedre's, tonight at 7:30." They assured him they wouldn't forget, and Buell ambled off. Ron watched him go, thinking how much he dreaded the coming evening. He went to talk to Janet.

Fleisher, meanwhile, was grinning in foolish gratitude, and shaking the professor's hand. But he was bewildered. "How did you know what I was up to, Professor?"

Benedetti shrugged. "It's what I would have done," he said.

"You mean you didn't know ... ?"

"Of course I knew. I knew you, therefore, I knew."

Ron, accompanied by Janet, rejoined them.

"Professor," she said, "did you mean that? About catching Hog within a week?"

"Niccolo Benedetti always means it when he stakes his reputation," the professor pronounced.

"How do we go about it, *Maestro?*" Ron asked.

"*Amico,* I haven't the first idea."

FOURTEEN

So BUELL TATHAM'S FIANCÉE WAS BEAUTIFUL, AND SHE could cook, too. Big deal, Janet thought, how many instruments can she play? She suppressed a giggle, and told herself firmly, no more champagne. Diedre Chester did know how to throw a get-together, even in the midst of a murder investigation.

Murder. The word sobered Janet. For the first time in weeks, she had gone an hour without thinking about Hog. There had been a tacit agreement to avoid the subject at table, and Diedre (who was practically incandescent) had been careful to steer conversation to other topics.

They talked about movies. Professor Benedetti, who had decided to come after all, turned out to be an avid fan of American westerns. Buell criticized them for not being true to life.

"What difference does that make?" Benedetti had replied. "They are not historical documents, they are entertainment. Do you believe the motion pictures produced in my native country show an accurate picture of the life of a roman gladiator? A motion picture is an illusion, possible only because of a defect in our perception; why should we ask more of it than diversion, eh? When real life offers so many more profound illusions." It was interesting.

Now, Janet could see, the conversation was being steered once again, this time *toward* the case that had brought them together. It was the professor who was doing the steering.

It didn't take much. Diedre Chester's eyes got brighter as the subject approached, and whatever she wanted, Buell wanted. Even Ron, while not looking happy, was accepting the inevitable. He looked like he was readying himself for something unpleasant.

Finally, Diedre asked straight out, "Are you going to catch him, Professor?"

The old man shrugged. "Five questions must be answered before we can capture Hog," he said. He ticked them off on bony fingers. "One. We must learn the significance of that missing scrap of metal, the one cut from the clamp that held the sign. Two. We must learn why of all the murders, those of the Bickell girl and Jastrow were made to appear self-inflicted instead of truly accidental. Three—and I cannot stress this enough—we must find Terry Wilbur. My intuition tells me he is the key to this case. Four, which we can answer, I am hopeful, when Wilbur is found. Why were those books defaced? Five. We must decide which, if any, of my young colleagues' researches, has relevance to the investigation. It is a shame Inspector Fleisher is not here to hear of them." He sighed. "Illusions. Politicians believe that a policeman must be miserable to be at work."

Diedre said, "What researches? What have you been up to, Ron?"

Buell wore the ghost of a smile. "Ron has been making vague references and asking cryptic questions of various people in the case."

"You get around," Ron said.

"I had a talk with Barbara Elleger. After that, all it took was a little checking up with the others. But I'm damned if I know what you're driving at."

Ron looked at him, appraisingly. Janet, who knew all about Ron's cryptic questions, was exasperated. "But what did you find *out?*" she blurted. "What's this all about?"

Ron looked at her. The professor said, "It is about pigs, Dr. Higgins."

"Pigs?" Diedre was incredulous, halfway to laughter.

"Pigs," Ron said. "As Janet can tell you, I spent all my time while the professor was on his way here in the library on the campus. I probably now know as much about pigs as anyone in this city."

"But *why?*" Diedre wanted to know.

"Because I knew the only thing we knew about the

killer was that he signed his notes 'HOG.' I mean, why that? It must mean *something* to him, right?"

Buell was skeptical. "Isn't that a little farfetched, Ron old boy?"

Diedre made a playful slap at him. "Oh, don't be a spoilsport," she said. "Just be happy he doesn't sign his notes 'GRITS.'"

There was laughter. Ron said, "No, I agree, it is far-fetched, but what could be more outlandish than the whole set-up of this case in the first place, with Hog's miracle getaways and snide notes?

"So I gave myself a cram course in pigs. Hogs. In all their glory, and their many, many applications."

Buell asked the professor what he thought of this.

"I applaud it," the old man said. "All knowledge is of value."

Ron smiled. "It was fascinating, actually. Pigs are an oppressed minority in the animal kingdom. They take a lot of unjustified abuse, especially considering their importance to man—actually *and* linguistically. They turn up everywhere."

"What do you mean, unjustified?" Diedre asked. "I always thought pigs were sloppy, messy animals."

"Not by nature, Diedre. Hogs don't sweat, you know, and their skin is very sensitive. That's why they wallow, to keep cool, and to protect themselves from the sun.

"Hogs are very commercial animals," Ron went on. "No animal turns feed to protein as fast as a pig. And it's not only meat they're good for, either. It's a cliché in the industry that they make use of everything but the squeal—they tan the skin for leather, make soap and cosmetics from the fat, fertilizer from the bones, brushes from the bristles.

"Biologically (I have learned) the hog is very similar to man. Pigskin is used for temporary grafts to humans in severe burn cases. Their eyes are like a man's. Their digestive system is the closest to man's of any nonprimate. Cannibals, who've eaten both, say human flesh tastes like pork. A cannibal term for human flesh translates as 'long pig.'"

"I'm glad I didn't make pork," Diedre said.

"Thanks," Ron said. "That leads to my next point.

"Now, everybody knows some religions—Judaism and

Islam, particularly—forbid their adherents to eat pork.
This was smart—improperly cooked pork can give trichinosis, and that was probably why the ancients of those
religions banned it. But at least *part* of the reason (according to the books I found) was superstition, based on
certain peculiarities of the hog's anatomy. In the first
place, unlike cows, sheep, goats, and other animals, but
like man, a pig has just one stomach. And in the second
place, pigs walk on cloven hooves.

"Now, given observations like this, and given the suf-
ferings the ancients saw of those who *did* eat the flesh
of pigs, and *did* come down with trichinosis, it's not hard
to understand how they would come to fear the pig as
the *earthly guise of devils and demons.*"

There was silence for a couple of seconds. They sat
around Diedre's coffee table like sitters at a seance. Janet
found herself murmuring, "It would fit. It would fit the
psychosis."

"There are echoes of it even into the New Testament,"
Ron went on. "Buell, doesn't Jesus save two demoniacs,
cast out their demons into the bodies of swine?"

"Well, yes, that much is right, Ron," he admitted.
"But—" he turned to the professor. "You don't honestly
think that this maniac, however crazy he is, actually
thinks he's Beelzebub himself, do you?"

The professor was grave. "What I think is of no con-
sequence. But I must say Hog has good credentials as a
demon. The murder of children and feeble old men; the
gloating afterward; and the suffering among all those the
tragedy touches; these are evil enough for any devil I
have heard of."

Buell was about to protest, but Dr. Higgins and science
were there to cut him off. "It makes sense psychologically,
Buell. Our killer is getting his gratification from a feeling
of *power*. It's a new experience for him; he revels in it.
It's a classic psychosis to delude yourself into thinking
you are God. If Hog is religious, or at least familiar with
religious dogma, he could easily prefer to be the devil.
As God, he ends their lives; as Satan, he has the added
power of tormenting their souls afterward."

Janet, the woman, listening to Dr. Higgins hold forth,
felt just a little appalled at what she heard herself saying.
This wasn't exactly after-dinner chitchat.

The effect of her comments rippled around the table. "That's something," Ron said softly.

"Again, I must say *'brava,'*" the professor said. "It may well be."

Buell was testy. "All right, that's enough of this for one night. I know all we have in common is the case, but have a little consideration for the hostess, all right?"

"Oh, Buell—" Diedre began, but Ron said, "I'm sorry. It just sort of snowballed. And anyway, in and of itself, it's no help at all."

Buell was relaxing, shrugging it off. "I'm sorry I snapped. But it did seem kind of irrelevant."

Ron raised an eyebrow. "That's what I thought, too, at first. But, on the not-altogether-ridiculous assumption that Hog just might be someone we've met in connection with the case, I took my new-found expertise, and tried to find applications to the people involved. I succeeded a lot better than I ever hoped I would."

Diedre gasped. "You mean you found someone?"

Ron took a sip of his champagne. It had gone flat; he made a face. "I found *everyone,*" he said.

FIFTEEN

RON POLISHED HIS GLASSES. "OR AT LEAST ALMOST everyone." Ron looked around at faces. They all, except the professor of course, had oddly uniform expressions of puzzlement. Ron knew better than to try to make anything important of it; the professor often said that controlled by a skillful liar, the human face was a deadly weapon.

Not unnaturally, they wanted to know what he was talking about.

"Well, as I said before, hogs—pigs—or something about them—turns up practically everywhere. With a little imagination you can tie in almost anybody. That's why I'm not so sure my little theory is worth anything. Though it has been interesting."

Diedre was impatient. "Well? Don't just sit there, *tell* us about it."

Ron leaned forward, elbows on knees, hands clasped together. "All right," he said, "let's take it crime by crime.

"It took me a while to get on to this. Hog's note about the first incident threw me off—it talked about Barbara Elleger's diaphragm. But *she* lived. Hog's first two *victims* were Carol Salinski and Beth Ling. Both girls were born in the United States, but one girl's ancestors came from Poland, and the other's came from China. Poland and China.

"It rang a bell when I first read about it, along with the story of the first note. And then, when I started my research, there it was, right in the encyclopedia, with a color picture. A Poland-China is a hog; a breed originated in Ohio that's known for its great weight-gaining speed. Don't ask me where the name comes in."

Janet was dubious. "That sounds a little farfetched."

Ron grinned. "That's what I said, at first. But it got me started. For old Stanley Watson, I admit, it was nowhere near a direct connection; the only thing that seemed to fit was that back in high school, Watson had been quite a football player. Scored four touchdowns once in one game."

"The old pigskin, Ron?" Buell was smiling. "Hell, if you call that a connection, you've connected up half the male population of New York State."

Ron nodded. "Including myself—I was a nearsighted I-formation fullback; carried the ball six times in four seasons. So we throw Watson's football career out because it's too general to be any help.

"That left me, after two murders, with one good tie-in, and one pretty weak one.

"The third and fourth incidents—accounting for the fourth and fifth murders, happened on the same night. Leslie Bickell was first. Follow me here. She was killed with heroin she bought with money she stole that night. The money was in the care of Harold Atler, but it was really the property of the members of that business class that Atler taught. That money was made through speculation in coffee beans and meat by-products. Guess what kind of meat by-products?"

Diedre guessed. "Pigs feet?"

Everyone but the professor laughed. The old man smiled indulgently.

"You're close," Ron told her. "It was mostly pork intestine."

"You mean chitlins," Buell told him.

"That's what they're called when people eat them," Ron conceded. "But these particular ones were earmarked for the pet food and pharmaceutical industries."

"That's an interesting combination," Janet said.

"I thought so, too," Ron said, "until I found out they make a drug called Heperin out of pork intestine. It's used in the treatment of phlebitis—breaks up blood clots or something.

"This was the best connection of all. This wasn't a pun, or a figurative connection—this was real, snorting pigs that actually lived. Or at least part of them. And it connected the Bickell girl and Atler at the same time.

"This was the same murder that gave us Herbie Frank.

I worried about him, until I found out he worked summers (as a clerk) in a foundry."

Janet said, "Oh!" then, embarrassed, said, "I remember you mentioned that." She scratched her head. "But I still don't get it."

"Metal comes to a foundry in the form of ingots," Ron said. "And my blue-collar source tells me these ingots—no matter what the metal is—are called pigs. As in 'pig iron.' "

It was probably the longest Benedetti had ever gone without talking. He broke his silence at this point to say, "Let us not forget, *amico,* that this was also the case that gave us Terry Wilbur."

"Yes, I'm interested in this," Buell drawled. "How does Wilbur fit in? Not another football player, is he?"

"No," Ron said. "I don't know if he ever played football. Wilbur ties in through those children's books he had in his room. The ones he told Mrs. Zucchio he had for his 'project,' whatever it was. You know about that?"

Diedre and Buell both nodded.

"Okay, then you're aware of how some of those books were defaced, and of how some of them were downright savaged. About the biggest book Wilbur had there, and one of the few that wasn't damaged at all, was *Charlotte's Web* by E.B. White. Are you familiar with that book?"

Diedre said, "Of course, I've had it since I was a little girl. I read it to Ricky."

"Well, Diedre, what's it about?" Ron demanded.

"It's about Charlotte, a spider, who can spell out words in her web and how—oh . . ."

"And how," Ron picked up for her, "she saves the family pig, whose name is *Wilbur,* from being killed and eaten."

Buell wanted to know if Ron had mentioned this to the police.

"No, I haven't. This could all be coincidence, you know. And not as wild a coincidence as it might seem."

"For those other things, I agree with you," the reporter said. "But the fact that he had a book featuring a pig with an identical *name* . . ."

"And the fact that he destroyed all those other books . . ." Diedre turned to Janet. "That's *crazy,* isn't it?"

"I can't figure it out," Ron said. "We know from his school record he wasn't much of a reader."

"What does the professor think?" Diedre wanted to know.

"I think the time has come to share this with the police," the old man said. "Perhaps they would take it more seriously if I told them, eh? We will talk it over later."

Ron was glad to hear it. It was bad enough looking Buell, Diedre, and Janet in the eye and saying these things as though he thought he meant them. Telling it to Fleisher would be murder.

He went on. The worst was yet to come. "Now we come to the murder of little Davy Reade—"

"That was horible," Diedre said, as though anyone needed to be told.

Ron ignored her. "Davy Reade's father sells motorcycles," Ron said. "A big part of his business is selling bikes to some of the police departments out in California where he lives."

"And policemen are called *pigs!*" Diedre said happily.

Ron shook his head. "You're getting ahead of us, Diedre. No. The point in this case is that close to a hundred percent of the motorcycle cops in this country—and a goodly portion of the motorcycle *gangs,* too—ride the same kind of bike—the Harley-Davidson Electra-Glide. It's one hell of a motorcycle, with an engine as powerful as some cars, and a price almost as big. But it will do one hundred thirty miles an hour, if you're crazy enough to ride it that fast. Hardly anybody ever calls it by the brand name though; it's a chopper—or a Hog.

"The last murder—"

"The last murder so far," the professor corrected him.

"So far." Ron sat back in his chair. "The last one so far, Jastrow, is almost too direct to be true. Diedre was onto it before. So was Shaughnessy in the police department, before Jastrow was even killed.

"Jastrow was an ex-sheriff's man, and a crooked one. If anything, he gave new meaning to the word 'pig.' "

"So there we have it," Buell began, but Ron said, "We're not finished yet. There are some hog-applications among the investigators too, you know."

Ron saw Janet get red, and drop her glass on the rug.

It was empty, but the stem broke off. Ron had been waiting for two days for her to catch on, but he never thought she'd take it like this.

When Janet spoke, though, he realized the red was not from embarrassment, but from anger.

"Of course!" she snapped. "Of course! Let's take me, first. I was born in Arkansas. I went to the University of Arkansas. As anybody knows, the athletic teams at the University of Arkansas are nicknamed 'the Razorbacks,' and everybody knows a razorback is a kind of wild pig. Right?"

Ron could only nod. What was she so upset about?

Diedre said, "How exciting!" and Ron could have strangled her. "How about me, how do I fit in?"

Buell was indulgent, "Now, Love . . ."

"It's okay, Buell," Ron said. "It just so happens that Chester Whites are another commercial breed of hog raised in this country, the same as Poland-Chinas." Diedre looked pleased.

"Now, when we come to the police," Ron went on, still wondering what was eating Janet, "we have a little more trouble. *Fleisher,* for example, is the German word for 'butcher,' and you can assume a butcher would be familiar with hogs . . ."

Buell laughed. "Not Fleisher's butcher."

"Exactly. As for Shaughnessy, Michael Francis Patrick Shaughnessy—well, it's reaching, but's that's a name that's as Irish as Paddy's pig."

"And you said it took a *little* imagination," Janet said quietly.

"As for myself, unless you want to count my football career, or lump me in with the cops as that kind of 'pig,' I'm ashamed to confess I can't think of anything."

Diedre was playing the game. "If people referred to you as 'Private Investigator Gentry,' you'd have the right initials."

Buell laughed again. "If he includes Fleisher because of the translation of his name, he's got to accept that one."

His fiancée looked shrewdly at him. "What about you, Buell?" Diedre asked. She turned to Ron. "There's nothing to link the professor either, is there? That doesn't seem fair, does it?" She smiled brilliantly. "Buell and the professor shouldn't be left out."

Ron looked at Benedetti, and saw in the black eyes a command to go ahead.

"Only the professor is left out, Diedre," he said quietly. He turned to the reporter. "Do you want to tell it, Buell, or should I?"

SIXTEEN

BUELL HAD KNOWN IT WAS COMING, NOT ONLY ALL EVE-
ning, but since the whole business started, and even before
that. He'd prepared and prepared, and it bothered him
that, now that it had happened, he still didn't feel ready.
He held it against himself; he considered it a weakness
in himself, all the worse because he hadn't known previ-
ously that it existed.

"You tell it," he said. He found himself hoping that
what Ron had found out wasn't what Buell had been con-
cealing, that instead it was something innocuous like all
the other foolishness Ron had come out with tonight. He
stepped on the hope and crushed it—if it *were* some silly
thing, they would have only mentioned it in passing, like
they had for everyone else.

Ron said, "Well, for one thing, your real name is Peter
Buell Chandler . . ."

That was enough to tell Buell he'd been right to stifle
that stupid little hope. "Tatham was my mother's maiden
name," he said.

"I know," Ron said. Buell met the professor's eyes. An
illusion of the light made them look like pits, like something you could fall into if you weren't careful. The old
man's look was unsettling but strong; Buell felt an almost
tangible snap as he tore his eyes away.

"You're from an old, and very rich family down south
in Knox County," Ron went on, "that has produced some
very successful evangelists, or popular ones, anyway. I
guess you'd have to measure an evangelist's success in
terms of souls saved, right?

"Anyway, both your father, H.P. Chandler, and his
older brother W. K. Chandler, became preachers, though
they didn't get along so well—"

"Buell has told me *all* about this," Diedre said.

"Buell's father wanted to sell off some of the land to the tenants at prices they could afford, and Buell's Uncle Willy didn't. And Buell's father preached to mixed audiences, when he toured the North, and that drove his uncle wild."

Ron nodded. "And coming back from one of those trips, H.P. Chandler's bus collided with a truckload of migrant workers, killing Chandler and his wife among others. Buell at first went to live with his maternal grandmother, but with his local political clout, and money judiciously spread in the right places, his uncle got custody. How old were you, Buell, ten?"

"Nine and a half." He gave a bitter chuckle. *"Tell me not in mournful numbers,* right? That is the mournfulest number in my life." Buell leaned forward and shook a finger at Janet ."You know, for all your expertise, Doctor, you can't tell me a thing about people exulting in power. I know all about that. You can't tell me anything about people trying to play God. Down in Knox County, Willy Chandler *is* God. I've seen him torment souls— and felt it, too. Do you know he used to let me believe *he* caused that accident; that he had it done? I didn't find out till years later it wasn't true. He used to mention my daddy's death, then tell me to keep in line.

"So nothing in this Hog case is really new to me, I can tell you. You want to study evil, Professor, you go down to Knox County and you study up on old Willy Chandler."

Buell never could have anticipated how good this was going to feel. It was like—like *testifying,* something he hadn't done since his daddy died. He was testifying, not to the truth of the Lord, but to the lies of Willy Chandler.

"He was evil, Professor—I meant to say he still is, though he is close to death now. He could go any day, and I know *one* person who won't be shedding any tears for him."

"You keep yourself informed, I see," the professor said.

"Lord, yes I do keep myself informed. I've kept myself informed from the day he threw me out. Making sure, you understand, that he'd be true to his principles, especially the one about not making wills. Because that's going to be my revenge. I swore then and I swear now, on my parents' souls, that I'd wait out that old bastard, and change Knox County into a decent and just place, the way it should have been long ago. And I'll throw out my uncle's damn Guardians when I do."

"Guardians?" Janet said.

Buell's apprehension was gone now, obliterated by the relief of letting his vow be heard. He explained, "The Guardians of America, Janet. Uncle Willy's answer to the Ku Klux Klan, American Nazi Party—that kind of filth."

"He came out with it in the early sixties," Ron said. "Backlash to the civil rights movement. In 1963, two members were tried for torturing, then killing two Rhode Island women in Knox County trying to get blacks registered to vote. Hung jury. There were other rumors, but nothing came of them. Chandler wasn't personally implicated." Buell snorted; Ron went on. "Since then, they've moved nationwide; they like to move into conflicts like busing, for example, emotional issues, but with decent, sincere people on both sides, then stir up hatreds for all they're worth."

"Which is horrible, of course," Diedre said. "But what does this have to do with *Buell?*"

"Well, according to my correspondent, the guy who dug up this stuff for me, when this organization was first begun in Knox County, it was called the Holy Order of Guardians of the South. H.O.G.S."

Buell got up, and walked to Diedre's bar setup. He got a tall glass, filled it with ice, then poured God's own clear water over it, and sat back down. "Put them all together, they don't spell 'Mother,' do they?" he asked. "Still, Ron, I don't know if I'm so thrilled with the idea of you hiring your fellow private eyes to check up on my past."

Ron shrugged. "It's not like it's so terribly sinister, Buell, or even so hard to dig up. And it's not a question of guilt—the name change was strictly legal."

"And I've been with Fleisher when most of the murders were committed, which is what you really meant to say."

Ron didn't bother to deny it. "The professor taught me to be a stickler for completeness. Once I started with the Hog tie-ins, I wanted to make sure I had everybody checked out.

"But the question is this: Why did I *have* to dig it out? You say yourself, you've kept yourself informed. Don't say Hog-H.O.G.S. never occurred to you. So what are you hiding?"

Buell finished his water, put down his glass. This was what he'd been afraid of. His life could go empty again with the next word he spoke.

He said it like a prayer. "Diedre," he said. "I'm hiding Diedre."

He saw hurt on her face, something he never wanted to see. To make it stop, he said quickly, "Diedre, Love, don't you see? If Uncle Willy ever found out about us, all my—all *our* plans for Knox County would be gone? That if anything could make him make a will so as to cut me out, that would? That *surely* would, Love."

"Oh, Buell," Diedre said, "of course I understand." She went and held him tight and cried on him. "It must be terrible for you."

"I can't give you up, Love, and I don't want to give up the dream. I . . . wasn't sure you'd understand."

"Well, I do understand."

"*I* don't understand," Janet said.

"Mrs. Chester's first husband," the professor explained, "by whom she has a son, was a diplomat—the ambassador to the United Nations from the nation of Liberia. A Black African nation, eh? I am sure Mr. Tatham was quite correct. The thought of his nephew marrying what the reprehensible Reverend W.K. Chandler would call a 'nigger lover,' and assuming guardianship of a racially mixed child, would surely seem sufficient cause to change his position about leaving a will."

"But still," Ron said. "You could have told us. Or at least Fleisher. I don't expect he'd go out of his way to help the W.K. Chandlers of the world."

"I was afraid of leaks, Ron," the reporter said. "Things leak. The press knows that better than anybody, just like we know how the cops work; that's why I was sure even before I got the first note that this was going to be a big case: I know how hard it is to fake an accident."

Benedetti scratched the back of his hand. "Since you know the police so well you must know that facts concealed at the beginning of an investigation are considered far more significant than they might deserve to be when they are discovered later on. I suggest you explain the whole situation to Inspector Fleisher, as soon as possible."

"You mean tonight?"

"This minute," Benedetti said. "I will go with you. I mean to speak to the inspector myself."

They said their goodbyes. It took a while, because Diedre was a great practitioner of the casual kiss, where you touch cheeks and peck at the air. It was a social convention that always struck Ron as a striving after intimacy, and it seemed even worse in the slightly strained atmosphere he'd caused with his little lecture.

It was arranged that the professor would go with Buell to the police station, and Ron would take Janet home, but outside, on the slushy sidewalk, Janet said, "It won't be necessary, you know."

"What won't be necessary?" Since they'd arrived at Diedre's, the temperature had gone up slightly, and the stars and moon were a little fuzzy around the edges; it was going to snow again. Terrific, Ron thought. In a thousand years, they'll finally catch Hog, frozen in ice like a mastodon.

He missed her answer. "I'm sorry, what did you say?"

Janet's *voice* was frozen in ice. "I *said,* it won't be necessary to drive me home."

"Why not? You're not upset, are you?"

"Upset? Of course not." Ron had never heard a more obvious lie. "It's just that now that I know I'm a suspect, there's no further reason for you to keep an eye on my reactions any more, is there? I don't want to take up your detective energies—"

Ron threw up his hands. "Oh, for God sake—"

"I'm surprised you let me get my hands on Mrs. Reade yesterday! Weren't you afraid the old razorback might cut her *throat?*"

"That's not funny. Hell, it's not even a good pun!" They were both shouting now.

Janet stamped her foot, making a small eruption of slush, which she ignored. "Of all the sneaky, amateurish—"

"Shut up!"

Ron was more than a little surprised when she did, until he saw that she hadn't shut up because he had said so, but because of the rage caused by the fact that he even had the nerve *to* say so.

He started talking while he had the chance. "Dammit, Janet, what are you so sensitive about?" She turned her back on him; he kept trying. *"Nobody* thinks you're Hog. My God, you're part of the team! The professor has accepted you!"

"Big deal," she said bitterly.

"It *is* a big deal!" *He* was getting offended now. "Whether you know it or not. I swear to you, you and I are the only two people in the Western Hemisphere to whom Benedetti has ever admitted having anything less than perfect confidence in himself. I never hope to see the day he starts baring his soul to people he thinks might be murderers!"

Nothing. He still had nothing but a long stretch of back and some windblown hair to talk to.

"It's not as though I singled you out or anything. I had some sort of stupid connection or other on everyone but the professor!"

She whirled on him, stamping her foot at the same time. *"You could have at least told me!"* The dramatic effect of this maneuver was somewhat diminished by the unfortunate accident of her foot's having come down on the edge of one of Sparta's multitudinous potholes, which had been concealed by slush. Janet's foot twisted under her, and she went down to the sidewalk like a felled birch, saying "Oh!"

Ron fought heroically not to laugh—and won, until Janet fought her way up to a sitting position and said, "Don't you dare stand there trying not to laugh at me!" He laughed so hard his glasses fell off, and he had to do a little acrobatic dance to catch them, at which point the woman on the sidewalk laughed, too.

"I'm such a klutz," Janet said at last.

"I'm going to hang a sign on you," Ron told her. " 'Dangerous When Provoked.' Are you all right?"

"I seemed to have twisted my ankle," she said, rubbing it. "Would you help me up, please?"

Ron knelt beside her. Janet put her arm around his

shoulders, and they stood up. "Can you walk?" Ron wanted to know.

She took a step, wobbled, said, "No." The shoulder was replaced.

Ron said, "I'm glad you're tall enough that I don't have to stoop to carry you. I'd be a hunchback by the time we got to the car. Do you want to go and have that X-rayed?"

"No—ow—I'm sure I just sprained it. I do it all the time."

"Okay," Ron said. "You're the doctor. Actually, I'm kind of enjoying this." He said it hoping to see Janet blush, and got his wish. But he also meant it. He smiled.

It was, in a comic way, like a three-legged race. Ron propped Janet up while she dug her key out of her purse, then helped her across to the couch. She sank down to it and wiggled out of her overcoat, while Ron slid an ottoman under her injured left foot.

It was a big room; Ron liked it. The sofa was a light green, the two chairs slightly darker. The window curtains were the same color as the sofa; the rug was a muted orange. One wall was all shelving, mostly for books, but it also contained a stereo and portable TV. There was a desk with an old-fashioned typewriter against the other wall. In the middle of the floor, standing like an altar, was an ebony baby grand, gleaming and obviously cared for. There was a complementary wood glow—a rich red—from next to the piano. It was a guitar, a Martin, in a stand, just waiting for a pair of hands to bring it to life.

Janet directed Ron to the bathroom, where she told him he'd find an Ace Bandage in the medicine cabinet. He went there, and chuckled to find enough Ace Bandage, gauze, tape, Mercurochrome, and liniment to set up as the trainer of a football team. He selected the right-sized bandage, and brought it back to the living room.

Janet spurned his offer to wrap her foot for her. "I've had plenty of practice," she told him, grinning ruefully.

Ron sat in one of the chairs. "The reason I didn't tell you about this pig business is that I didn't believe it myself. I probably never would have said it to anybody, but the professor egged me on—probably to torment me. Or Buell. He gets like that sometimes."

She was shaking her head. "Don't explain. I was childish, really." She laughed. "That's the only advantage of being a psychologist—it doesn't stop you from acting irrationally, it merely lets you talk intelligently about it later on."

"Which is nothing to be sneezed at," Ron said. He changed the subject. "That's a beautiful guitar."

"Thank you. I bought it for myself the day after I gave my last piano recital."

"Why did you give that up, Janet?"

She scratched her head. "It's hard to explain. I guess it's because I love music too much to want to work at it."

"I don't follow you."

"Well," she said. "When I play . . . even practicing . . . I don't like to come to the piano because I *have* to. And I didn't like to have to justify my existence by playing before a crowd—the regimentation of it made me start to think of it as drudgery. Sometimes it was anyway, and that was ruining the whole joy I got from playing. Can you understand that?"

"I think so," Ron said.

"What about you?" Janet asked. "Why are you a detective? I've been trying to figure you out for weeks."

Ron laughed. "You and the professor; only he claims he's been at it for years. Am I really so puzzling?"

She just looked at him.

"All right, all right," he said, "I'll talk. Turn off the cold professional gaze. It's a 'Purloined Letter' solution— I puzzle you with my very simplicity. I'm a detective because I hate mysteries."

"You mean you *love* mysteries."

"No, I hate them. I love *answers*. Life is so damn confusing, and it's all mysteries: what's going to happen in the Middle East; what can be done about the energy crisis; why do people do such rotten things to each other?

"That last one is Benedetti's question—his studies into 'Evil' with a capital 'E' amount to just about that.

"But I'm too simple a guy for that. When you think about it there's only one important question I'm equipped to answer—only one important question with a simple answer: Whodunit? I'm not saying it's simple to *find* the answer to that, but when you do find it, there it is.

"Hey, this is wrong. *I'm* the one who should be on the couch."

Janet laughed.

"Can I take a closer look at your guitar?" Ron asked. Janet said, "Sure," and Ron shed his coat, put it on the other chair with Janet's and went to pick it up.

Janet was eager to hear him play. She had a theory that the way a person played a musical instrument, regardless of skill, could give the psychologist a significant insight into a subject's personality. She had tapes; one day she was going to do a paper comparing the piano style of Harry Truman with that of Richard Nixon.

Ron picked up the guitar, checked it for tune, then started strumming. He started playing a series of A-minor chords. It suited him, she thought. Inquisitive, a little ominous. Then he started to play.

His playing surprised her. It was far more sensitive than she had expected. He was playing "I'll Follow the Sun," an early Beatles song and, keeping with his perception of himself, a simple one. Technically, he was adequate at best. There was an awful lot of fretting-fuzz. But his phrasing was expressive, and more important, he was enjoying it.

She was now certain that Ron Gentry wasn't the poking, probing inquiry machine she first thought he was. At least, that wasn't all he was. If Professor Benedetti played guitar, or any other instrument, she was sure he would play it with an icy perfection. She was astonished at how pleased she was to find out that Ron wasn't like that.

He finished playing, and Janet applauded him softly. She was astonished again to see him actually *blushing*.

He effaced himself. "Don't try to pretend you're not just being nice," he said. "My playing is a lot better suited to a thirteen-dollar Stella than to a beautiful piece of wood like this."

Janet pointed to the far wall and said, "Would you get me that gray case, please?" He got it for her. She opened it and took out her current pride and joy, a custom-made twelve string that cost her a little over three weeks' salary.

She realized suddenly she hadn't had her hands on it since Hog first came into her life. She threw the strap over her head, tuned, and looked up at Ron. Even bi-focal lenses couldn't diffuse the glow in her eyes when she said, "What do you want to play?"

It was a leading question. Maybe. He didn't want to press the issue. He was enjoying himself. Janet loved music enough not to make her living on it; he loved it enough to enjoy doing it badly.

He liked this girl. He liked her clumsiness, her open-ness, even her temper. And he liked the basic paradox of a self-conscious shrink. He was more than a little weary of omnipotence and cynicism and froth and crusading; of the Benedettis and Fleishers and Diedres and Buells.

Tall, angular Janet gave him a happy and comfortable feeling that could have been falling in love, for all he knew. So he just smiled at her and said, "Just start picking, and when you come to a place where a chord I know fits in, I'll play it."

She liked that. She led him on a guided tour of the folk scene (1960-63), one of Ron's favorite eras, playing and singing (in a sweet contralto) Dylan; Peter, Paul and Mary; the Limeliters; and some he didn't even re-member.

It was better than a vacation. For the first time, *he* could almost forget about looking for and at, and under, corpses. He told Janet so, and could tell she was pleased.

"You know," she said, taking off the guitar, "the last time I—*Ow!!*"

"What's the matter?"

"I am such a *fool!*" She had her right hand up to the side of her head.

Ron was still at a loss. "What happened for God's sake?"

"It's so embarrassing!" she said, then, seeing a look of pure exasperation on Ron's face, she went on. "Oh, all right. I caught my earring on my stupid guitar strap! I hope I didn't tear my ear." She took her hand down to look at it, put it back, looked again. "Ron, would you please see if it's bleeding?"

Smiling and shaking his head indulgently, Ron joined her on the couch. He lifted the thick, grey-brown hair to assess the damage to her earlobe. "It's a little red," he reported, "but I'm happy to say still in one piece."

"That's good," she said. "Sometimes I wonder if *I* shouldn't go look up a good psychologist." She shook her head at herself. "What a dope!"

It was, Ron supposed, proximity. Or possibly just his way of impressing on her that to Ron Gentry, for one, there was nothing whatever seriously the matter with Janet Higgins, Ph.D. In any event, he discovered that she was not uncoordinated when it came to kissing. Nor, for that matter, uneager or uncooperative.

There came a point, though, when she started making urgent noises, and broke off the kiss to speak. "We're going to scratch our glasses," she warned.

Very solemnly, Ron removed Janet's bifocals, then his own glasses, and placed them gently on the coffee table. "Now where were we?" he said.

The time soon came when they both realized a move to the bedroom was indicated. "But I can't *walk*," Janet protested.

"I'll carry you," Ron said. And before she could say anything about her being too big, he had lifted her off the couch. She just had time to reach down and scoop up the two pairs of spectacles.

In a combined spirit of scientific curiosity and biological necessity, Dr. Higgins had, from time to time, "had men." The Janet part of her, though, where her emotions lived, was a virgin. So as she came closer and closer to the "Big Moment," she found tormenting little questions spinning down like maple seeds through her brain. What is he *thinking?* What is he thinking about my stupid bumpy nose? What is he thinking about my stpuid flat chest? What is he thinking about my stupid bony shoulders, and my stupid big hands and feet, and my stupid—

But then he said, "You have the back of a goddess," and she knew it was going to be all right.

SEVENTEEN

JANET WOKE WITH A GUILTY START WHEN THE PHONE rang. She groped for it, gave up, turned on the light, picked up the receiver. Before putting it to her ear, she squinted at her digital clock—it was six-thirty-something.

"Hello?"

"Hello, Dr. Higgins? This is Sergeant Shaughnessy."

"Yes, Sergeant?"

The sergeant hesitated for a few seconds, then said all at once, "Look, I hate to bother you, but is Gentry there?"

It was a two-stage blush; it deepened when she realized she had no neckline for the blush to stop at.

Ron was awake. Janet covered the receiver with her hand and said, "It's Shaughnessy. Are you here?"

Ron didn't smile, but there was a twinkle in his gray eyes. "It's your reputation," he said.

"That's right," Janet giggled. "It is." To the phone, she said, "He's right here," and handed Ron the phone.

Whatever it was, it was bad news. Ron's face went from happy to stern in the space of a few syllables. He said, "Great," twice, very bitterly, then, "Oh, that's really great!" then, "Okay, fifteen minutes."

He gave Janet the phone to hang up, and said, "Hand me my glasses, please?"

As she did, she said, "What was that about?"

"I don't know," he said. He started to dress. "He was upset. Apparently, the professor has gone back to his easel, and won't come out to see what they have to see. So I'm elected." He shrugged. "I might as well; I'm going to lose my license pretty soon."

Naturally, Janet was concerned about that. Ron told her about Atler. "It's not so much the charges," he concluded, "as much as the fact that it's going to come out

147

that I got my license through a very loose interpretation of the law."

"What do you mean?"

"You're *supposed* to have three years experience as an investigator with a peace-keeping organization or as an operative for a licensed private eye, to get your own license. What happened with me was we got somebody in Albany to call Benedetti a special case, and that my three years with him let me qualify. But that was two administrations ago."

That reminded Janet that her days as a member in good standing of the faculty association were numbered. "I'll go with you," she said, and started to get up.

"No you won't," he said. He was fully dressed now. He pushed her gently back to the mattress. "I'll tell you all about it later, *whatever* it is—I promise." He tucked her in. "You just stay here and take care of that foot, okay, Funnyface?" And before she could say anything, he kissed her, right on the bump of her nose, and left.

Funnyface, huh? she thought happily after she had heard the outer door close behind him on his way out. Disregarding Ron's instructions, she got out of bed, and hobbled to the mirror. She'd always thought of it as an enemy; the merciless mirror.

She squinted into it. She'd forgotten her glasses. Scolding herself, she hobbled back to the bedside table, put them on, and hobbled again to the mirror. She turned around and looked back over her shoulder at her reflection. That *was* a nice back. It was a *very* nice back.

Then she saw her face. Her face didn't look as bad as usual, and she wondered why. It wasn't because of some "glow"; she didn't believe in glows. Then she realized it was the smile—it was the first time she'd ever seen herself in that mirror when she didn't have a look of dread and/or despair on her face. The smile made a lot of difference.

Fleisher never would have been on the scene when the body was found if some overachiever in Traffic hadn't given Shaughnessy a buzz on the phone.

The inspector had been sitting in his office, going over reports. These were the most recent reports, but this was already the eighth time he was going over them. They told him nothing new. The bolt cutter couldn't be traced. If they ever found it, of course, they could match the cutter with the cuts in the clamp; but it wasn't like guns —nothing useful could be learned just by studying their marks. They were no kind of lead.

The other report was about Jastrow. They'd traced his movements for the years between the times he was making trouble in Sparta. He had drifted West, first to Cincinnati, then to Chicago, still working at his first love, petty extortion, only without benefit of a badge. The last three years he had been in the clink out there for it. He'd been released around Christmastime. That had been reasonably interesting, the first time Fleisher read it.

Right now, though, the only question the inspector was interested in was how tired he had to get before he could die. Goddamn the mayor, anyhow.

And God bless Shaughnessy, stays with me like a leech —no, that wasn't right, and to hell with it anyway, because here he was.

"Thanks, Shaughnessy."

"You're welcome, Inspector." The sergeant was tired, too. It took a couple of seconds for him to add, "For what?"

"Never mind, never mind. What's up?"

"I just got a call from Winkel, in Traffic. They've got guys out now doing crowd control at a fire at the shopping center out on Huron Street."

"So?"

"The fire—and Winkel says the buzz is it's arson—is the Clockround Market."

"The bastards who first started selling those pig masks, and all that crap?"

"Yes, sir."

"Arson, huh? Think it might have something to do with our boy?"

"Can't hurt to have a look," Shaughnessy said.

Clockround Market was a modern supermarket—it sold everything from fennel to fan belts. It was a low, sprawling, modern-looking place, and, thanks to the recent striking down of an ages-old city ordinance, it was open twenty-four hours a day. It did a better business than one might expect in the early hours of the morning —night shift people on their way home, university students with the midnight munchies, insomniacs, and the people who just preferred to do their shopping at night.

These people (and others) were standing around the vast parking lot watching the Sparta Fire Department battle the blaze. It wasn't a big fire, but it was a nasty one—there was a lot of plastic and rubber in the place, and the fumes were bad.

Fleisher got out of the unmarked car. He had to half-skate over leakage from the firemen's hoses that had frozen to the blacktop. He slipped once, and fell, and Shaughnessy offered to help him up, but he barked, "I can do it myself, for crysake!" He did so, and made it without further incident to the man in the white fireman's hat.

Fleisher and the chief exchanged greetings. "I didn't know you were a fire watcher, Joe."

"This place I am. This was the outfit that started cashing in on Hog. Maybe he resented it or something."

The fire chief spoke some instructions through his bull horn, then turned to Fleisher. "Didn't you know?"

"Didn't I know what?"

"We caught the arsonists already. A couple of juveniles."

Fleisher was impressed. "Yeah? How'd you do it so fast?"

The chief laughed. "They were standing there watching the fire, holding matches and a can of lawn-mower gas when we got here. One of our tougher investigations."

"Where you got them?" the inspector asked.

The chief gave a head jerk toward the rescue truck. "Couldn't spare anybody to haul them in, yet."

"Everybody get out okay?" Fleisher wanted to know.

"We think so. I had a few men look around inside, but the smoke was too thick. If there *is* anybody in there, they came alone—all the employees are accounted for, and families and friends are all matched up."

"Good." Fleisher watched the smoke pour out of the ax-holes that had been smashed in the huge plate glass windows in the front of the store. He refused to believe it was just a coincidence. He had stopped believing in coincidence.

"I want to speak to those juveniles," he told the fireman.

"I don't want to tell you your job, or anything," the chief replied, "but you know the rules. If you talk to them without their parents' knowledge——"

"Yeah, I blow the whole case," said Fleisher. He spat on the ice. "As though you can get a juvenile punished for anything in the first place, right? We got fourteen-year-old murderers walking the street, for crysake."

He got the key to the rescue unit and went in with Shaughnessy. The two kids inside were giggling over their accomplishment. A redheaded kid with freckles was saying, "I never thought it would go up so *fast!*" His companion, who had dark hair and a runny nose, said, "I *toja* not to put it in the car section. They got gas treatment, they got oil . . ."

They noticed the inspector, broke off their review, and giggled some more. Fleisher was going to cow them into being quiet; he started by drawing himself up to his full height, which caused him to bump his head on the roof of the boxlike vehicle. The boys, whose age Fleisher put at fifteen, tops, found that hilarious.

Fleisher squatted on a heel and looked at them, with Shaughnessy standing behind him doing the same. The kids kept laughing, but after a while they began taking sidelong looks at the cops. They met nothing but those cold stares, and after a while, they shut up.

"I wish I could be that happy in so much trouble," Fleisher said.

The boys seemed surprised at the idea they might be in trouble.

The inspector let Shaughnessy handle the preliminaries. He found out the redhead was William Smith—with documents to prove it (and here you go, Ickes, Fleisher thought) and the one with the runny nose was Marc ("with a 'c' ") Goodsite. They both lived on the same street about five blocks from the shopping center, and they were in the ninth grade.

"Why did you do it?" Fleisher asked them.

Smith was indignant. "Waddaya mean, why did we do it?"

Goodsite wiped his nose. "Somebody hadda do it," he said reasonably.

"Why?" Fleisher persisted.

"This place was cashing in on people gettin' *killed,*" Goodsite said.

"Somebody wearing a mask chased my little cousin home from school, gave him nightmares," Smith said.

"My kid brother, too. Last night, my mom said somebody ought to burn out the you-know-what that was selling these things. So this morning, Billy and me got up early, 'cause we thought it was a good idea."

"Jesus Christ!" Fleisher exploded. He lunged at the kid, but the sergeant held him back. "Your mother tells you to pick up your goddamn socks from the floor. I bet you're not so quick to do that! But setting fires, that's different, right? That's *fun!* You little—"

Shaughnessy said, "Sir . . ."

Fleisher stopped, and shook his head violently to clear it. I'm getting too old for this crap, he thought. Not enough sleep. Too many nuts running around.

"Okay, Mike," he said. "I'm all right." There was nothing else he wanted to ask these two punks. He was just about to say, "Let's get out of here," when he heard the thump of a hand slapping the metal exterior of the truck, and the chief's voice yelling, "Hey, Joe, come on out. Looks like this might be your baby, after all!"

Fleisher cursed, expressively and sincerely, then turned to the boys and said, "Well, I hope your mother will be very proud of you. Her little suggestion has gotten somebody killed."

They'd already gotten a lot accomplished by the time Ron Gentry, in response to Shaughnessy's phone call, arrived at the scene, so they could take the time to berate him for what they considered Benedetti's lack of manners.

"Look," Ron interrupted, "I've known all about that guy for years. I'll tell you exactly what he said. He said, 'I have no time for repetition—' "

"He said 'redundancy,' " Shaughnessy corrected him.

"Okay, redundancy. Then he said, 'I will not be interrupted!' then he made a snide remark about me, told you where I was, and said you should bother *me.* Right?"

Shaughnessy was forced to admit that was just about it,

and Ron said, "All right. So don't complain to me when the professor gets difficult. What have we got?"

What they had was the body of Gloria Marcus, Mrs. Xhema Marcus, who was a charwoman at Sparta's biggest downtown office building. She often stopped in the Clockround Market before going home to fix breakfast for her husband, who had a small watch-repair shop in town. The couple was childless; Mrs. Marcus was forty-five.

They'd found her body under a jumble of twenty-eight ounce cans of Tahiti Delight Fruit Punch; the cans were the remains of an eighteen-foot pyramidal display that had taken an hour and a half to put up, a store employee told them sadly. She was the only person in the store who hadn't gotten out. The fire department made a careful check after the fire had been extinguished.

According to Dr. Dmitri, of the Medical Examiner's Office, the victim had died of lack of oxygen as a result of smoke and toxic fumes from burning hydro- and fluorocarbon products in the store. He also said, however, that Mrs. Marcus sustained a blow to the skull that probably would have sufficed to render her unconscious long enough for her to be overcome by the smoke.

"He says," Fleisher concluded, "that there's no reason it couldn't have been an accident." Fleisher's voice was calm, but Ron noticed his hands were clenched in tight fists.

"I can see how it could have been an accident," Ron said. "There's smoke, the alarm, confusion—she might panic and run blindly into that stack of cans, bringing it down on her. One hits her in the head, there you are." Ron had been straddling a fire hose and had to make a quick little jump out of the way as the firemen gathered it in. "Oops! Now where was I?"

"How you could see it might be an accident," the inspector said sourly.

"That's right, thanks. On the other hand, if it was murder, this could be the one that busts it open."

"What do you mean?"

"Well, do you think Hog was standing around this store at what? Five-thirty in the morning? Pricing pig masks or something, when the fire just happened to break out?"

"No," Fleisher said. It was the flattest "no" Ron had ever heard.

"Well, then, maybe we better talk to those two juveniles again and ask if anyone other than their mother had a hand in inspiring the fire."

EIGHTEEN

"I NEVER SAW ANYTHING LIKE IT," RON TOLD THE PRO-
fessor later that morning. "This one has got to be an accident. If it *was* Hog, which God forbid, either he
bribed those kids with something *extremely* special, or
he pulled off another miracle!" Ron took another spoon-
ful of cereal. "This guy scares me, *Maestro*."

Benedetti sipped his tea and nodded sympathetically.
Ron had come home ready for another shouting match
with his mentor, but the professor's painting frenzy was
over—at least for the time being. Ron found him
downstairs, watching *Seven Ways from Sundown,* with
Audie Murphy, on television, happy and conciliatory.

"Good morning, *amico,* I hope you spent a pleasant
night?" The expression on his face wasn't quite the
usual leer. For all his continental charm and advanced
intellect, Ron found the professor's mind distressingly
locker-roomish when it came to women.

Wondering why the old man seemed so happy, Ron
dashed upstairs for a look at the canvas. New York State
was gone—the fat part was now completely round, and
the long part was much longer, with the smooth edge on
the top instead of the bottom. It took Ron a few seconds
to figure out what it was because he was still thinking of
it as a map. Finally, he realized it was no longer a map
at all, just a painting of a gold key on a blue background.
He shrugged. If it meant anything, the old man would
tell him when he got around to it.

When he came downstairs, the old man told him,
"Ronald, did you know it is possible in this country to
send flowers to a lady and have them added to one's
telephone bill? I took the liberty of sending some to our
hostess of last night."

On my telephone, of course, Ron thought. Oh, well. "A bouquet from both of us, *Maestro?*"

"Of course not!" The professor was stung. "Niccolo Benedetti does not use half-measures. Mrs. Chester this morning will receive a lovely bouquet from *each* of us!"

Ron grinned. "Thanks for thinking of me, *Maestro,*" he said.

"Non é niente," the professor told him graciously.

Ron brought him up to date, telling him about the bolt cutter and Jastrow results, then about the fire and its aftermath.

". . . and you would never believe such virtue in a pair of teen-age arsonists," he concluded. "Fleisher questioned them for a solid hour and a half. Nobody told them to torch that place; nobody helped them; nobody paid them. It was their own idea—they did it as a public service. Fleisher offered them immunity if they'd talk, and they still wouldn't say anything. That's what convinced Buell—he met us downtown. Here the inspector is, giving them the perfect chance to lie their way out of it, and they don't take it."

"Well, perhaps as you say, their reward from Hog was enormous. Have the police intercepted a note?"

Ron tilted his bowl to get the last of his milk. "Fleisher no longer waits for notes. He has started large-scale investigations into the eleven customers and three employees that were in that store when the fire hit, solely on the basis of the pig masks the place sold. You must have done an excellent job selling my Hog-pig connections last night. Which reminds me. How did the inspector take Buell's revelations last night?"

"He accepted it as yet another thing that had come along to complicate his life. He had, by the way, already checked into the possibility that the Guardians of America might have been behind these deaths."

Ron was surprised. "That wasn't in the reports," he said."

The old man grinned. "He was embarrassed to tell us because he thought it was 'too wacked-out' as he put it." He stopped grinning. "It makes little difference, however. I believe I have an idea how to find Terry Wilbur."

Ron dialed the 401 area code for what seemed like

the hundredth time. Richard Bickell had to be the hardest man in all of Providence, Rhode Island to speak to. He was out. He was in conference. He was not to be disturbed. *But it's about his daughter's murder.* Sorr-ee, Mr. Bickell was not talking to reporters, *click.*

Ron tried a different approach. Using his full catalog of tricks, he pried loose the Bickells' unlisted home phone number. A female answered the phone. She told him curtly that it was strictly against doctor's orders for Mrs. Bickell to speak to anyone, especially about *that,* and how did he get the number, and if he called again, there would be trouble.

"Well, if she changes her mind, have her call me, all right?"

"I don't think she'll change her mind."

"But if she does . . ."

"Yes, goodbye."

The professor, at this moment, was upstairs taking a nap. Ron held it against him. True, the old man had stayed awake all night coming up with the idea that Ron was trying to follow up, but this was a lot more difficult than he expected. It probably wasn't Bickell that was the problem, Ron knew; it was some middle-echelon gatekeeper obsessed with following orders to the letter, the kind that, if you send them to the store, you have to remember to tell them to come back.

In his frustration, Ron was starting to doubt Benedetti's idea had been so good in the first place. One had to consider the source after all; it had been inspired by Herbie Frank and his talk about Terry Wilbur and his jingling keys.

That was the "one significant thing" the professor had gleaned from the conversation with Herbie. It got the professor's mind working on Terry Wilbur and keys, and it had finally worked itself out on the old man's canvas last night.

Leslie Bickell had given Terry a key to her apartment. Perhaps, just perhaps, she had duplicates made of *all* her keys to give to Wilbur. It was possible. The idea now was to find out just what she had keys *to.* Instead of looking for Wilbur in the places one might expect to find him, as the police had been doing, maybe they'd be better off looking for him in a place they might expect to find Leslie. If they could get somebody to tell them where that might be.

Correction: if *he* could get them to tell. Ron was in this alone. For some reason (pure damn conceit, if you asked Ron), the professor had forbidden bringing the police in. Not, he had to admit, that it would make much difference. He had already claimed to be a policeman three times to three different secretaries.

He decided he needed a break, so instead of dialing the area code, he dialed a local number.

It was answered on the first ring. "Hello?"

"Hello, Funnyface."

"Ron," she said. She made it a happy word.

They talked. They talked about fire and death in lovers' tones; it was what had brought them together. As he had promised, Ron told her all about recent events, right up to his unsuccessful phone calls. The professor had only said not to tell the police—he hadn't said anything about Janet.

She was sympathetic. "I can see why those secretaries and whatever won't put you through, though, especially when you say you're the police. Not that he would, of course, but Bickell could probably buy and sell the police—"

"That's it!" Ron said. "Janet, I love you. Beauty and brains both. I'll call you later, 'bye now."

By now he had the number memorized. "Providence Seafood," the operator said.

"Give me Dick Bickell's office," he said gruffly. He should have know. Benedetti was the only one who could get things accomplished by being polite. It was something you had to be born with.

When Bickell's secretary, or whatever he was, picked up the phone, Ron said, "Let me talk to Dick."

"Whose calling please?"

"I can't afford to have underlings know I'm calling. Put Dick on the phone. If he wants you to know, he'll tell you."

The voice wavered, but held firm. "I'm sorry, but Mr. Bickell is in conference. Can I take a message?"

"Yeah," Ron barked. "You tell him he's got a hell of a nerve trying to keep that merger with Con Foods a secret, especially from his friends."

"Ah . . . Hold on a second, would you please?"

Ron timed it. Twenty-five seconds until he heard a friendly baritone in his ear. "What's all this nonsense about a merger with Con Foods?" He should have realized that the way to crash a fence built around a businessman is with business. No one would ever protect the boss against a chance to make money.

"Dick?"

"Yes," the voice said. "What do you want?"

That accomplished, Ron apologized for his imposture, and in five minutes had found out what he wanted to know. "Imagine them thinking I wouldn't want to help you with this," Bickell said sadly. "I'm going to have a few people reexamine their values around here."

"Good idea, Dick." Bickell had told Ron to go on calling him Dick.

"And Ron?"

"Yes?"

"When you find Wilbur, let me know. I—I want to *talk* to him. I've got to try and . . ."

"He may not be the Hog," Ron pointed out.

"Even so."

"Okay," Ron said. "But if he is, the professor gets first crack at him."

Inspector Fleisher was experiencing a literal agony of fatigue. He couldn't remember the last time he was home; all he could remember was whenever it was, he hadn't been able to sleep. His brain had had enough abuse and ceased to function. He seemed to be able to *feel* it, inside his head, clenched tight like a fist and somehow detached from its usual moorings.

His eyes still worked, but his brain refused to interpret the signals they sent him, so what good was it? He walked through a world where meaningless colors and shapes jumped around the way tongues of fire did.

It surprised him that his hearing worked so well. He recognized the voices of Shaughnessy and Tatham, who kept asking him if he was all right.

"Of course I'm all right, for crysake!" he snapped. "Who the hell would run this investigation if I wasn't all right? The commissioner? Ha! Benedetti? Hell, he don't even care any more!"

"We don't really know that for sure, Inspector," Buell pointed out.

"Well where is he? We've all been here all morning, and where is he? This is what, the sixth victim?"

"Seventh," Shaughnessy corrected.

Fleisher thought he would have remembered that, but after the weeks of grinding, frustrating routine, the days ran together, and the crimes with them. Fleisher had, in fact, forgotten all about the professor's timely intervention with the press yesterday, except for the boast that Hog would be in custody within a week. He says that, the inspector thought, then he goes home and dabs canvas, for crysake.

There was a horrible wailing from the main room. It was old man Marcus—he'd been going on like that all morning. His beautiful Gloria, his wonderful Gloria, okay already. Marcus's lamentations had exactly the same effect on Fleisher as the rasping of an electric alarm clock.

"Shaughnessy," the inspector said, "go out there and shut him up, or I swear to God I'll shoot him." Shaughnessy went.

Fleisher looked blearily at the pile of shapes that produced Tatham's voice. "Buell," he said, "after I drop in my tracks on this case, you write my obit, all right?"

"Don't talk like that, Inspector." The reporter sounded very uncomfortable.

"This is my last case," Fleisher went on. "I'm going to die, right here, reading that last report that alibis one of those jerks in that store this morning."

"You're just down from fatigue, Inspector—you're dead beat, that's all."

"Dead beat? I'm beat dead for crysake." On sheer nerve impulse, not strength, Fleisher got up and started to pace.

"Some good news will perk you up," Buell said cheerfully. "Maybe the lab will find something about that note."

The note. They already had the note, only a few hours after the murder—the post office had fallen in with the spirit of the thing and spotted the latest note before mail from the various dropboxes was mixed together. This one came from the box on the corner of State and Harriman streets. Right in front of the Public Safety Building. Insult to injury; which brought him back to Benedetti.

"And the goddamn professor! Doesn't he even care about the note, for crysake? Nothing to say at all?"

"He doesn't know about the note," Buell said. "Gentry's line has been busy all morning."

"Oh, for *crysake!* Don't just stand there, try it again!"

Buell mumbled something, and left the office to find the phone.

Fleisher stood in the middle of the floor, rubbing his eyes. My God, he thought, did I actually do that? Am I actually ordering Buell around like he was a cop? And he's *humoring* me, for crysake. You're in bad shape, Joe.

Do something constructive. You're a detective-inspector. Inspect. Detect. Read the note again. The lab has the note, but you've got a photo to look at, right? So look at it.

It was the hardest thing he ever did, but Fleisher forced his brain to make sense of that note. It was the same format as the previous ones (except for the one with the blood spatter). It read:

TATHAM—
    THIS SHOULD HELP THEM SELL THEIR MASKS, SHOULDN'T IT? I USED TAHITI DELIGHT TO HELP THAT WOMAN ESCAPE THE SNOW AND COLD. I LOVE TO HELP PEOPLE. TILL NEXT TIME.
                              —HOG

I'll help you, you bastard, Fleisher thought. He tried to read the note again, and burn it into his memory, but it was no good; might just as well have been alphabet soup, the way letters went swimming around.

Then *everything* was doing it, and Fleisher was on his knees with his hands flat on the desk for balance. This is ridiculous, he told himself, and tried to get up, but his legs couldn't stretch down far enough to find the floor, and he fell unconscious on his own linoleum.

NINETEEN

◆◆ ◆◆ ◆◆ ◆◆ ◆◆ ◆◆ ◆◆ ◆◆ ◆◆ ◆◆ ◆

THE TOLL OF THE WOUNDED WAS CATCHING UP WITH the toll of the dead. Janet was *hors de combat* with her twisted ankle, practicing walking with a cane. Four persons connected in various ways with the Hog case were occupying beds in St. Erasmus Hospital: Barbara Elleger, Bizarro, Joyce Reade, and now Fleisher. What a bridge foursome *that* would be, Ron thought.

Ron and the professor had come to the hospital to visit Fleisher, but since he was out cold paying back the interest on the rest he owed himself, they wound up talking with Buell Tatham and Sergeant Shaughnessy, who had come for the same reason.

"Have you spoken to the doctors?" Ron asked.

"Yeah," the sergeant told him. "He'll be okay, but he's totally worn out. You have to remember that he was going not only on the Hog stuff, but on every single damn fatal accident in the area for three whole weeks."

"So, I understand, have you and Buell, Sergeant," the professor said.

Buell made a face. "Don't forget," he said, "Fleisher's got almost twenty years on me, and I'm not exactly a boy."

"Not only that," Shaughnessy said. "This case just got to him. Sometimes they get to you, you know?"

"Indeed," the professor said. "And I understand now the case will have a chance to 'get to' that *ciuco*, the commissioner."

"Yeah, he's taking personal charge of the case," he said with a bitter grin. "He even chased me. He goes, 'Rafferty'—didn't even know my right name, the jerk— 'Rafferty, you look like you could use a few days off. Come back Monday, maybe I'll have the case wrapped up by then.' Then he patted my ass and laughed."

162

Shaughnessy then launched some speculations about the commissioner that would probably have resulted in a libel suit, if they ever got back to him.

The professor cut him off. "I can sympathize with your frustration, Sergeant, but it might be for the good after all. Had you any plans for this weekend? No? Excellent. Perhaps you might like to accompany my young associate."

"Where?"

"To the place where Terry Wilbur is, I have every hope."

Buell was excited. "You know where he is?"

The professor shrugged. "I have an opinion; Ronald is planning to check its validity."

"Where is he?" the reporter asked. "This is big. A whole lot of people are convinced Wilbur is Hog."

"It's my belief Wilbur is holed up in a cabin in the Adirondacks that is used by the father of Leslie Bickell on his hunting trips."

Now Shaughnessy was excited. "Yeah, but where is it? We can call the troopers and get them to haul him the hell out of there!"

"No," Benedetti said. "I do not want a show of force. I do not want Wilbur killed in a gun duel (since he may have a gun), and I do not want him to commit suicide. If I cannot solve the puzzle of Terry Wilbur, I may never solve this case.

"Perhaps I was unwise." The old man narrowed his black eyes. "You do have your duty, after all, Sergeant. But I ask you, in all humility, to follow my wishes in the matter. Ronald knows the place; he will tell you just before you depart. Will you agree?"

Shaughnessy's freckled face broke in a grin. "Try and keep me home. My wife's not going to like you for this, though."

"Diedre won't either," Buell said. "I'm coming along."

The professor looked at him. "It may be extremely dangerous, Mr. Tatham."

Buell laughed. "I think I should feel insulted." His face became serious. "Look, professor, I was in on the very beginning of this case—if you remember, that's why our boy gave me the dubious honor of being his go-between. I am going to be in on the end, if Terry Wilbur *is* the end."

Black eyes met blue eyes for a long moment. Finally the old man said, "I understand. Go along, of course."

Diedre's eyes grew wide. "Where did you get *that?*" she asked breathlessly.

Buell was cleaning a gun that looked like something that should be carried by Wyatt Earp or somebody. "It belonged to my granddaddy, who carried it up Kettle Hill in the Spanish-American War. I took it when I left home."

"But, I mean, why are you cleaning it?"

"It's dirty," he said.

"But you told me the professor said——"

"The professor is not going to knock on the door of a man who has killed . . . Besides, he said we should protect ourselves if necessary. Shaughnessy's bringing his gun, too."

"I don't like the idea of you getting in danger like that. What would happen to me and Ricky?" She sniffed.

"Hey," Buell said softly. "Don't worry, Love, it probably won't even be necessary. I'm sure it won't." He held her. "He probably won't even be there." He gave a little reassuring laugh, but his eyes were worried. He tilted her head back, pinched her chin. "Help me pack, all right, Love? It's going to be cold out there."

"You're getting pretty good with the cane," Ron said.

"I can get around, at least," Janet conceded. "Want me to come help you pack for the trip?"

"All packed," he said. "The evening is free. The professor is busy on another painting."

Janet, finished with her walking practice, took a chair. "What's on the canvas this time?"

"Too early to tell."

"Oh," she said. Something wasn't exactly right. She felt cheated of helping Ron pack. It was . . . it was almost like he was going away to *war* or something, which she didn't want to think about. It would be just her luck, just after he had (finally) turned up in her life for him to get himself—but she made herself stop.

Ron snapped his fingers as though he just thought of something. "Do you have any Vaseline?" he asked.

Janet thought, hmmm. "Why?" she asked.

Ron had his head back, laughing at her. "Janet," he said, shaking his head, "never change, all right? Please?" He took off his glasses and wiped his eyes. "I need the Vaseline for my trip. I don't have any at home."

She told him, with a blush (could she ever stop that?), that he was welcome to the Vaseline. She wanted to ask him if he had to go, but stopped herself. It would do neither one of them any good if he had the "yes" dragged out of him. Instead she said, "I hope you're bringing a gun."

"Wouldn't help me any," he told her. "I never fired a gun in my life. I was never in a situation where I'd be justified in shooting anybody."

Janet didn't know what to say. She had thought private detectives carried guns the way nurses carried thermometers. "Well, you just be careful!" she snapped.

He laughed at her again. "You can count on that," he said.

The time was coming, Janet knew, when she would have to say it, not as a joke the way he had this morning, but seriously. She would have to look him in the eye and say "I love you"—but not yet. Because then *he* would have to say something, and there were thousands of things he could say, from "Goodbye," to "Oh, my God," to "That's nice," to what she hoped she *would* hear. And she wasn't ready to buck those odds. Yet. Whatever the relationship they had now could be called, she liked it too much to risk making it grow too fast, or trying to.

Ron looked at his watch.

"You're leaving very early tomorrow morning, aren't you?"

"Five o'clock. It's a long drive."

"When will you be going back to your place?"

He looked at his watch again. "Pretty soon," he said.

"Not too soon?" she asked. She had her pretty, wistful, self-conscious, little-girl smile on. She didn't know it was there. Janet had no wiles.

Ron could not refuse that smile anything. "No, not too soon, Funnyface."

They drank coffee from Shaughnessy's thermos as they headed east into a rising red sun. Ron squinted at it, took a hand from the wheel to lower the sun visor. He owned a pair of prescription sunglasses, but hadn't thought to bring them along—Sparta residents don't see enough of the sun to worry about it.

There was a little bit of trivial conversation when they first got underway. Shaughnessy had the morning's *Courant,* and held forth for a while on the fortunes of Sparta's minor league hockey team, but that soon died out, and they rode in silence.

Ron left the Thruway for Route 81 in Syracuse, and followed that north and east until Watertown, where again he pointed the car dead east. The sun wasn't so bad now, it had risen above the windshield.

About fifteen miles from the small motel that was their destination, Ron said, "Buell?"

The reporter had been gazing out the window at the snow. It covered everything; the world looked like a Christmas card gone wild.

"Buell?"

Buell turned away from the window. "What?"

Ron said, "I just wanted to tell you I wasn't being vicious the other night, and I'm sorry if I caused you any trouble."

Buell was a man about it, a gentleman. "Nothing I couldn't handle," he said. "I was worried about what Diedre would think, that's all. You don't have to apologize to me, I know what this case can do to your mind."

"I'm glad to hear that," Ron told him. They rode on a few more miles. Once, an animal darted from the trees on one side of the road to those on the other.

"What was that?" asked a startled Shaughnessy. Ron and Buell had thought he was asleep.

"I don't know," Ron said. "It went by pretty fast."

"If I didn't know better," Buell said, "I'd think it was a mountain lion."

"It's just barely possible that's what it was," Ron told him. "There used to be mountain lion populations all over North America, but they've mostly been wiped out here in the East. Still, there are parts of the mountains up here that are wilderness as wild as you can find anywhere.

There are eagles up here, bears, even the occasional wolf. All kinds of predators."

"Just as long as there are no hogs," Shaughnessy said, and they all laughed.

"You know, Mike, you've given me a thought," Ron said. "Buell, did it ever occur to you that Hog might be aiming this whole thing at you?"

He seemed surprised. "Me?"

"You get the notes," Shaughnessy pointed out.

"And you were the only witness to the first murder," Ron added.

"If you remember the first note, though," Buell said reasonably, "the fact that I was a witness is why he sent the notes to me in the first place."

"Even so," Ron countered, "it was one of his more miraculous crimes, followed by a miraculous escape—he got away without leaving a trace on the overpass or anywhere else. Maybe he hoped you'd be watching. Then there's Jastrow; you were a big thing in his past. And your Uncle Willy with his GOA, formerly HOGS. Somebody might be arranging things with you in mind."

"Nah, that won't work," Shaughnessy said. "You're saying Hog maybe knew Buell would be on that road the day of the accident. Okay, maybe he did. We know he knew the girls would be there. But it's not possible he knew they'd both come under that bridge at the same time, with Buell just far enough behind to see the accident. That kind of thing can only be worked out by God."

Ron supposed he was right.

Buell said, "As for Jastrow, I've been twenty-five years a reporter in Sparta, and you meet a lot of people in the newspaper business. I bet if you picked *any* seven people in Sparta at random, the chances'd be better than even I knew one of them.

"And as for my Uncle Willy, well, you got into it the other night. There's a hog tie-in for everybody if you look hard enough."

Ron was glad the professor wasn't there to see this. Defeated on all fronts. Maybe I'm slipping, he thought. Or just distracted. Maybe the old man is right about staying away from women while he's on a case. He didn't have time to dwell on it, though. There was the sign—

Mac Dougald's Adirondack Inn, then below, FISHING, HUNTING, GUIDES, BEER, FOOD, and painted sloppily below everything, SNOWMOBILES.

"We're here," Ron said.

Ron had the old tube-filled radio on the scarred bedside table warmed up enough just in time to hear a nasal-voiced over-friendly announcer saying, ". . . North Country weather, clear and cool today, with a high of about minus fifteen"—*cool,* for God's sake, thought Ron —"but with the wind-chill factor, it feels more like minus fifty-five."

For a mad moment, he wished he was back in balmy Sparta, where it rarely got colder than ten below, but he put aside the thought as unworthy of him. He had a job to do.

Last night he had checked his companions' gear to make sure they had brought everything he had told them to bring, then had held a quick lesson on how to dress for the cold.

They tried to tell him that they'd lived in Sparta long enough to qualify as experts at dressing for the cold, but he pointed out that Sparta was full of buildings you could duck into to warm up, and that buildings around here were kind of sparse, and that improperly protected, you could lose fingers and toes to frostbite in a surprisingly few minutes.

So Ron dressed, following his own advice. He started with a loose fishnet t-shirt. Over this he put a regular cotton t-shirt, then another fishnet, then another cotton shirt. He was building up bulk, with very little weight. Most people equate heavy clothes with warmth, but Ron knew that fabric doesn't insulate you from the weather, the air it traps does. If you can isolate enough air between you and the outside world, to be warmed by your body heat, you can stay warm.

Ron followed with tops and bottoms of thermal underwear, rolling the legs in with thick white socks. Then came a shirt and pants, then the artic survival gear developed by the Air Force, the parka part of which is popularly known as a snorkel coat. With that, and fleece-lined, waterproof snowmobiling boots, he was almost ready to face the outdoors.

He walked down the hall, checking on his two companions, just in case. They'd been able to buy or borrow all the stuff they needed in Sparta, but there was still a chance they'd put it on incorrectly.

They were all right, though, and Ron went back to his room to finish up. He rubbed Janet's Vaseline on his face, especially around his nose and lips, pulled a black ski mask with an oblong opening for both eyes over his head, slid his glasses between mask and head, placed dark-yellow bubble ski goggles on (he'd had a hard time finding a pair that fit comfortably over his spectacles), pulled on his fleece-lined gauntlets, and was ready to go.

Buell and Shaughnessy were similarly ready, except, Ron knew, somewhere in there, they had bundled lethal weapons in with them. They just had to hope they didn't need them, he thought, or if they did, that no fast-draw work would be required.

Mac Dougald had cheerfully rented them snowmobiles, good powerful big ones, which (Ron was thankful) all three of his little group knew how to operate. The machines, two Ski-Doos and a John Deere, had key-start ignitions, Ron was happy to see. There is no lonelier feeling than being miles away from anything, pulling again and again on the rope of a snowmobile motor that won't kick over.

"All set?" he asked. Getting two nods in reply, he said, "Okay, let's go." They roared off, leaving the frozen air smelling faintly of gasoline fumes.

"There it is," Buell said. His words, carrying the moisture in his breath, froze instantly against the wool of his ski mask. Dressed according to Ron's instructions, he was comfortable enough, but you could tell just how cold it was. The air seemed not so much to part against him as he chugged forward on the snowmobile, as it seemed to crack open under his momentum.

"Yeah," Ron said, "Bickell gave good directions."

For obvious reasons, Ron had declined Mac Dougald's offer to guide them. Buell was all for that, of course, but he'd been a little nervous about getting lost up here. Ron had been right about wilderness. This was God's country, all right.

But here they were, at the edge of a surprisingly large

and surprisingly flat (after what he'd seen today) clearing, and there at the other edge was a strong-looking stone cabin that stood up bravely under the weight of snow several feet deep on its roof. The snow on and around the house, and in drifts in the clearing, looked decorative, sculpted by the wind into graceful curving shapes.

"What do you think?" Buell asked.

"Tracks outside, looks like," Shaughnessy said.

"Old ones," Ron said pessimistically. "And no smoke coming out of the chimney. It could be he's been and gone, and it could be the old man was just full of hot air."

"No smoke from the chimney doesn't mean anything," Shaughnessy said. "My brother-in-law's got a place like this with gas heat; has a tank in back of the house, gets it filled up at the end of the summer."

"True," Ron admitted. He started his snowmobile and started forward.

It was no use, Buell knew, to try to sneak up on the house. The noise of the snowmobile was unavoidable, and the snow was too deep to walk in. A snowmobile is built to ride on the surface of snow the way a boat rides on the surface of water. It will take a man places where a man trying to walk without snowshoes would disappear under the snow.

The prevailing wind was from the far side of the house, so the cabin formed a windbreak. Consequently, there was a teardrop-shaped area in front of the cabin where the snow hadn't drifted as deep. Where Buell dismounted, it came only up to his calves.

In case of a shot, Shaughnessy suggested they spread out to approach the house. They did so, with Ron in the middle, Shaugnessy on his left, and Buell on his right.

Buell was afraid. He could admit that to himself. It was a feeling of being in the wrong place. The trail of Hog had begun on superhighways and in city and suburban streets. He felt out of his element knowing it had taken him here, where there were no roads, only depressions in the snow.

Ron walked up to the door. He pounded on it, and yelled, "Wilbur!"

Inside, Buell heard panicky, tentative scratching noises. He zipped his parka partway down, not feeling the cold.

"Wilbur!"

That Gentry boy has more courage than smarts, Buell thought. He pulled his grandaddy's gun out of his belt, and saw it tremble in his hand. He closed his eyes and offered a silent, sincere prayer. The trembling had stopped by the time he was finished.

Ron called one more time, getting only more scratching in reply. What is he doing in there? Buell asked himself.

Shaughnessy also had his gun out. "I'm going in after him," he said. "Follow me, Buell."

It wasn't locked. The cop crashed in, yelling "Freeze!" Buell, holding the gun ready, followed, holding his breath.

Inside the door, Buell saw Shaughnessy lowering his gun. The disgust on the sergeant's face was discernible, even behind a ski mask and goggles.

"Oh, for crysake," the sergeant said.

There was no shock of warmth as Ron went inside the cabin; the only difference he could feel was that he was shielded from the wind. Ron closed the door behind him and saw what Shaughnessy hadn't shot at; what had made the scratching noise.

It was a raccoon, standing in a corner and eyeing the three men suspiciously.

"He was fooling around with that stuff," Shaughnessy said, pointing to a large bundle of bedding on the floor in front of a cold fireplace.

Buell was puzzled. "I thought they hibernated."

"Not exactly," Ron told him. "They wake up from time to time to eat. The way bears do. Probably in here looking for food." Ron looked at the raccoon. "He's scared. Let's let him escape, shall we?" He opened the door again, and stood away from it. The raccoon scampered across the cabin and out.

Ron took a quick survey of the cabin. One big room, but a nice one. A stove and a refrigerator (probably warmer inside *that,* he thought), three beds, stripped, a rough-hewn wooden table, two wooden chairs, and by the far wall, a big rectangular affair with a subdued metal-flake paint finish. A gas heater. It looked fairly new, but there were big dents around the bottom of it, as though it had been kicked in anger. The used contents of a box of wooden matches were scattered on the floor around it.

"As long as we're here, we might as well have a look around," Shaughnessy said. "How about if I turn on that heater and try to get us some heat?" He didn't wait for an answer, but strode across the room to do it.

Ron was trying not to think of his disappointment. He thought instead of how strange they looked dressed the way they were. No wonder the raccoon had been scared. He laughed, adding a new layer of ice to his mask.

Shaughnessy was having trouble. "How the hell do you . . . Oh, I see." There were instructions printed on the inside of the little metal panel that opened to reveal the controls of the heater. " 'Saf-T-Lite,' " Shaughnessy read. " 'One. Strike match. Two. Press green button at top of panel to allow gas flow and unlock regulator handle.' Okay, where the hell is the green button? Oh, here it is, like in the doorjamb part of the top of the panel." He pressed it. " 'Three. Turn regulator handle to right as far as it will go.' Oh, great, somebody busted the handle off!"

It didn't prove to be much of a handicap, though; there was enough of a stub left to let the sergeant turn the handle with little trouble. " 'Four,' " he said, " 'drop match in hole marked with arrow.' 'Bout time! My glove is about to catch fire." He dropped in the match, and there was a satisfying *whoosh!* of the fire taking hold.

The heater was surprisingly efficient. Considering the temperature the room was, it was practically no time at all before the three men could remove their masks and gloves, though coats were still required.

"I'll get this stuff from the floor," Buell volunteered, bending over the sheets and blankets the raccoon had been playing with. He grabbed a corner of a quilt and pulled, then yelled and jumped back as though he'd gotten an electric shock.

Ron had been checking the cupboard for signs that the cabin might recently have been occupied and had just about decided it had been, when Buell yelled. "What's the matter?" he said.

"Look!" The reporter was pointing. They followed his finger to the line of the blankets. Buell had disarranged the bedding enough to reveal a pair of men's shoes. With a man in them.

Shaughnessy and Ron joined Buell at the bundle. They had trouble separating the body from the blankets—not only had he frozen to death, he had very nearly frozen solid. When they finished, they had the body of a well-built young man, who appeared to be curled up for a peaceful night of sleep.

"That's Terry Wilbur, isn't it?" Ron asked.

"It sure is," Shaughnessy said. "Damn, I wanted to take him alive."

"We all did," Buell said.

"Easy enough to see what happened. He put all this stuff on the floor, and curled up in front of the fire. The fire went out, and he froze to death in his sleep."

Ron was sitting on one of the wooden chairs. He was shaking his head adamantly. "No. It's not that simple at all. For one thing, there's no more firewood in the bin in this cabin. For another thing, this is a big table, you can bet there'd be more than two chairs along with it. Obvious inference, he busted up some chairs for firewood.

"Then he curled up in front of the fire under the blankets and quilts from all three beds, to try to keep as warm as he could."

Buell was impatient to interrupt. "But—"

Ron nodded. "Exactly. All we've got to do is figure out why Wilbur went through *any* of that—why he even bothered to *build* a fire in the fireplace when there was a perfectly good gas heater here a child could operate— one that would have kept him as warm as his mother's embrace.

"In other words, *we have to figure out why Terry Wilbur chose to freeze to death.*"

TWENTY

❖❖ ❖❖ ❖❖ ❖❖ ❖❖ ❖ ❖❖ ❖❖ ❖❖ ❖❖ ❖❖ ❖❖ ❖

THERE WAS A MESSAGE FROM DIEDRE WAITING FOR THEM back at the lodge. Mac Dougald told them she said it was urgent, so Ron let Buell make the first call, with the stipulation that he would mention nothing of what they had left back at the cabin. Benedetti had to be the first person in Sparta to hear about that.

Buell wasn't on the phone long, only about three minutes or so, but in that time Ron heard him come out with three whoops of triumph, laughter, and one "Love, that's great!" It clashed badly with the detective's mood.

Buell looked ten years younger when he stepped out of the cubicle that housed Mac Dougald's antique telephone. He hugged Ron and patted him on the back in sheer exuberance.

"I made it, Ronny!" he said. "Diedre got the word only a little while after we left, but she had to ask the professor where we were." He laughed. "And he didn't want to talk to her on the phone because he's expecting a call from you, and doesn't want the phone tied up!" Buell slapped Shaughnessy on the back. "That's something, isn't it?"

The sergeant seemed to be in no more of a mood for celebration than Ron was. "What was it she got word of?" he asked dryly.

Nothing could bother Buell. "My *dear* Uncle Willy finally went to join the devil, where he's belonged for years."

"Oh," Ron said. Normally, he would have said such happiness at any man's death was not in the best of taste, but knowing the history, he could understand Buell's reaction. The world didn't cry when Hitler died; Uncle Willy had been Buell's personal Hitler.

"Then he never found out, right? About Diedre? Didn't leave a will?"

"That's right," Buell smiled. "I am a rich man, Ron. This money will give me the power to do so many *good* things." He clapped his hands, walked to a window to look out at the snow, then turned back to Ron and Shaughnessy. "But you know the best part? The best part is now I can stop all the lies and deceit; I won't have to go skulking around any more—"

"It wasn't that bad, was it, Buell?" Ron asked. "After all, it isn't like your Uncle Willy was having you watched."

Buell seemed a little taken aback. "Uh—of course, of course, that's very true," he said, then made himself smile. "In fact, Diedre says the authorities down there are starting to look for me already. It—it's just—well, *you* know you're hiding, even if nobody else does."

"That," Ron said, "is probably very true." His mind presented him with a very clear image of Terry Wilbur, and what had happened to him in *his* hiding place. He gave Buell hasty congratulations, and placed a call to the professor.

Ron wondered why it was that he always got a better connection calling long distance than calling another office in the Bixby building from twenty feet down the hall. He had the leisure for such speculations because the professor was off on an extended spate of his rapid, incomprehensible Italian incantations. They had started immediately after Ron told the old man the news that Terry Wilbur was dead. That was the first time. This current monologue was the result of Ron's telling him of the circumstances.

Benedetti came to the end of whatever he was saying; the unexpected silence that followed startled Ron.

"Maestro?"

"I am here, *amico*," the professor said softly, and a little sadly, as though his innermost desire was to be somewhere else.

He sighed heavily, like a Venetian escaping his mistress's husband on that bridge, Ron thought. The detective asked his mentor, "What do we do now, *Maestro?*"

"La storia, una volta piú, per favore," he said. "You have no doubt Wilbur died of the cold, eh?"

"There wasn't a mark on him, *Maestro.* It could have been natural causes, or even poison, but Wilbur was young and healthy, and who was around to poison him? For what it's worth, Shaughnessy, who's seen plenty, says it looks like a freezing to him."

The old man sighed again. *"Basta, basta,* I accept the sergeant's word. The denting in the body of the heater, the breaking off of that handle, had no effect on the function of it, eh?"

Ron shook his head at the phone, realized the futility of that and said, "No, *Maestro.* Shaughnessy had the thing lit in fifteen seconds, even without the handle."

"I see chaos, *amico.* I do not like it. Niccolo Benedetti can see nothing but chaos. Evil will keep this day a holiday, Ronald."

The old man was giving up. Ron couldn't blame him, but he wanted to cry.

"There was sufficient fuel?" Benedetti asked in a hopeless voice.

"Ninety-eight percent of capacity, *Maestro.* We checked it before we left." If only the professor hadn't shot off his mouth about catching Hog in a week, Ron thought. *That* was the worst of it. People do fail occasionally. It's no big disgrace.

And still, Ron couldn't get over this last inexplicable horror in a case that seemed to be nothing *but* inexplicable horrors. "If it's any consolation, Shaughnessy and Buell are convinced that Wilbur was the man."

"Hog?" the professor said.

"Of course!" Ron said. "Who else?"

"What are their reasons?"

Ron snorted. "Analogy, *Maestro.* Hog is obviously demented, and what could be more demented than sitting in front of a dying fire and freezing to death when all you have to do to light the heater is open the panel, read the instructions, and drop in—"

To this day, Ron swears he received an electric shock at that moment, that the telephone transmitted Professor Benedetti's brain impulses to him. Janet scoffs, and says if it was anything, it was telepathy—that Ron had become attuned to the old man's psyche. The professor says nonsense to both of them—that Ron, at that moment, was doing subconsciously what the professor was doing consciously: solving the case.

"Come home," the professor said.

"What?" Ron said taken aback.

"Come home," the professor said again. "At once."

"We haven't even told the authorities about Wilbur yet."

"Shaughnessy can deal with authorities. I need you."

"Buell will probably want to come with me."

The professor thought it over for a second. "Let him come, by all means," he said at last. "But no word of our discussion on the trip home. I will be expecting you."

"I'll leave immediately, *Maestro*."

"*Va bene*," the old man said. "And, *amico*," he said confidentially, "we will let evil find its holidays elsewhere, eh?"

The sky over Sparta was lightened by a false dawn when Ron and Buell finally arrived there. A couple of hours had been added to the trip by the traffic pileup behind a truck that had jackknifed across the highway south of Watertown.

"Where do you want me to drop you?" Ron asked. "The paper?"

Buell rubbed his eyes. "Not necessary," he said. "I called the story in after you spoke to the professor. The *Courant* has its scoop on Wilbur's death. I can do the follow-up in my column for tomorrow. Sell more papers that way."

"Where then?"

"Better make it my apartment. I'm too tired to do anything but sleep—I'm going to phone Diedre, tell her everything's all right, then I'm going to sleep as long as I can, then I'll write my column, then I'll get me a lawyer and see about that estate."

"Does that mean you're through with the case?"

"Of course not," Buell said. "I'll stick through the formalities. But I think we've seen the last of Hog with the death of Terry Wilbur. I have a feeling about it."

"I hope you're right," Ron told him. Buell knew nothing about the professor's brainstorm, not even that the old man had told Ron to come home. Not wanting to arouse anyone else's curiosity before his own was satisfied, Ron had put it to Shaughnessy that Buell had to be home to handle his important business and it would be safer if two people went, to share the driving. He pointed out that the sergeant would be the logical one to leave behind to talk with his fellow law officers.

Ron attributed his getting away with it to fast talking and a blithe disregard for what the state police and upstate local officials would think about his disappearance. They left Shaughnessy grumbling, but agreeing.

The trip back into town took them under that unfinished overpass where the first two girls had died. Ron could sense a shudder from the man beside him. Buell had really been through a lot, Ron thought. Well, if the professor knew what he was talking about, the case would soon be over. If? O, ye of little faith—the professor *always* knew what he was talking about. Just ask him.

Then what had the old man seen? Who was Hog? Ron would have to bludgeon his instincts into submission before he could get them to accept the idea that Terry Wilbur had been unfindable in Sparta for days on end, then had run off to the Adirondacks to hide after the seventh death—the very day the professor had decided to look for him there. But if it isn't Wilbur, what do those books mean? What was his "project"? And, in the name of God, how had he come to die the way he had?

Too many questions. He'd be better off asking them of the professor than of himself. He forced himself to think of other things until he dropped Buell off and went home.

Ron heard a very unprofessorial gasp as he let himself into the house. Before he even had a chance to wonder about it, he had arms around his neck, and was being kissed by a very relieved psychologist.

"I've been so worried," Janet told him.

"Why?" Ron asked. "Not that I mind. What are you doing here? Not that I mind that, either. Shall we repair to the sitting room and discuss it?"

She smiled at him. "No, I'd like to, but we can't. You're supposed to go upstairs and see the professor as soon as you get in. He's painting. He called me up a few hours ago—woke me up. He said you would be home any minute, and when you did, he was going to start the last phase of the Hog case, and that he thought I might like to be in on it."

"I *told* you you were part of the team," Ron said. "How's your leg?"

"Not bad, as long as I use the cane I'm all right. What about you? I was afraid something had happened, you were so late."

"Something happened, but not to me," Ron said. He told her about the truck on Route 81. "Has the professor filled you in?"

Janet nodded. "He told me about Terry Wilbur. I—I can't understand about his death. It doesn't make any *sense.*"

"What does make sense about this case?"

"Nothing," Janet said. "It seems physically *and* psychologically impossible." She smiled sadly. "Frightening, isn't it?"

"Yes. What else did the old man say?"

"He said Wilbur was the Hog."

"He said that?" Ron was surprised, for more than one reason. For one thing, he never really believed it. For another, it just wasn't like Benedetti to state the solution to a case straight out. He liked to build up to it, deviously. Ron asked Janet for the professor's exact words.

"Well, he said, 'The death of Terry Wilbur brings the case to a conclusion,' and he said, 'Wilbur fled because he knew he was a killer.'"

I'll be damned, Ron thought. He said, "I'd better go see the professor." He took his arms from around Janet and ran up the stairs.

He found the old man (yet again) bent over his easel, painting by the feeble sun that had just struck its rim over the horizon. The old man looked up smiling at Ron and said, "Ah, *buon giorno, amico!* You arrive at precisely the right moment. I have finished." He gestured at the painting.

Ron looked at it. Against a neutral, translucent purple-grey background, the professor had painted two spheres in collision, one black and one white. The painting showed in great detail the flattening and fragmenting of the spheres at the point of impact. Huge gouts of red spurted from the openings. It would probably turn up in a museum—it was one of his better canvases. Simple, but powerful somehow. And a little frightening.

"What is it, *Maestro?*"

Benedetti beamed. "What is it? Why, it is a portrait of the killer's soul."

By this time, Janet and her cane had made their way up the stairs. Ron heard her voice behind him say, "Terry Wilbur's soul?"

The professor scowled. "Of course not," he said. *"Hog's* soul."

TWENTY-ONE

JANET'S CONFUSION WAS GROWING BY THE SECOND. THE professor happily admitted making the statements, "Terry Wilbur's death ends the case," "Terry Wilbur was a killer," and the seemingly contradictory, "Terry Wilbur was not the Hog." That wasn't logical.

And he wouldn't explain, either. He was apologetic about it, saying, "You must keep in mind that my colleague is still my pupil. In fairness to him I must give him every possible opportunity to arrive at the solution. Usually, all that is necessary is for me to point him in the right direction, eh?"

The right direction, apparently, was the one that led to St. Erasmus hospital; that's where the professor had told Ron to drive them. He sat in the back seat, puffing on a cigar. Once, Janet turned around to look at him, and he *winked* at her. Ron had *said* he was a rake, but that had been a little raw, she thought. Unless he was kidding.

Ron drove grimly, deep in thought. Janet sat beside him, feeling strangely lost. She strove desperately to see the sense in *something,* so she worked on the coincidental puzzle of why the streets of downtown Sparta were so deserted at the start of what should have been the morning rush hour, until she realized that it was Sunday. She had lost track. Sunday, the eighth of February. The end of the Hog case, according to the professor. *I wonder*—

"*Whore!*" Ron yelled, "Of course!"

"What?" asked Janet, startled.

"*Bravissimo, amico, bravissimo,*" the professor said. "You make me more reconciled to the unpleasant fact that I cannot live forever."

"But what—?" Janet asked.

"*Shhh!*" the professor told her. "My young friend now

181

must have time to consider the implications—to fill in the rest of the story."

Her first instinct was to protest. Nobody had shushed Dr. Janet Higgins in quite a while. She put a hand on the back of her seat to turn and give the old man a few chosen words on etiquette, but when he gave her a significant look, then a small smile, and patted her big hand with his bigger, bony one, she subsided.

Janet could tell Ron was distracted, she could almost feel the tension of concentration in him. When they were challenged at the hospital entrance, the professor had to remind him to produce their credentials.

Going up in the elevator, Ron's eyes opened wide, and he whispered, "Oh, my God."

"You have it now, eh, *amico?*" the old man asked.

"Oh, my *God*," Ron said again. "Why, *Maestro?* What was behind it?"

"I do not know," the old man said.

Ron sputtered. "Then—then this makes less sense than *anything!*"

"I hope to know before the day is over," the professor said. "Let us do what we must do here, eh?"

Janet forbore asking any questions, but she would have given years of her life to know what they were talking about. I must really love him, she thought ruefully, as the elevator stopped. She meekly followed down the hall to the room that housed Jorge Ruiz Vasquez, aka Juan Bizarro, aka the Pope of Dope.

"He's probably asleep," the patrolman guarding the door said. He was living proof that a man cannot serve two masters, Ron thought. If he lets us in, the hospital will be on him; if he doesn't, it's the department.

Loyalty to the force won. On the assurance that the professor would assume full responsibility for the state of health of the prisoner, the patrolman let the three of them in. No medical personnel happened to see them.

Ron turned on the room's fluorescent lights. The brightness brought the figure on the bed to squinting wakefulness. Ron was glad. He didn't want to touch him. Ron looked at the Pope of Dope, and marveled to think how much damage he had been able to do immobilized in a hospital bed.

Vasquez blinked at them. "What the hell do you want? What time is it?"

The professor scratched the back of his hand. "It is time you told us the truth, eh? Your spite has cost enough lives."

"Go to hell," Vasquez said. He looked as though he wanted to spit.

"Who beat you up, Bizarro?" Ron asked.

There was silence from the bed.

"Wilbur beat you up, right? That's why you tried to make us think he was Hog, but he wasn't, was he?" More silence, broken by a gasp from Janet.

"You're crazy," Vasquez said at last. "I'm going to ring for the nurse!"

Ron took the buzzer away from him, leaned over the bed. "Later. Right now we talk."

"What happens if I don't?" the pusher sneered. "You break my legs?" He glanced down at where his legs were in traction.

"I don't even like to smell you, let alone touch you," Ron said. This was his department. The professor was counting on him to get Vasquez to talk. It was a loose end that had to be tied before they could breech (and God help us all, he thought) the person who really was Hog.

"I'll tell you what happens if you don't talk, your Holiness. First all the charges against you will be dropped."

"That's a threat?" Vasquez asked.

"I'm not finished. First all the charges are dropped. Today is Sunday. Tomorrow, Frank Pompano is arrested. Tuesday, Leo Hertz is arrested. On Wednesday, I open a bank account for you with twenty-five hundred dollars in it, that sounds about right." Vasquez was sweating, had panic in his eyes. Ron went on. "On Thursday, we go to Rochester, and arrest Manny Gill—"

"Jesus, you're out to murder me, man! You—you can't do that!"

"No? On Friday, I put another six, seven hundred bucks in your account."

Vasquez was trembling. Ron was threatening to make him look like a class "A" stoolie, talking about the big boys. "They'll *kill* me," he protested.

"Of course," Ron went on. "I'm putting you right on the bull's-eye, Bizarro. After the lives you cost I'm only sorry I can't think of anything worse. On Saturday night that cop outside your door is going to get something in his eye and have to leave the door unguarded while he gets one of the nurses to take it out."

"Bah!" the professor said in disgust. "Leave him alone, before he soils the bedding. The sophisticate. The graduate of the university. *Verme. Codardo.*" Now the old man leaned menacingly over the bed. "Now, Jorge Ruiz Vasquez, *I* will recount what happened the night of January 27–28. If I make any mistakes, you will correct me. Or I shall send my colleague out to start getting the charges against you dropped. Do you understand?"

Vasquez nodded.

"Va bene," the professor said, straightening up. "One of the things I have learned in my researches is that while not all evil is cowardly, all cowardice is evil. A good individual, an honest man or woman, is heroic in his very honesty—a life like *that* one"—he gestured toward the bed—"is too often rewarded in today's world.

"But I digress. The night Leslie Bickell died." He addressed Vasquez once again. "It has been established that Leslie Bickell stole the money from Atler's office, obtained the heroin from you, and returned to her apartment.

"We know Terry Wilbur came to that apartment, in haste, and we know that he shouted *something* while he was there, after which he ran away, and was never heard from again—until yesterday afternoon."

Vasquez looked surprised.

"Oh, yes," the professor said. "He has been found. And from him I have learned enough to solve the case— and to discover your part in it."

Ron looked to see if the old man's bluff was working. It was the best kind of bluff—the truth.

"Now Herbert Frank, that most valuable of witnesses, told us that Wilbur was angry at Miss Bickell—that he called her a 'whore.' I didn't realize until quite recently that it is very easy to mistake shouted words, especially when heard through walls. Only the strongest syllables are likely to be heard . . ."

That's what stuck in the old man's mind at Reade's

house, Ron thought. When Reade found his wife after her suicide attempt, he'd yelled for Dr. Higgins but all they'd been able to make of it was "rig." An increase in volume led to a decrease in precision of articulation.

". . . and once one realizes that," the professor was saying, "it is a simple thing to put a new construction on events.

"Leslie Bickell has broken her hand. She cannot administer her needle to herself in the only vein she has isolated. She is understandably reluctant to go searching for a new one—she may miss, giving herself a subcutaneous injection that wouldn't suffice for her needs.

"So. She needs that shot. But she needs help as well, to get it. She calls Terry Wilbur, who loves her. I think it probable that Wilbur was not aware of the effect your influence had on her, Mr. Vasquez.

"That would account for the other things Herbert Frank heard Wilbur yell. We can reconstruct the conversation. 'I have become a narcotics addict, through the influence of your old friend,' says Miss Bickell. Mr. Wilbur invokes Jesus Christ. Miss Bickell says, 'You must give me this injection of heroin, I need it, and I am suffering greatly.' Wilbur yells her name, in anguish and disbelief, but he can't stand to see her suffer, so he does as she asks.

"He couldn't know that was part of an extremely potent batch of poison. All he knows is that before he had even finished emptying the needle, Leslie is dead.

"He knows it is your fault, and he yells. *Your* name, Mr. Vasquez. He has known you since the day you left Puerto Rico—you yourself told us Wilbur is the last person to call you by your baptismal name, pronounced the Spanish way. Herbert Frank's misguided passions made 'whore' the only word that made sense. But it wasn't 'whore' he was shouting, it was *'Jorge'*; 'whore-hay.' The second syllable would easily be lost—it is little more than a breath, as the name is pronounced.

"Wilbur was a killer, and he knew it. Because of you, he killed his own girl. He dumped the heroin in the bathroom sink, leaving the water running to flush it away, then looked for you and found you."

The eyes of Jorge Ruiz Vasquez blazed. "He was *crazy!*" he said vehemently. "He should have been locked up years ago. He tore into me like old man Timmons, but there was no one to pull him off. He left me for *dead,* man, he had to suffer for that."

"You *knew,*" Ron said. "You knew that Wilbur had killed her accidentally, but you didn't tell us, hoping we'd pin the whole Hog thing on him."

"I hoped they'd find him and gun him *down,* Gentry. And don't be surprised someday if it happens to *you,* either."

Ron smiled at him. "I'll be ready, George."

The professor said, "I will never know why, but Wilbur thought he had killed you, and felt guilty about it— that was why he ran away. One who kills the likes of you should be awarded a medal." The old man turned to Ron and Janet. "Let us go, eh? Our Sunday morning has been sufficiently profaned."

Hoping she didn't appear hopelessly backward (though that's the way she felt) Janet, very politely, asked the professor to explain how he had arrived at the conclusions he had just outlined.

The professor didn't look at her when he answered; he appeared to be hypnotized by the elevator lights. "When once I had determined that Terry Wilbur was not and could not be the Hog, it was easy."

"But that's what I don't *understand,*" Janet protested. "Just because he killed Leslie Bickell accidentally doesn't mean he couldn't have been Hog. He could have added her in the note to cover up, or try to. And what about the books? And the way he died?"

The professor's black eyes blazed as he spoke to Ron. *"Siamo tutt'e due idioti.* Those children's books *screamed* the right answer, and we couldn't see it."

"I'm going to scream," Janet said loudly, just as the elevator doors opened in the lobby. A guard asked her if she was all right, looking suspiciously at the professor and Ron.

"No, no, I'm fine," she told him. Embarrassment chased her across the lobby and out into the cold, with Ron and the professor just behind.

Ron caught up with her outside the door. "I'll explain, Funnyface."

"Please," she said sincerely.

"Look, in order to be Hog, Wilbur had to have sent those notes, right?"

"Of course," Janet said.

"Well, from the very beginning, the evidence has been blindingly obvious that *Terry Wilbur could not read!*"

The professor had caught up with them. "Precisely. We had his school records to study—they were quite bad, yet everyone (especially the lovely Mrs. Zucchio), told us how personable and bright he was.

"Evidently, Terry Wilbur suffered from dyslexia, or some other learning disability. That is more your field than mine, Doctor, but what I understand of it, it is a tragedy of the first magnitude."

Janet drew a long, soft breath. "Of course. *I* should have seen—And you're right, professor, it *is* tragic. For some reason, the brain simply cannot make sense of the written word. Someone once called it a 'blind spot in the understanding.' It's only come to the attention of the public in the last few years."

The professor spoke bitterly. "All the more tragic for Terry Wilbur that he was attending school during that 'enlightened' time when children were passed from grade to grade, regardless of their accomplishment or lack of accomplishment, in order not to *embarrass* them, *buon'-Iddio,* rather than being detained to ascertain why they did not learn and doing something about it. Stupidity, eh?"

"With understanding, and little special help, dyslexics can get along fine," Janet said. "From what I read in the journals, they're often very bright children, with good memories, and high IQs."

"Nelson Rockefeller was dyslexic, I read somewhere," Ron put in. "And look what he did for himself. Of course, he had the wealth and influence to draw on."

Benedetti nodded. "Terry Wilbur, though, had no such influence, nor, I am sure, such understanding instructors. He was simply passed along, from grade to grade, knowing he was somehow less than the other children, unable to decode the information locked in the school books. Can you imagine the loneliness he must have suffered? Each year growing farther and farther behind? Being the stupid one; the slow one?

"I am inclined to believe that teacher, Mr. Timmons,

did Terry Wilbur a favor by touching off his frustration in high school by calling him stupid, and getting beaten up. Outside the school, working as a gardener, Wilbur could achieve something positive, eh? From a poor student, he had become a good gardener."

"Then he met Leslie Bickell," Janet said. She could see it; she could almost feel it. The gardener fell for the heiress; the dropout wanted the graduate student. All the feelings of inadequacy would come back. Wilbur would feel he would have to measure up.

"That, of course, was the sinister 'project' Wilbur told Mrs. Zucchio about," the professor said. "That was the purpose of the children's books. Wilbur was devoting the winter to one last effort to learn how to read. Inspired by love, he would learn by sheer force of will. But it is not always so easy."

Again, Janet could feel the pain Wilbur must have felt, poring over books designed for children, silly stories and fairy tales, painstakingly copying the letters and words, underlining a word he might recognize ("No, I do not like *them,* Sam; I *do* not like green eggs and ham"), but not being able to make any progress, not being able to keep the letters from moving around, or showing themselves in different shapes. Defeat. Humiliating defeat.

"He defaced the books in frustration," Janet said. "The same way he lashed out at that teacher. It explains so much."

They had reached Ron's car. He unlocked doors, they got in.

"It even explains *Charlotte's Web,*" Ron said. "Probably the one thing Wilbur could recognize on sight was his own name. When he was buying the books he was going to use, he probably spotted it, and bought it on a whim. Of course he never got to try it because he never got past the simplest books."

Ron started the car, pulled into the street. "It explains how he died, too," Ron said tonelessly. Janet could tell he felt the tragedy of Terry Wilbur, too.

"He couldn't get that gas heater started because he couldn't read the instructions," he said. "He couldn't find that stupid green button. He kicked those dents in the thing in frustration, tried to force the handle and broke it. He might have had enough firewood, but you'll recall, four days after he must have arrived at the cabin, the blizzard hit, blanketing the whole Northeast. Not only did it force him to use more firewood, it buried any he might have been able to find in the woods. He broke up the furniture for a while, but eventually, the cold and fatigue got to him."

They were silent for a while. Janet thought about the tragedy; it was, she realized, totally peripheral to the Hog case. Even if there had been no Hog, Leslie Bickell and Terry Wilbur would still have died. But . . .

"But if *Terry Wilbur* killed Leslie Bickell . . ." She spun on Ron and the professor, *"Who sent the note? That was an authentic Hog note!"*

"It was," Ron agreed. "Hog wrote that note, of course."

"But—" Janet was coming to grips with an idea the ramifications of which she couldn't comprehend. "But if Hog wrote a note . . . *if he didn't kill Leslie Bickell . . ."*

The professor smiled like a cat, and said, "For the third time, Dr. Higgins, *bravissima.* You have a certain undeveloped talent for this sort of thing. It is a pity I did not meet you when you were younger. Training a female protégé would have been interesting.

"For you have a knack for asking the right question. If Hog didn't kill Leslie Bickell . . . just whom *did* he kill, eh?"

TWENTY-TWO

✦✦ ✦✦ ✦✦ ✦✦ ✦✦ ✦✦ ✦✦ ✦✦ ✦✦ ✦✦ ✦✦ ✦✦ ✦✦ ✦

THE PROFESSOR NEVER GOT A CHANCE TO ANSWER HIS own question (not that Janet expected he would), because Ron had a sudden thought.

"You know, *Maestro,* Buell Tatham may, right this minute, be writing a column that will perpetuate a lot of wrong ideas about Terry Wilbur."

"We mustn't allow that," the professor said. "Is there anything else we must do before we inform of what we have . . . deduced?"

"I can't think of anything," Ron said.

"On second thought, I can." The old man took out a cigar. "I believe Inspector Fleisher has been sent home from the hospital. I firmly believe we should offer him the opportunity to be in on this conference."

Ron grinned. "As opposed to, say, the commissioner?"

"Precisemente."

"Good morning, Inspector, I hope you are feeling better," the professor said.

"I'm okay," Fleisher said irritably. He had recovered sufficiently to resent things. Most of all he resented being taken off the case. But there was plenty of room left to resent being awakened at eight o'clock on a Sunday morning and having to entertain the professor. What had gotten into his wife, anyway?

"You look well," Benedetti said amiably. "By the end of the day, you will doubtlessly feel much better."

"Why?" the inspector asked.

"Because of three quarters of an inch of iron. Among other things." And the professor began to talk. When he finished, Fleisher dashed up the stairs to get dressed like a man who had never been sick a day in his life.

He figured it out, the inspector said to himself. I don't

190

believe it, he figured it out. Of course, it makes *me* out the sap of the decade, for crysake, but *still*.

"I'll be right with you, Professor," he called.

"Of *course* we're going to celebrate tonight, Love," Buell told Diedre over the phone. "I'm taking you to the best restaurant in town. Uh-huh. Because in a week, maybe two, we're leaving this town. Got to get things squared away up here, then we'll go down and get my identity established, and start work."

He loved the way you could hear happiness in Diedre's voice. Like little bubbles. "Oh, Buell, I'm so excited!"

"I'm excited, too, Love."

"The only thing is, you're kind of leaving the case in midair, aren't you?"

He was patient. "Well, we can't wait forever, can we? Some cases are never solved. Besides, they've got their best people on it, I'm not that important—"

"You are so."

Buell laughed. "All right. Hog will just have to send his letters to someone else."

"Well, it would still be nice to know how it all turns out."

"We can keep in touch, Love," he said, but Diedre didn't seem satisfied. To reassure her, he added, "I'm sure the professor will come up with something."

The doorbell rang. "Someone at the door, Love, I've got to go now. See you at six-thirty. 'Bye."

Buell opened the door to find Fleisher, Benedetti, Ron, and Janet. "Well," he said. "Come on in. Dropping in on your way home from church?"

"The professor has some ideas," Ron said. "He wants to fill you in before you write your story."

Buell threw open the door wide. "By all means," he said. "I can always use facts. Aren't you coming in, Ron?" The detective had held back.

"No," he said. "Janet and I have something to do." He took her hand, pulled her back from inside the room.

"Are you sure, *amico?*" the professor asked. "You deserve to be present, as does Dr. Higgins."

"What purpose would it serve, *Maestro?* No, I'm sure."

The professor shook his head, smiling. "A *very* complex man," he said.

Buell had no idea what they were talking about. He shrugged and closed the door.

Janet was beginning to think there was a conspiracy to keep her from ever finding out what was going on. She was arranging the words to express her irritation, when Ron took her other hand and held both of hers in both of his.

"Janet," he said, "let's get married."

"What? What's the matter with you?"

"I want to marry you, so there's something the matter with me?"

That wasn't what she'd had in mind when she asked, but now that he mentioned it—oh, what was the use? She could feel herself blushing.

"I mean—why don't—how come you didn't go in?"

"It would make me uncomfortable. The professor can tell me anything I want to know."

"I thought you had it all figured out."

"I do."

"Then why should the professor have to tell you anything? Certainly it wouldn't make you uncomfortable just to hear him explain to Buell what you already *know*."

"He's not explaining things to Buell."

"He's not?"

"No."

"What *is* he doing?"

"Collecting his fee," Ron said.

"Fee?"

"Two hours," Ron said. "With the killer."

"Buell?" It was impossible. "He—he has all kinds of alibis! He doesn't match the profile."

"Yeah." Ron grinned ruefully. "How about that. Look. *I* can fill you in, everything except why. Or you can go back inside. They're probably just getting started."

Of course, no good psychologist would pass up the chance to study the reactions of a killer as his guilt is brought home to him; she owed it to science to go inside. The fact that she had known the man socially (however briefly) could only help to provide additional insights.

"Oh, go to *hell,* Dr. Higgins," she said fiercely.

"What?"

"Nothing. Nothing at all. Let's go somewhere else. Then you can tell me all about it."

They went to Ron's office in the Bixby Building, where Benedetti found them several hours later. The old man didn't explain how he knew they were there, and (to Ron's surprise) he had managed to join them without incurring any expenses the younger man had to pick up.

"You certainly will require further study," the professor said, smiling and shaking his head at Ron. "At the moment of triumph you lose interest in the case. Fascinating."

Ron shrugged. "The simple question is answered," he said.

Janet was impatient. "Did he talk? Why did he do it, Professor?"

"He had reasons he considered sufficient."

"But it's so *horrible*," Janet said. "It's almost worse than if he really did kill all those people."

"It has been . . . enlightening," the professor said. He took some papers, folded once lengthwise, from his coat. "Here you are," he said, giving the pages to Ron. "I believe this will answer your questions. It does, however, pose a difficult ethical question for *me*."

Ron didn't ask him what it was. He opened the folded sheets of typewriter-sized newsprint, and, with Janet looking over his shoulder, began to read.

for Feb 9

THE HUMAN ANGLE

by Buell Tatham

(SPARTA)

This column is being written under the wary eye of Police Inspector Joseph Fleisher and the all-seeing eye of Professor Niccolo Benedetti. They have graciously honored my request to have the final story about the "killer" —HOG, who has been terrorizing the city.

"Where did you get this?" Ron demanded.

The old man chuckled softly. "It fell from the inspector's pocket. I happened to catch it before it hit the floor."

"You mean you *stole* it?" Janet was aghast.

"Niccolo Benedetti does not steal," the old man said haughtily. "I have merely borrowed it until I can resolve my ethical question."

Now Ron asked what ethical question he was talking about.

"We will discuss that after you have finished reading."

Ron returned to the typescript.

The truth is HOG was a hoax. There was no HOG. I was HOG.

Carole Salinski, Beth Ling, Stanley Watson, and Davy Reade died at the hands of none other but God. Their deaths were purely accidental. Leslie Bickell and Gloria Marcus died as the result of human perversity. I merely sent the notes, and (in the first case) changed the evidence to make it look to the police like murder . . .

"I can't get *over* it," Janet said. "That missing scrap of metal—"

"Was, in reality, *two* scraps of metal," the professor said. "It was, of course, the key to the whole case. Buell had been planning to study accounts of recent accidents and sent himself a note claiming some as unprovable murders. That day, however, when he was driving behind the unfortunate young girls, he was presented with an almost miraculous opportunity, eh?

"Because here was an accident he could not only claim was a murder, here was one he could *prove* was a murder, and better yet, a murder he could not have possibly committed."

"Sure," Ron said. "He stopped, helped the girls as much as he could, as long as he was sure one was dead—"

"What if she wasn't?" Janet asked.

"I'm sure he would not have finished the job," the professor said.

Ron continued. "He helped the girls as much as he could then took a bolt cutter and *cut the naturally broken snapped ends off that clamp*. An instant-miracle murder."

"As were they all," the old man said. "As were they all."

Ron shook his head. It was all so simple. They had wondered, so hard they had wondered: How did Hog get behind Watson on the stairs? How did he get in between Davy Reade and the garage with that piece of ice? And the answer: of course, he hadn't.

"I'd like to have a quarter," Ron said, "for every time in this case somebody said, 'We'll never be able to prove it wasn't an accident.' Hell, they all really *were* accidents!"

More or less, anyway, he thought. Once the professor proved that outside of the note, Hog had had nothing to do with Leslie Bickell's death, *all* the deaths became suspect. Then it became easy to see that only one death could *not* have been an accident: Jastrow's. But if the first instance, the car crash, had been an accident, Buell and only Buell had to have faked it. He was the only one there. Simple. Assisting in the hunt for himself.

. . . because I needed a smoke screen, a number of "killings" horrible enough to cover the murder of Jeffrey Jastrow.

Jeffrey Jastrow deserved to die. I'm not sorry I killed him. I have important things to do, very important, and Jastrow, who lived his life by victimizing innocent people, tried to put me in a position where I either had to sacrifice my task or the woman who gives meaning to my life . . .

"What is he talking about?" Janet wanted to know.

"Ah, yes," the professor said. "Indirectly, Buell was the cause of his own dilemma." He picked up a letter opener from Ron's desk and started playing with it. "After Jastrow was forced to leave this county he went from place to place, eventually going to prison in Illinois. While he was there he met a fellow inmate, who happened to be a ranking member of the Illinois Chapter of the Guardians of America, and was serving a sentence for setting fire to a day-care center. Charming, eh?

"In any case, over the course of many months this inmate told Jastrow all about the organization, of which he was quite proud. He lauded the illustrious founder of the organization to Jastrow, and told him of the entire family history.

"'The Guardian was inexhaustible on the sbuject, and eventually the story of the missing nephew came out, coupled with the fact that Tatham had been his mother's family name.

"We can certainly appreciate how Jastrow would be sensitive to that name, eh? So when Jastrow was released he planned to reveal Buell's connection to the founder of that organization—if nothing else, than to tarnish Buell's humanitarian image.

"But it was not hard for Jastrow to discover Buell's impending inheritance. *You,* starting with even less knowledge than Jastrow, found it out in just a few days, did you not, *amico?*"

"My correspondent did, yeah."

The old man smiled. "What your agents have accomplished, you have accomplished, *amico.* Do not be ashamed to take credit. When your agents fail, you are surely blamed for the failure."

Benedetti scratched his hand. "To continue. Once Jastrow knew Buell's situation he tried to find a way not only to exact his revenge, but to line his own pockets."

"And he discovered Diedre," Ron said.

"Exactly," said the old man. "Mrs. Chester was the motive. Buell loves her . . ."

Janet shook her head.

"Yes, Doctor?" Benedetti asked.

"What? Oh, nothing, Professor. Please go on." She bit her lip. She had been wondering, frankly, what Buell saw in Diedre that was so wonderful, but made herself stop. Who could say? Anyway, that kind of thinking would lead to speculation about what Ron saw in *her,* and she wasn't interested in that at the moment. The bare fact he *did* see something was sufficient.

"As I said, Buell loves her," the old man went on, "but not enough to renounce his uncle's money and with it his lifelong dream of a posthumous revenge. So when Jastrow, about a month ago, met secretly with Buell and presented his ultimatum, Buell decided he had to die."

"What was the ultimatum?" Janet asked.

"It was actually quite ingenious," the professor said. "Jastrow must have planned it for a long time. He wanted to force Buell to write, in his own hand, a document saying that Buell had lied about Jastrow's activities as a deputy sheriff, that he had wrongfully and maliciously deprived Jastrow of his livelihood and his 'good name,' and in voluntary expiation of this wrong, he would pay Jastrow twenty-five percent of any income he would receive from any source in the next ten years."

"Ouch," Ron said.

"Precisely. Certainly, sometime in the next ten years W.K. Chandler would die (it proved to be within ten weeks), and Buell would come into an inheritance of something over eleven million dollars. He decided it would be worth a try, to attempt his threat to make W.K. Chandler aware of the history of the woman his long-lost nephew intended to marry."

"He was an idiot," Ron said flatly. "Why didn't he have the famous letter-revealing-all as life insurance?"

The professor shrugged. "Jastrow simply didn't think of it. Neither did Buell, eh? Or none of this would have happened."

Ron read on.

I knew that if I simply killed Jastrow the police would dig into his background and find the secret he was using to torment me. I would fall under immediate suspicion.

Then I thought I would make it look like an accident, or suicide. But my parents died in an accident, and I have been a reporter for many years, and I know how thorough even a routine investigation of such a mishap is. I couldn't be sure I could fool the police. The best thing, I decided, would be for Jastrow's death to be part of a series of murders, where my connection would be simply another of thousands of irrelevant facts turned up in an investigation. Of course, my long friendship with the Sparta Police and the fact that it would seem to be the "killer" who involved me with the case, would serve to minimize suspicion and give me access to the facts.

But this, too, was unacceptable. Jastrow was an evil man. I am not. In killing him, I would only be doing what had to be done, what someone should have done long ago. But no power on earth could, just to protect myself, cause me to do anything that would bring harm to an innocent person. I'm just not made that way . . ."

"He wouldn't harm an innocent person," Ron said with the bitterest irony he was capable of. "He's not built that way. What does he call Joyce Reade, for God's sake? Gloria Marcus? That death grew out of the whole Hog phenomenon! So did the young guy that was shot by his wife, and the pig farmer's brother-in-law!"

"He's sick, Ron," Janet reminded him gently.

"I think *I'm* about to be sick," he said. "Let's see what else he has to say."

I found it very easy to establish the idea of HOG in the minds of the police and the public. Somehow it captured the imagination . . .

"It sure as hell captured mine," Ron admitted, shaking his head. "Did I really come up with all that garbage about football and Poland-Chinas and pork intestines? You'd better find a new pupil, *Maestro.* Buell played me like a violin."

"You shouldn't feel so bad, *amico.* It is amusing to note—" he looked significantly at Ron and Janet. "Amusing only for the three of *us,* you understand—that I discerned the truth about the first incident the moment I discovered the missing piece of the clamp. I discounted it because of Leslie Bickell's death—a definite non-accident. I knew that Tatham was incapable of wholesale murder. That is why the explanation of Miss Bickell's death revealed Buell's guilt."

"If you'd only mentioned it at the time, Buell might have broken down. Or at least been scared away from any more notes," Janet said.

The professor shrugged. "I am guilty as charged, Doctor. We all have our blind spots: our private learning disabilities, eh? Mine is that I cannot remember that Niccolo Benedetti is never so often wrong as on those occasions he convinces himself he cannot be right. I am hampered by the conviction that I am not omnipotent."

Most times, Ron would not have let that pass without a remark, but his mind was on something else.

Once HOG was established, all I had to do was stay with Inspector Fleisher. This gave me the secret details to make my notes authentic, and it gave me alibis for the "murders." After my innocence was established, it was safe to spend less time on the investigation, giving me the time to give Jastrow what he deserved. My foresight was proven in that—though I tried to make Jastrow look like a suicide, the police immediately knew otherwise.

I had to make HOG as horrible as possible to be sure he distracted the attention from the "victims" as individuals. And all I had to do was scrawl those notes. The last one was written at home and mailed just before I entered police headquarters to join Inspector Fleisher.

It was a good plan. It hurt no one who was innocent . . .

And Ron shook his head again.

. . . but it accomplished what had to be done. My only mistake was an attempt to make HOG too horrible, when he claimed to have "murdered" Leslie Bickell and young Davy Reade in the same night. I accepted too soon the inspector's judgment of the Bickell girl's death as a routine drug overdose. There were complications in the situation (which, I am sure, you will find elsewhere in today's Courant*), that led Professor Benedetti to the truth.*

"It is the first time," the old man said, "that I have ever unmasked a murderer by proving him innocent."

So, my friends and longtime readers, there you have it. I can't say I'm sorry for what I have done, but I do apologize for any inconvenience I may have caused. You can take comfort, though, in the knowledge that the problems of the last few weeks (and it was only an illusion, after all) will be a very real help to thousands of people who have suffered under a very real *evil.*

"He's *crazy!*" Ron said.

"That is hardly a revelation, *amico*," the professor said.

Janet, professionally, as Dr. Higgins, was theorizing. "He wanted to kill his uncle. He *always* wanted to kill his uncle. But the idea of wiping out everything his uncle stood for appealed to him more and for that, the old man had to die a natural death." She started walking around, as if dictating notes.

"But when Jastrow came along," she continued, "he was a perfect substitute. Abuse of power . . . yes, and the direct threat to Buell's loved ones! His parents, then Diedre.

"I'm not saying Buell didn't have a sincere desire to do good—"

"Never have I seen more terrible evil from such a desire," the old man said.

"Your painting," Ron said. "The good and bad colliding, and resulting in blood . . ."

"Of course he wanted to do good," Dr. Higgins said impatiently, "Hog even said so in that last note. But I say the deep-seated reason Buell felt he had to kill Jastrow (that's what he always says in the article; he *has* to kill him) is because then he could feel he was really killing Uncle Willy. It could even be—"

She never told them what it could even be. She was interrupted by a knock at the door of the office. Ron went to answer it and opened the door to Diedre Chester.

Diedre had been crying. Janet felt sorry for her, naturally, but she couldn't suppress a little bit of jealous irritation when she saw how attractively Diedre wore a red nose and bloodshot eyes.

"I have a message for you, Professor," Diedre said.

"Yes? From Buell?"

"Yes. I—they wouldn't let me see him, but his lawyer told me to tell you he has no hard feelings." She sniffled. Ron opened a desk drawer and gave her a Kleenex.

"I am gratified to hear that," Benedetti said.

"Yes," Diedre said.

Janet said, "If there's anything I can do . . . If you want to stay with somebody for a few days . . ." Diedre couldn't *help* it if she was beautiful, after all. Silly thing to hold against her.

"No, thanks." She seemed to lose her balance; staggered around a little. The professor led her to a chair. "I can't *believe* it," she said. "I just can't believe it."

The old man showed her a sad shrug.

Diedre looked up at him. "Buell will still get his money, right?"

"What happens if he doesn't?" Ron asked.

She looked angry. "It doesn't matter to *me!* I'm standing by Buell no matter what! But it means everything to Buell. He didn't kill his uncle, right? There's no reason he shouldn't inherit. He'll die if he has to go to prison without accomplishing what he had to do."

The professor grinned more enigmatically than he ever had before. "It may be," he said, "that Buell might not have to go to prison."

Diedre gasped. "Tell me!"

"I must warn you, the alternative is not especially attractive."

Janet could almost hear Diedre's hopes crash. "You mean kill himself?" she said contemptuously. "What good does that do anyone?"

"None at all," he said. "That was not what I had in mind." He held up the stack of newsprint. "This document," he said, "might well be the basis of an insanity plea, eh? It will not get him acquitted, that I know, though I am not an *avvocato,* a lawyer. However, there is in this state a concept (a foolish one, but still the law) known as 'diminished responsibility.' With this, he might, just might, be penalized less severely, and get the intensive psychiatric care he needs.

"However, if he does plead insanity, *he will not get his uncle's money.* The insane do not inherit. An interesting dilemma, eh?"

Diedre swallowed a couple of times. "Let me see that," she said. She read it through, then again, then said, "But this is supposed to be for the *Courant.* Aren't you going to give it to them?"

The professor shook his head. *"Non é possibile.* Once this were made known, it would be impossible to empanel an impartial jury on this case, and it has been carnival enough without that.

"No. This is a valuable opportunity for my studies. Eventually, you will be allowed to see Buell. Tell him this, please. If I give this to his attorney, it is possible, with skill, he can minimize Buell's punishment. But if so, he forfeits his inheritance, as he has already forfeited the other thing he sought to protect; the chance of a happy lifetime with you."

Diedre started to cry softly into her hands.

The professor ignored her. "But tell him this, also. A

confession is not needed from the police. In Inspector Fleisher's possession is the pen used to write the notes, and even more incriminating, a glossy photograph of you, your son, and Buell. Jastrow induced you to mail it to him with a spurious advertisement; Buell recovered it the night he killed him. It was to be evidence against Buell to his uncle—now it is evidence against him to the state of New York. It has Jastrow's fingerprints on it.

"The rest will follow. Buell may have no doubt of that. Now that the police know the nature of the evidence they seek, they will find it. The bolt cutter, for instance. Did he own one? They will learn.

"So tell Buell that if he chooses to be tried and judged as a sane man, and keep his vow and control of the money from his prison cell, that Niccolo Benedetti will have no qualms about destroying this story. I will answer to Inspector Fleisher and the law itself, if need be."

The old man laid a big hairy hand on Diedre's shiny blonde head and tilted it back, until his eyes met hers.

"Will you do that?"

"I'll—I'll tell him," she whispered.

"And bring me his reply."

Diedre nodded, rose, and walked to the door. She looked back as though she were about to say something, but didn't. She left the door open. Ron got up and closed it behind her.

TWENTY-THREE

"Do you think she really will?" Janet asked.

"Really will what?" Ron said.

"Stand by him."

Ron shrugged. "For a while, I guess." He turned to his mentor. "Ramifications upon ramifications, eh, *Maestro?* Buell has really painted himself into a corner."

"Ah, that reminds me." The old man lit a new cigar. "Tuesday morning the workmen will come to paint my room. I had forgotten to tell you. The color the walls are now is no longer bearable."

Ron raised an eyebrow. "So you'll be staying in Sparta?"

Benedetti shrugged. "Does your brain retire when a case is through, Ronald? I will be *forced* to stay for the trial, no? The three of us will be the star witnesses." He grinned. "Besides, I have promised Mrs. McElroy, Mrs. Zucchio, and our own Mrs. Goralsky that I would improve my acquaintance with each of them at the earliest opportunity. Niccolo Benedetti does not break his word!"

He said it with an air of such righteousness that Janet couldn't help laughing. "Sounds like a busy spring, Professor," and everybody laughed.

Ron said to Janet, "Hey, you never answered my question, you know."

Janet's eyes were bright. "What question?"

Ron made a noise. "What question! *Will you marry me?* of course!"

"I just wanted to be sure you meant it," she said playfully. "Yes, Ron, I will marry you. I love you very much." He kissed her.

"Mmmm," the professor mused. "We shall have to

take steps, then, to prevent Ronald from losing his license, since he will have a wife to support."

"And a stingy old philosopher," Ron murmured in Janet's ear.

Just then she thought of something.

"Professor!" she said.

"I am right here. What is it?"

"Hog! You've explained everything but that. Why *Hog?*"

Ron shook his head. "I forgot all *about* that," he said, wondering.

"Ah, yes," the old man said. "That is perhaps the biggest mystery of all, eh?" He heaved a deep sigh, and became very grave.

"Unless Buell says so," he went on, "we shall probably never know for certain why those notes were signed the way they were.

"But I have an opinion.

"My opinion is based on several things. The victims Hog claimed. Human beings, from an innocent child to a sexually precocious young girl—hardly the most terrible of people. Aside from Jastrow, of course, and he does not count. Victims of accidents, or in Leslie Bickell's case, of vice. The great horror Hog caused was the fear of an individual who could cause such inoffensive people to die so horribly.

"Buell had the same horror of his uncle, eh? Until he found out his parents' deaths were truly accidental. But does that lessen the horror, really? To find that instead of the result of an evil design, your loved ones have died at random? Arbitrarily?

"I think not. And noticing that Buell, in his notes and in his confession, always rendered the name in upper case, I have decided that the word is an acronym, as so many have suspected all along."

"But what does it mean, *Maestro?*" Ron asked.

The professor took the cigar from his mouth and blew smoke through a humorless grin. "Buell himself has told us," the old man said. "Look again at the confession. Hog was a truthful killer. From the first, the taunting notes told the simple truth about the agency that struck down the six innocent victims—the same agency Buell convinced himself struck down the seventh guilty one as well . . ."

The grin fell from the old man's face, to be replaced by a look of weariness. "All were killed by the Hand of God."